THE LAST REMAINING ROSE

LESLIE CARDIX

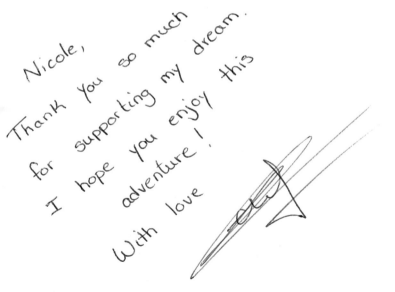

Nicole,
Thank you so much
for supporting my dream.
I hope you enjoy this
adventure!
With love

LESLIE CARDIX BOOKS

THE LAST REMAINING ROSE

For more information visit:

Cover design by Sam Hayles

Editing by Katie Wolf

ISBN: 979-8-9855481-0-5

For all those who encouraged me, supported me and loved me through the years. I would not be who I am today without you.

CONTENT WARNINGS

- Sexual Assault
- Physical & Mental Abuse
- Suicidal thoughts
- Gaslighting
- Domestic abuse
- Grief

CHAPTER ONE

The date was 1772. A young girl lay bleeding, dying on the floor. A man silently left the barn's shadows, bending by her side to remove the spike from her abdomen. His face gave the impression he must have been in his early thirties. His cold, blue eyes, however, showed a great deal of power, intelligence, knowledge, and weariness, proving he was, in fact, a lot older than he appeared to be.

The barn had been on fire for a few minutes, causing the place to fill up with smoke and making it harder for her to breathe. Her eyes watered, her lungs burned, and her legs had given out. He picked her up in his arms while warm, red liquid poured out of her stomach and carried her out in the open.

"Alia," he said, his voice soft, "you have lost too much blood. This moment is your death." He placed her sitting upright against a fresh pile of hay outside of the fiery chaos and kissed her forehead as her breath became irregular. She held her shaking hands to her wound, looking up at him, eyes wide with fear. The full moon made his pale skin shine brightly, making it easy to see the worry in his eyes.

"Save me, Malcolm," she whimpered. "I beg you, don't let me die. Take the pain away."

He approached her calmly, putting his mouth on her neck. He drank her blood until she was seconds from dying, then cut his own wrist, encouraging her to drink his own. As her memories flashed before his eyes, he expected she had experienced his. The blood ritual had been completed, and in just a few hours, she would be a part of his world.

A vampire.

I was no ordinary girl. I looked young, yet my charisma was one of an elder. I walked down the dimly lit corridors just as I had done countless times before, my duffel bag hitting the side of my leg. Corner after corner, the hallway never seemed to end. I glanced at my watch—my plane was boarding in ten minutes. I began running, my long, black hair violently slapping against my face and back. People's heads turned to watch me. They always did, with an equal mixture of desire and fear.

As I settled into a large, comfortable seat, I was offered a glass of champagne that I politely turned away. I was grateful for the UV protection window tints that allowed my kind to fly safely. I watched the safety instruction video for the millionth time, and soon, the plane began to roll down the runway. The engines made noises I had never heard. I could only describe them as a sawing or drilling sound. Did the other passengers hear this as well? Had I ignored signs warning me not to board? But the machine began to increase in speed and lift itself up. I looked back at the people sitting further down the aisle. An elderly man formed a cross over his body and prayed, something he must do with every flight. I laughed to myself. If tonight was our time to go, God would not be here for us.

Excitement and relief washed through me. I had waited too long to visit. Eventually the crew brought out some food; the meals were smaller than I remembered. Not that I would eat it in any case, since regular food didn't generally agree with me. As most people began shutting their eyes and nodding off, I didn't sleep, not one minute of the eight-hour flight. I waited patiently as ever, watching a comedy and then a thriller. My muscles ached, and I felt frustrated. I was not a good flier. Time passed by, and eventually we arrived. My heart began to race again. I did not have any luggage and quickly passed customs.

The air outside the airport was surprisingly cold, even to one such as myself, and a heavy smog covered the sun; with no direct sunlight touching my skin I had no problem walking around. I quickly grabbed a cab.

"Où voulez-vous aller?" asked the driver.

I looked above my black, oversized sunglasses and read his name tag. "I don't know, Florian, why don't you drive me around Paris? I haven't been here in a very long time and I have time to waste. Show me the city of lights."

My heart began aching and I frowned, looking out the window. This was not how I remembered it. Paris had changed tremendously. The smell of gasoline invaded my nostrils, turning my stomach, and the once gorgeous monuments I remembered were now covered with a thick layer of pollution. However, the beautiful golden statues remained shining all over the city. Police officers avidly watched every street corner in attempts to fine speeding motorists. Traffic was the worst— hours of waiting just to cross a few miles. Paris was a beautiful city to visit, but in my humble opinion, too stressful to live in. The driver brought me to my hotel, wishing me a good rest. I took a hot shower and lay in bed watching television. I hadn't spoken French in years, but it quickly came back to me while sitting through various game shows. Paris would always be dear to my heart, but I struggled to find any resemblance to my past.

When I awoke, hungry and disoriented, the sun hadn't risen yet; a fog lingered around the trees and the sky was a dark blue. As long as no sun touched my skin directly, and with some extra precautions, I could walk around during the daytime. So, unwilling to risk any burns, I put sunscreen on my face and hands, dressed myself in a white turtle neck and tight black jeans. The clothes hugged my skin, emphasizing my curves and covering most of my body. I stepped outside and, closing my eyes, enjoyed the rare peacefulness of this busy place.

Later that morning, I was driven to the train station and left for the South of France. Trains were my favorite mode of transportation, not only because all windows were equipped with UV filters, but they also brought memories back. Happy memories of family members gone too soon. I watched the landscape fly by and smiled to myself, remembering a time I hopped on and off trains, getting to see so much of the world. But this was not a vacation; I had a specific reason for being here and I did not step off until we reached Marseille.

Unfortunately for me, and as I anticipated, the weather was as Mediterranean as it could get—sunny and warm. I rubbed myself with sunscreen and waited for my chauffeur to greet me with an umbrella. He took me to the nasty side of the town, which is where I wanted to go. A part of the city tourists never saw, where all the houses had bars on their windows, their walls completely tagged, and where women did not walk alone at night. An ancient house presented itself on top of a hill—a retirement home. It was such a strange notion for this respectable establishment to be located right here.

The car had to be buzzed in through the gate and I walked into the lobby, feeling unsure of where to go. The receptionist greeted me with a warm smile.

"Hi, I'm—" I began.

"I know who you are, Ms. Henry. I was told you'd be coming today."

"Please, call me Alia. How is she?" I asked.

"I'm afraid it's not going to be much longer," she answered with a sad smile. "Follow me. I'll take you to her room."

I followed the woman down deserted corridors, but I could plainly hear the televisions turned on inside the closed bedrooms. She left me outside a door and I knocked, waiting for a frail voice to approve. "Bonjour, Madame Lucette," I gently greeted an elderly woman as I entered the bedroom.

A tiny woman sat in a wheelchair facing a window opposite to the door. She didn't respond to the greeting, so I walked around to face her. The little lady stared hard, not recognizing my face. Then, suddenly, her eyes grew wide with surprise and excitement. Her head fell back; she couldn't catch her breath and held her hand to her chest. I laughed tenderly.

"It's alright, it's only me. No need to be so shaken up."

My heart tightened and sadness overtook me. She had gained an unhealthy amount of weight since the last time I'd seen her many years ago. The woman was very sick. "Alia, what are you doing here?" she stuttered.

"I came to surprise you. I told you I'd be back before your adventure came to an end."

She gave a contented smile, and I quickly scanned the room. Pictures of Lucette's deceased family decorated the walls. A family tree was framed and at the top was my brother's name. The elderly woman was my last living descendant, my grandniece a few times removed.

"How are you, ma belle?"

She smiled again and whimpered. "This isn't a life for me. Old and handicapped."

I brushed the little lady's short hair with my fingers. "I'm so sorry, honey. Life has a funny way of twisting around. I did my best to accommodate you. I hope it was enough."

"There is nothing more you could have done, except what you refused to do years ago. And it sure is too late for that now."

I exhaled, choosing to let her comment go, and kneeled down so we could be at eye level. "I've missed you, little woman. Time has gone by, hasn't it?" I could hear her heart beating erratically.

"Yes, it certainly has." She watched me. "You haven't changed. You're still beautiful, whereas I'm ready to die." Her gaze undeniably held animosity, although she quickly tried to hide it. I didn't want her to be so angry with me and my guilt resurfaced. "You've been taking care of me for too long," she continued. "All in good time. Let's lie down like we used to." I easily carried her fragile body to the bed and rested my head on the pillow next to her so I could watch her breathe. "I love you, ma chérie," I whispered, just as I did when she was little. Her heartbeat was irregular still and she had trouble getting enough air.

Lucette had spent all her life in France. Her parents had died in a hit-and-run while she was in middle school and when no family member had stepped forward to take guardianship, I had seen no other alternative than to take up that role. I had moved to France and done my best at taking care of a pre-teenager when both our lives couldn't have been more different. It hadn't been easy. I hadn't always known how to be nurturing or motherly towards a young human who wanted to be given immortality.

She met her husband when she was nineteen and he was twenty-three, and they were soon married. At that point, I had no more reasons to stay in Europe and moved back to my home in America. When her husband died of a very early heart attack, some thirty years earlier, I had hoped she would move to America where I could take care of her personally. She had refused; this was her land and her home. Although I had not stepped in this country in decades, Lucette and I spoke over the telephone often.

After she survived a stroke at the age of seventy-one and became partially paralyzed, I had no choice but to place her in a retirement home where others were paid to watch and care for her. She had the largest room in the entire facility, which overlooked a splendid garden. However, when one loses reasons to go on, the battle is often already lost. Her health had quickly deteriorated, and she was dying. My eternal youth and presence had seemed to become upsetting to her, and I had decided to stay away, until I received the nursing home's call.

When she awoke, I pushed her wheelchair downstairs to the cafeteria where I was introduced to her friends as her granddaughter. I sat down with them as they ate and listened to the gossiping of old women. We then returned to her room where she watched a soap opera—she on the bed, and me on a chair. Lucette criticized the actors and I found her bitterness endearing; she was a harsh critic. She fell asleep before the end of the episode and I caught a hitch in her breathing, which quickly slowed as her chest stopped moving. The old lady died peacefully, and I hoped my visit had been of some comfort. I was jealous of her ability to die.

Within the next couple of days, I fulfilled her wish to be cremated and to have her ashes thrown into the wind at the very top of the Garlaban mountain. This was her city, where she had been born, where she had learned to love and grieve. She would now forever be a part of it. I had loved her, this small child that life had already taken so much from. I had been proud of the woman she had become and her tenacity, even when death came knocking at her door again. I loved her still when she began resenting me for not having changed her, and now she was gone.

I dried the tears that had fallen down my cheeks and looked out to the city below once more. It was so strange to me, how one's life could just putter out like a candle. I would never experience the danger of time. I did wonder, though, whether I would perish if I jumped off this mountain now. The pull was strong, but I wouldn't yet.

I went in the direction of Carry-le-Rouet, a nice little village up on a hill near the ocean. It was peaceful and beautiful. I was dropped off outside the gate and realized I hadn't stepped on this property in possibly two decades. The trees and plants had grown over the house. I stepped over many brambles to get to the door. All was as it had been left inside, but with a thick layer of dust and mold. Lucette had owned this house with her husband, and she would have been heartbroken to see its condition today.

I did a walk through, inspecting drawers, boxes, and closets keeping important documents and other memorabilia. I found a picture of me and Lucette when she must have been around thirteen or fourteen years old at Christmas dinner. I was in the middle of handing her a tightly wrapped gift with an enormous bow on it. Our neighbor had snapped the candid picture and the look on Lucette's young face was pure delight. I put the picture in my jacket's inner pocket, close to my heart.

I collected some wood and lit the ancient fireplace. I prayed the chimney wouldn't catch on fire as a chimney sweep hadn't been done in a very long time. The wood cracked and crackled. This house was filled with spirits and energy. The fire hypnotized me, the magic of the flames leaving my mind open to the voices. Maybe I was a tad crazy. *Everyone you've ever loved and cared for is gone, why are you the last one? Take your life. End it.* I shook my head and chased them away. Should I have changed her like she had requested as a teenager? It had been such a strain on our relationship when I refused to, but she couldn't comprehend the ways in which she would change. I couldn't have done that to her, to my own blood. I lay on a dusty chaise lounge and drifted off into an uneasy sleep.

The next day, I closed the house. I would sell it and never return.

Going through the travel process once more, I was back on

a plane, heading "home" to America. The last of my bloodline had vanished. It had pained me to see her go. What purpose did I have in life now? I buried my heart long ago and now found myself longing for it all to end. Life had not been good to me; perhaps death would be somewhat better. Then again, I was not truly alive or dead. All I'd ever been, was a monster.

CHAPTER TWO

1767

Witchcraft was forbidden, yet Alia practiced it thoroughly, and neither her family nor her friends knew about it.

The daughter of new American settlers, she was always very obedient, or so it appeared. She'd had an easy childhood. She lived alone with her father in a small village where everyone knew each other and knew everything concerning their neighbor's life. God was very much involved in everyone's lives, and all were expected to attend Sunday sermon, lest they be accused of devil worshiping. A Bible was found in every bedroom and thoroughly studied. It was a place where the best she could hope for was being married off to a good man who would provide for her while she took care of their children. But she was too stubborn, too outspoken, and had received no marriage proposal yet.

At the age of eighteen, she was considered a spinster. Her mother had died of cholera when Alia was only a few years old. Her older brother had married and had three children of his own. He was preparing to return to France with his new family, finding their life in America too tough. As she was yet to be married, she took care of her father and their house: going to the market daily, cooking their food, doing the laundry in the common basin, and catering to the farm animals' needs.

But *he* somehow knew of her practices. This stranger had arrived from nowhere and decided to settle here. Foreigners were not welcome inside the village, but no one dared ask him to leave.

She was young and beautiful. He stood tall, powerful and raised thoughts and feelings from her she'd never had before. She wanted him. The villagers took it upon themselves to warn her about him, asking for her to stay away. And though he only seemed to be around at sunset, her eyes searched for him when she was out and about.

Every full moon she escaped her house and ran deep into the forest to worship the Goddess, careful to not ruin her white ankle-length tunic, lest her father take notice. The grass was covered in a light frost, her breath fogging the air in front of her, and she wore a sheepskin cloak as she made her way outside and walked deep into the forest.

Tonight, however, she wasn't alone. As she started her ritual, he stepped out of the darkness and interrupted her. She couldn't stifle the scream that escaped her lips and chided herself, afraid it would echo through the valley. She began panicking, realizing one way or another she was caught, and imagined all the terrible ways the villagers would kill her: she would be burned, pushed over a cliff, drowned, or hung. She held her breath, eyes wide with fear.

They stared at each other for some time before he finally spoke. "I was looking for you," he said, circling her like a shark circled its prey.

She knew from his clothing, from his deep brown coat, waistcoat, and breeches, all the way down to his black riding boots, that he was a noble and that she ought to avert her eyes. Something told her to stand very still. "For what reason were you looking for me?"

"You are a powerful sorceress. Your power reached for me, called for me to come to this rotten village."

His voice was pleasing to her ears. "Who are you?"

"It's not who, but what am I?"

"I don't understand. What do you want?" She really shouldn't be so rude if she hoped to live through this night.

"I am not what I seem. I search for power."

He came to a stop, facing her, and the night stood still. She noticed she could no longer hear the crickets or any other nocturnal animals around her.

"Are you a witch hunter?"

"No, I believe I wouldn't be very good at it. The light is... unpleasant to my skin. I saw you sneaking around tonight, and every part of my being bade me to follow you here."

"What will you do? Will you tell the villagers?"

"No, no, madam, you mistake my intentions. My only will is to watch you practice."

"Watch me practice?" she repeated. "Aren't you afraid?"

"What is there to be afraid of? No, I am not afraid of you, and I am not like anyone else. I'm... evolved."

All her senses screamed she should be fearing for her life. His eyes seemed to glow in the dark and suddenly, she knew without a doubt what he was. She had heard stories about such beings.

Vampires. A cold sweat broke over her body. She would not go unscathed after all.

"You're an eternal!" She took a step back, and he lifted an eyebrow.

"I am Count Malcolmian Istvan." He bowed down awkwardly, clearly unused to the gesture. "I didn't come to bring you harm. You needn't be alarmed."

She focused on controlling her breathing, but her instincts were shouting a warning. She felt her magic dissipate; she had only halfway connected herself to the Goddess. "I must finish my ritual. If you're going to watch, you may sit over there." She jutted her chin towards a boulder.

He gestured for her to continue while sitting down. She went into a trance. Her head fell back, and her eyes, while opened, were unseeing. He watched her. Minutes passed, then close to an hour before she came to and she knew what she looked like: exhausted, but also fiercely euphoric. She glanced down and her skin glowed with life, with the energy she had absorbed from the earth. The air around her was charged with electricity; it crackled as she stood up.

"Marvelous," he whispered, looking at her with interest. His deep blue eyes shone through the night. "I should be honored to have your company in my home." He smirked and she nodded in acceptance.

He led her quietly to his property and while she wanted to ask him questions about himself, she remained quiet, not wanting to be a bother. She wrung her hands nervously. The air was cold and humid; she enjoyed it very much—it refreshed her burning skin. And although walking miles must have taken a while, she was still feeling hazy from her spell, and time moved differently for her then.

He didn't live in a tiny wooden cabin like she did, but in an enormous mansion hidden behind the mountain, many miles from the village. His entire residence was decorated with weapons from all eras, paintings of stern-looking men and women, and other valuable objects. All of these unusual items excited her, taking her away from her uninteresting life. Maybe that was why she found herself so attracted to a vampire.

They came across a few servants, busying themselves with lighting the many torches in each room. The shadows added mysteriousness to her surroundings. She slightly brushed a sword's edge, piercing her skin. A small cry escaped her lips in surprise as a red line appeared on her finger. She hadn't realized he was so close to her, and she gasped as he gently raised it to his sensuous mouth, licking the trail of blood. She watched his tongue move with hypnotized eyes and wished he'd use it all over her body. The sensuality that radiated from him nearly drove her crazy.

"Count..." she whimpered.

He raised his eyes to meet hers. "Your blood is exquisite, unlike anything else I have ever tasted before."

"Do you want more?"

"Only with your permission."

"You won't take too much?"

"Never."

She nodded, and holding her hand tightly in his, he led her up some stairs to his bedroom. A fire blazed in a stone chimney and an enormous four poster bed, the curtains pulled open, sat in the corner of the room. Still, the room was drafty, and she shivered. The bed was covered in pillows, and as he quietly laid her down, she was surprised at the softness of the mattress. This was a far cry from the straw she slept on at home. She felt panicked but also excited, not knowing what he would exactly do with her. She watched him take off his coat and vest, carefully placing them on a chair, and she held her breath when he approached her. He lay down next to her on his side and tilted her neck upward. "Will it hurt?" she whispered.

"Not at all. It'll be but a kiss."

He closed his mouth on her flesh, kissing her at first. She felt the moment his teeth punctured the skin and he began taking her blood. She gasped, arching her back, and he placed his left hand around her waist to stop her from moving. His lips were soft and his tongue sent electricity through her veins. She couldn't help the moan that escaped her. It was fire and ice combined. Pleasure and pain. She wrapped her right hand in his hair while the left one gripped at the sheets by her leg. He soon pulled away, getting off the bed, and she wished she could bring his mouth back down to her neck.

"I hope this was as good for you as it was for me," he said, handing her a glass of water and cleaning her small wound. She nodded, still unable to find the words. They talked about her life, about the village, and he had a servant bring up some grapes for her. She knew she had to return home soon.

"I should walk you back," he announced, grabbing his coat.

"No, it's alright. I know how to find my way and I do not think it'd be good to be seen together this late."

"Will you come back to see me?" he asked, walking her to the front door.

She nodded with a small smile. He kissed her cheek, and she felt her skin burn up. The walk home was almost as joyful as she felt during her spells. What an intriguing evening.

"Where were you?" her father screamed as she attempted to sneak into her home quietly.

"My mind was troubled, and I took a walk."

"Alia, you cannot be out all night, especially during a full moon. Do you want to be charged with witchcraft?"

"Father, please stop yelling. I ran into the newcomer; he can vouch for my whereabouts."

"You *what*? Alia, there are stories being told about him. He has been seen with other girls. This will not end well. The devil has many shapes."

"Please do not listen to the slanders of envious men."

She returned to Malcolm almost every night. She felt unsure at first, but he always met her halfway to his mansion. If she hadn't come to him, then he would have gone to her.

The tension between them grew steadily over the next year until they decided to take their relationship to a deeper level. He had just finished feeding off her, and instead of getting up from the bed to hand her some water as he normally did, he remained lying by her side. He tilted her face to his and looked at her in a way he never had before: with tenderness and eagerness.

"I want to kiss you," he told her.

She inhaled sharply, her heart beating against her chest. His lips met hers softly at first, tentatively, as he wrapped his arm around her waist, bringing her closer. She melted into his body, opening her mouth to his. It was passion and fire. It was madness and her undoing. All in one kiss.

He moved on top of her, never breaking the kiss, and she felt him harden against her leg.

"Malcolm, you know I haven't..."

"I know. But do you want to?"

"Lord, yes!"

He removed his shirt, letting her run her fingers along his defined stomach. He then hiked her dress above her stomach and began tasting her, getting her wet. His tongue was inside her and she didn't know what she should be doing with her hands. He massaged her breast while also holding her firmly in place. These sensations washing over her made her wish she hadn't waited so long to experience this. Finally, he unbuttoned his breeches, and she glimpsed the length of him. Too nervous, she returned her gaze to the ceiling and felt him settle back between her legs. There was a sharp pain and she cried out, trying to crawl away. This did not feel the same as when he fed on her.

"It's okay," he murmured, rolling his hips into her. "It won't hurt for long." She nodded, starting to move her body to his rhythm. "You are mine now. There will be no other. Is that clear?" he said, grabbing her chin and forcing her eyes to meet his. "Of course."

She hadn't known what to expect, and she didn't enjoy her first time with him, but he assured her it would feel better the more they did it. All she could think of as she returned home was that she was no longer a maiden. She smiled.

Every night for five years, she would join Malcolm. She was his confidant, his friend, and his lover. He took care of her, fed her, and protected her, and she never once wondered what he would ask in return. Admittedly, she would have given him everything—he only had to ask.

I woke up with a gasp, holding a hand to my throat, where the faint traces of a scar remained. Each time I dreamt about my sire, I relived my memories through dreams, and the two puncture marks on my neck seemed to burn.

I lay back in bed, breathing heavily, then closed my eyes and listened to my surroundings. Although my room was on the third floor, I could clearly hear my cleaning lady vacuuming the lobby. The clock on my dresser informed me it was 5:37 p.m. I hadn't gotten that much sleep, not that I needed very much sleep to function. The sun would set in a few hours, and I would have to go to work; DJ Velvet Kiss would be performing at my club tonight, and I had to be there to welcome him.

Something woke me from my slumber, but it wasn't the woman downstairs. I threw the sheets off me, stood up, and looked around, noticing a frame on the floor. With cold, delicate fingers, I picked it up, wondering how it could have fallen off its shelf, and looked at the intense eyes staring back at me. *Malcolm.* Memories tended to fade over time and his face was not one I wanted to forget. My throat tightened and a feeling of grief overwhelmed me. Although he had died over ninety years ago, time had not eased the pain. I distinctly remembered the way his cold but beautiful eyes would study my figure, the way his strong hands would touch every inch of my skin. The set of his defined jaw as he became aroused. If I tried hard enough, I could still smell him on me, feel him inside of me. My body responded to the memories of our wild nights together. Sometimes I could still feel his gaze upon me. More importantly, I clearly remembered the brutal ways he and the rest of our clan had been murdered. Pure hatred gradually replaced the grief as I had never been able to find out the responsible parties, but a movement outside my bedroom door interrupted my thoughts.

"You may come in, Lidia."

The twenty-two-year-old woman entered, holding a cup of blood on a tray. Her long, golden hair was tightly pinned into a bun, enhancing her sharp features. Her green eyes pierced through the darkness in search of me. Lidia was a very attractive and bright young woman, and I had decided to go ahead and pay for her classes at a very refined culinary school.

The Sanchez family had worked for me, living inside my manor, for generations. I offered them wealth and in exchange they were my eyes and ears when I slept, and they handled emergencies that took place during the day. Somewhere down the line, we also developed a familial bond. They were more than employees to me, and I hoped the feeling was reciprocal.

The Sanchez family had always known I was a vampire, even before we announced ourselves as real creatures, not something from a storybook. Vampires had been accepted as part of society about ten years ago. But were we really accepted? That was debatable.

The smell of blood nearly brought me down to my knees. I relied on holding on to my desk chair to remain standing.

"Good morning, Alia." She glanced at me, and I clenched my teeth while waiting for her departure. "I'll just put this here." She set down the tray and left the room hastily. We had been through this many times. When I struggled to keep control over myself, having a human in my room only made it worse. I lashed out at my breakfast, drinking the liquid in one large, endless gulp, immediately feeling better. I hated the need to drink blood and I refused to feed off humans, solely dining off animals. It satisfied but didn't quench. Only one type of blood got rid of the thirst, for a little while...

I opened my shutters, letting the setting sun touch me. It was painful, stinging and burning my uncovered skin, but I thoroughly enjoyed it. Pain was about the only emotion I was able to feel these days, and it always amazed me how much of it I could endure.

I had to get ready and quickly took a shower, curled my hair, and put on a sexy black dress and some makeup. I had been turned in my early twenties; I had to consciously work on looking older because I didn't always get the respect I deserved as a businesswoman who looked so young. I realized I was running late and approached the veranda, then jumped down and lightly landed on my feet. If I wouldn't feed my demon any human blood, I could at least satisfy it with an adrenaline rush. I exited the house and walked to my chauffeur George, Lidia's father, and to the black Mercedes awaiting me.

I lived about thirty minutes outside Boston. Although my business took place in the main city, I resided deep within the forest. I couldn't tolerate the constant hustle and bustle of this century. I couldn't accept the pain everyone was in while losing their humanity, constantly looking down at a phone, scrolling social media, pretending to be alright. I didn't mean to be quiet the entire ride and only became aware of it when I looked up and realized we had almost arrived. Perhaps it was because my mind was never quiet. As the car approached the establishment, people waiting in line could be seen from around the block.

"Looks like tonight will be a good night," George said.

"Yes, I expect it will be."

The vehicle parked out front and I waited patiently for my driver to open the door. I was all about dramatic entrances. I walked down the red carpet and entered my palace. When I first opened, almost eight years ago, people came hoping to witness or participate in some illegal, freaky vampire business. I quickly became tired of that crowd and made this club exclusive to the elite. People who were used to being observed and needed a safe space to enjoy themselves. As they spent thousands of dollars, I owed them the very best, and unless you had money, you would never set foot in my kingdom. With four floors and seventeen rooms playing different styles of music, my club quickly became the number one spot for celebrities to party in.

As I finished putting money away in the safe, my guest DJ arrived. While I escorted him through the building to the room I had set up for his set, I felt his hand sliding from the small of my back to my ass. I had to give it to him, he had big ones. I grabbed his fingers in a swift move, ever so slightly twisting his wrist down.

"If you want to keep your hand, you'll never take liberties like that again," I warned, leaning into him and letting him feel some of my power. The air became charged with electricity, which zapped him where I touched his skin. He nodded with a groan, and I released him, shoving him away from me. I made my rounds, saying hello and offering bottles to some of the elite clientele. I danced with some and decided to leave around two in the morning, a relatively early time in the club world.

"Already done?" George asked, looking back at me from the rearview mirror as I sat in the car.

"I grow tired of this place and these people." I stared out the window.

"Is something wrong?" he questioned.

I was distant, caught up in my thoughts. "I'm old and I'm tired. I am emotionally drained. I see all these humans enjoying their nights, every night, without any real trouble in mind. They take pleasure in living because they know death is coming. I envy them. I envy them for having a reason to live every day like it is their last."

"Maybe you could meet someone like you. Vampires are no longer a secret to the world, you know that."

"Don't be foolish—too many vampires are still in hiding. Even if one did approach me, my power would scare them."

He understood the conversation was over and focused on the road. I rolled down my window, leaning my head against the seat and letting the fresh air touch my skin. Once we left the city, I enjoyed being driven through dark winding roads and when we reached the manor's gates, I tapped George on the shoulder. "I would like to walk the rest of the way."

I watched the car disappear into the darkness and closed my eyes for a moment, letting the cold air relax me. The gates creaked shut and I knew I shouldn't have gone out tonight; I was now in a terrible mood. All around me, nature whispered sweet words of sorrow. At an early age, when I was still human, I learned that everything had a life, had a spirit and a voice. I had been a witch turned into a vampire. The voices constantly tried to talk to me and I usually blocked them out, but not tonight. Let them have me.

All I could see for miles was all sorts of different trees swaying into the night: pine trees, cypress trees, and sycamores among them. The wind picked up, and I smelled an air that was pure and healthy. I felt safe and almost at peace in this environment. I took my shoes off and dug my toes into the dirt, letting Mother Earth fuel and rejuvenate me, absorbing the energy she provided and letting it settle deep in my bones. I had a good ten minutes of walking ahead of me and I loved using this time to focus on the here and now. I filled my lungs with fresh air, breathing in deeply and releasing my anger and frustration. Maybe a bit of loneliness too.

I watched various animals scurry around and listened to a distant owl hooting, crickets chirping into the night. Mostly I acknowledged the voices all around me, the ghosts of my past, their despair. I listened to their enraged whispers, felt their sadness deep in my gut, and wished them on their way. This was my punishment for the atrocities committed in my life. I would never be totally free, but I could accept it, accept them, and move all these emotions along peacefully.

CHAPTER THREE

1772

The sun had set on this valley hours ago and a light fog was settling in. A night earlier, a farm girl had died.

Alia had become careless while spending time with Malcolm over the years, feeling untouchable. She had an overly confident sense of safety within his arms and had ignored the suspicious glances from her neighbors, as well as her father's constant warnings. She chose to dismiss the ill-natured gossips as she returned home with bite marks that she no longer cared to hide. Her behavior, although not affecting others, had become unacceptable and sacrilegious towards God. This incited the villagers into attacking her, wanting to get rid of the devil inside her, and they set fire to her barn, thinking she would perish. Little did they know she was about to rise from the dead.

Alia was buried outside the village's gates along

with witches killed throughout the years. No cross and no flowers marked her coffin's location within the woods; she was to be forgotten. At midnight, everything stood still, and nature remained silent, as if it knew evil was awakening. Scratches, screams, and pounding came from underneath the ground, and then, suddenly, an arm emerged from the earth. Like the animal she had become, she crawled out of her entrapment. She put her bleeding hands to her mouth and studied her environment with new senses. Everything looked much more vivid. She could hear and smell things she had never noticed before. A sob escaped her lips. She couldn't understand what was happening to her. She rubbed her face for a moment, and her skin felt cold and numb to the touch. She looked down at the dirty clothes she did not remember putting on. In fact, she couldn't remember much at all. A fire, smoke, a stake, and then what? The only thing she understood was her need for a familiar face.

She recognized these woods, for she had spent many hours playing here as a child, and ran to her house, faster than she ever had before. The cabin was plunged in darkness when she opened the door, nearly ripping it off the hinges. The welcome she received was not what she expected.

"You are the devil!" screamed her terrified father, running outside. "You should be underground! Stay back, demon!"

"Father, please, I do not understand. Why are you so afraid of me?" She breathed hard, stumbling over her words as tears streamed down her face. Her hands were held forward in a pleading motion.

The despair and confusion in her voice stopped him in his tracks, although he kept his distance. He looked at her for a long time, not knowing whether it was a trick.

"Where did you go, Alia? Where have you been?"

She put her hands in her hair, shaking her head violently from side to side. "I don't know. I woke in the ground and I don't know how I got there. What is happening to me?" Her eyes were wide and manic. He then approached her, took her hands away from her face, and flinched at the coldness of her skin.

"You don't remember?" She shook her head. "You died. You can't stay here; you must leave before the villagers see you."

She began remembering the previous night's events and as she realized what she had become, her heart shattered. She felt as though she would throw up. Thoughts crossed her mind so fast; she couldn't focus on just one.

"Father, it's still me. Don't send me away, please!"

"No! It is against all rules of nature and if the villagers see you awake, God have mercy on your soul. I should have the strength to put you back in your grave, but I can't bear to lose you a second time. I'm sorry, Alia, but you cannot remain here. Live, prosper, but leave. Please." His voice broke, and with a look of torture on his face, he walked back into the house, closing the half-broken door behind him.

She remained out in the cold, heartbroken and reaching a level of despair unimaginable. Maybe if she stayed put long enough, he would change his mind—he had to. Where was she supposed to go? The thirst soon invaded her thoughts. A thirst so intense, so deep in her throat, like an itch that refused to go away until scratched. Her body began to shake with the need of it, and she recognized it exactly for what it was, thanks to Malcolm's description of his own need. She decided to leave the village and look for shelter. Why was she alone? Where was Malcolm?

A week passed, yet she was still alone. She had gone to Malcolm's estate, but it had been closed down, and he was long gone. She knew him, on a personal level; he wouldn't have played her for a fool... would he? She hadn't known where to go, so she stayed hidden within the forest where she could see her village.

The thick trees covered her from the sun, and she watched over her father. Her brother having moved back to France some time ago meant her father was now alone. He seemed to be having a hard time completing all the tasks his land required without her help, his body too old and tired. The farm was not going to hold up much longer. She wanted to return home so badly but knew things would forever be different, that part of her had died.

Alia understood what she had become and had attempted to fight the urge to drink blood. However, a few days earlier, she had been spotted walking through the village by the priest. He had almost alerted everyone, but she had caught up to him, and his fear had awoken the thirst inside her, this animalistic predator instinct, until she sank her teeth into his neck. He had been the one to lead the hunt against her, impaling her with a stake, and she had enjoyed watching the life leave his eyes. She was unsure how the villagers made the connection; maybe someone else had seen her, but soon the whole village blamed her father. They slammed their fists on his door until he came out and stood on his doorstep.

"We know your daughter is walking. It is your responsibility to get rid of her," a man said.

"Never! You fools are the reason she died!"

Alia watched it all happen atop a nearby cliff she had stationed herself on. A deep, forbidding feeling overwhelmed her.

Eventually, her father's house was set on fire while he was trapped inside. The sun was high in the sky and although she attempted to rescue him, a stolen sheet covering her body, the flames burned too hot, and he perished in a great deal of pain. She soon learned exactly how long she could stand in the light before her skin would start burning. Not long enough.

Alia became enraged, revenge overtaking every other emotion, and once the night arrived, she set out to kill everyone in the valley: mothers, fathers, children, elders—none survived her wrath. They had to have known it would end this way. How could they take something from her and not expect retribution? She took pride and joy in seeing the fear in their eyes, in bathing in their blood. But when the anger subsided, she was left with a bitter taste; she felt shame and was disgusted by her actions. This was what she had become? She had watched over some of these children, played with them and catered to them.

The sky became lighter, the air became dryer. The sun would rise in a matter of minutes, and she awaited it by the edge of the forest, welcomed it. This was not how she wanted to live the rest of her life. Suddenly, a strong pair of hands encircled her waist and dragged her into the shadows.

"What are you doing?" Malcolm exclaimed.

"I just murdered my entire village! I couldn't control myself! You changed me into a monster! I want no part of this!"

He kissed her lips, licking the dried blood from them, and held her. "Pardon me, my love. I was forced to leave in a hurry, but I came back for you. You'll learn to control yourself with time, but you don't have to. We are gods."

"Where did you go? Why did you leave me? Look what I've done!"

"I had to move my assets so we could leave this place. I didn't expect it to take so long. Listen, these people didn't matter. They are of no importance. We are together now and will be for all eternity."

She always let him sweet-talk her into anything he wanted. She relaxed for a bit and gazed at the valley. She made a promise to herself that eventually she would build a home in this precise location in honor of her father.

I slowly opened my eyes, shaking away the dream. I had fallen asleep on my rooftop underneath the starry sky, and the sun was moments from rising. I spent my nights practicing magic, and I needed to meditate every day to keep my powers under control. It was like having a fiery ball of energy under my veins at all times that just wanted to implode. It would be catastrophic for this energy to go unchecked.

I often considered taking a stroll down to the valley during the day and ending this eternal misery, yet I couldn't help feeling like something was about to happen. I was meant for more. Something either good or bad was coming my way and I knew I had a big part to play in it.

After checking all my accounts, scheduling new performances for the club, and paying bills, I spent most of my time painting, a habit and skill I started developing in the mid-1800s and continued to work on today. Many of my pieces recollected my past and scenes that were forged in my memory. I worked primarily in oil paint, but also used pastels. Most of my canvases now hung in museums all over the world, as they gave new generations an honest look into the past. My experiences were infinitely valuable, opening a side of the world humans had known nothing about until vampires had come to light, so to speak. I had had lessons from masters and all the time in the world to practice and hone this skill. I was one of the most well-known vampires to have come out, yet I was terribly bored with my life. Even if the club hadn't been doing so well, I had been alive a long time and my bank account reflected that. I sponsored various charities and research across the world which helped world hunger, medical advances, homelessness, and education in underprivileged neighborhoods. I worked hard at ending the stigma against vampires, and yet I felt completely uninspired.

My cell phone rang, and I had to fish it out of my purse. I didn't often receive calls. "Hello, Alia speaking."

"Ms. Henry, this is Detective Thompson. I hope I am not disturbing you."

"Of course not, Detective, what can I do for you?"

"I was wondering if you were available to come into the morgue this evening to identify some markings we've found on multiple victims. They are unlike any others we've come across before and we're a bit stumped."

I knew that what he meant by markings was in reality teeth marks, but the fact that he couldn't identify them, when I had shared all my knowledge with him over the years, had me more than curious. "Absolutely, I can be there within the hour."

I asked George to drive me down to the city. He held an umbrella over my head, shading my face from the sun, and I kept my sunglasses firmly positioned over my eyes as I entered the building, my heels echoing on the polished floor. Detective Thompson, a fifty-three-year-old man, awaited me at the reception. I noticed the tan line from his missing wedding ring as he shook my hand.

"Thank you for coming on such short notice, Ms. Henry," he greeted me. He was accompanied by whom I guessed to be the medical examiner. A third person entered from a different room—probably the morgue diener who would have assisted in the autopsy. A strong odor of formaldehyde emanated from both men—it was a little off-putting. Once all introductions were done, they walked me to the back area.

Two bodies lay under white sheets on two respective aluminum tables. As I got closer, the medical examiner removed the sheets down to the victims' collarbones so I could see the bite marks.

"What do you think?" Thompson asked. "Have you ever seen anything like it?

"Both the man and the woman alike were completely drained of blood. And not because of the wound on their necks. There wasn't even a drop of blood found at the scene. Something bit them and sucked them dry. Muscle, tissue... it's almost all gone. There is almost nothing left but skin and bone," the medical examiner explained.

"Bite mark" was too light of a term for the savagery displayed. Their necks had also been nearly taken off, with huge chunks missing. And I had absolutely seen this before. My heart began beating faster, my breathing accelerated, and I felt panic rising.

"Ms. Henry?"

It took me a moment before coming back to myself and being able to answer. "I believe this is an Astaroth vampire's doing."

"Ast... what? Is this a new breed?" The detective was taking notes.

"No." I chuckled in disbelief, not at the man, but at the situation. "It's one of the oldest breeds. And they're supposed to be extinct, so this has me as baffled as you." Decades ago, after what happened to my clan, vengeance had pushed me to look for these beasts, but I found no trace.

"Well, apparently there is at least one left."

"Yes, it would appear so," I whispered, falling back into traumatic memories. "While they can kill easily with their claws, this is how they feed. Everything is gone."

"How do we arrest it if we run into it?"

"You don't. If you run into it, you kill it because it will not hesitate to kill you and everyone in its path, and this is coming from me. You kill it. You may want to send a special vampire unit out for this one."

"Do they have the same weaknesses as other vampires?" I would normally feel irritated at being asked this question by a human. I would feel as though I was selling out my species, but I trusted the detective.

"Yes, same weaknesses: sun, decapitation, stake through the heart, taking out the heart. But they also have doubled the strengths. They're even faster and stronger than a regular vampire. They're hungrier. They heal faster than even we do. Can you tell me where these two were found?"

"By the bay, just found in an alley."

I nodded absentmindedly. "Can you please keep me updated as to what you find?" I asked. "You have my cell phone number."

I left the morgue with thoughts whirling in my head and as the night approached, I decided to go out dancing at the bay myself. I would keep my eyes open, hopefully catch the Astaroth's scent, and see an old friend at the same time.

A few months ago, I had been intimate with a vampire named Paul, a DJ who had been turned recently; I had shown him the ropes and taught him the rules. Our relationship didn't last long because I just couldn't open up. He wasn't what I was looking for, but we still kept in touch. Tonight, I would watch him perform at a club near the water. I braided my hair and wore a sexy yet elegant one shoulder, long-sleeved mini dress.

George dropped me off and as I entered the building, I instantly recognized the style of music being spun and danced my way through the crowd to the front. The energy in this place was already high, full of bodies grinding on each other. The security guard moved to the side and let me dance on the stage for hours next to my DJ friend. All spotlights were directed on Paul and me. While I danced, it was as if nothing else mattered. The past, the present, and the future had no hold on me.

When he finished his set, he grabbed my hand and led me away. I was breathing heavily, still feeling the rush. We remained talking by the bathrooms where the noise was lessened, although we could still feel the bass in our chests. His full mouth was dangerously close to mine. He held me tight to his body and I ran my hand down his muscular back, feeling the sheen of sweat on his deep brown skin. "Let me get you a drink," he said in my ear.

"You know I don't like drinking alcohol."

"I'm not talking about that kind of drink," he replied.

He took my hand in his and walked me to a back room. Even though it was entirely dark, I could see as clearly as daylight. The room was empty but for two sofas that were positioned against the far wall. On one of them lay a man and straddling him was a young woman—a vampire. Soft moans escaped both their lips, and blood dripped down his neck. I stiffened. I wasn't shocked; such displays were often found in clubs. However, I wasn't ready for my thirst to resurface with such power.

"Is he willing?" I asked.

"Of course he is. I don't need the cops on my ass."

"Have a taste," the female said while getting off her meal, and I took a step back.

"I can't. I won't." I looked at Paul with pleading eyes.

"Oh, Alia, are you still on that vegetarian diet of yours?" He slowly brought me closer to the couches and sat me next to the limp man, who was barely conscious.

"When was the last time you actually fed off a human? Don't lie to me. I can sense your hunger; you reek of it. You need human blood and we're not talking about killing him. He willingly offered himself. It's like a donation!"

I found resisting had become an impossible task. I felt my composure slip before I even accepted what I was about to do.

"I won't be able to stop myself. It's been too long. I will kill him," I whined as I looked at the small streak of blood running down the man's throat. It smelled so good.

"I'll stay here and make sure that doesn't happen," he rebutted.

I searched for a way out of my predicament. I wished to find strength within myself but found none. Maybe a taste wouldn't hurt anyone. Finally, I let go of my principles and lashed out at the man's neck. I hoped I hadn't damaged him too much, but that was not my main focus at the moment. He tasted so good. He tasted... different? After a few minutes, I still could not quite place what the strange taste in my mouth was and pulled myself away.

"What the hell is in his blood?" I gasped, trying to regain my self-control.

"It took you longer to notice than I expected," Paul giggled and I noticed how out of it he sounded.

Then it dawned on me. "Heroin. You drugged me with heroin?" I exclaimed.

"It's alright, Alia, calm down. It'll be fun. Come here." He gently pulled me into his arms, licking the blood off the corner of my mouth.

"Fun?" I violently pushed him away. "I cannot lose control of myself! You don't know what happened the last time I tried heroin! This is not going to end well!"

I wanted to hurt him for drugging me, but I was becoming a danger to everyone, myself included. I ran for the door. Reality hit me as the club's lasers and strobe lights blinded me, and the music pounded in my head. I realized the drug was already taking effect. If I lost control, this place would become a blood-bath. No one would survive it. Everyone continued dancing, bodies against bodies, making it harder for me to leave. I tried my best to rush to the exit, literally shoving people out of my way, and once outside, I collapsed to my knees. My body felt heavy, and a nauseous feeling settled in my stomach. I was swaying. Heroin was one hell of a drug, one I never liked. I felt more powerful than usual, although my mind was in a complete mist.

One of the club's bouncers approached me. "Ma'am, are you alright?" he asked with concern on his face.

He lifted me in his arms before I had a chance to protest. My head rested on his shoulder and it only took a second for the demon in me to attack. The feeling of power washed through me as I sunk my teeth into his flesh; I felt as if I could break him like a twig. While vampires didn't have "fangs" as portrayed in the media, our teeth were still sharper than humans' and could cut through flesh easily. I somehow stopped myself before severely hurting the man and wobbled away.

I had already thrown up a couple of times, but the nausea wouldn't go away. I arrived in a park and collapsed. I itched all over and lying in the grass didn't make me feel better. Whenever I closed my eyes, I'd fall into horrible visions, and terrifying thoughts would materialize in my mind. I lay on my side, waiting for it all to end. I felt as though a dark figure was over me; I couldn't tell whether it was real or not. My head was a complete mess and I couldn't focus on one idea. The sun would rise in a few hours, and I would not be able to get into a covered area.

CHAPTER FOUR

1773

Being intimate with Malcolm was about the only time she felt connected to him anymore, the only time he did not make her feel dysfunctional. She wasn't simple-minded; she saw the red flags. She had thought being eternal with Malcolm would be different, that she'd get to live wild adventures and see the world, but instead he only craved violence against humans. What could she possibly do?

"Do you know who made you?" she asked with her head on his chest, playing with his hand, half expecting to receive no answer at all.

"Yes, of course. I was in love with her. She was a beautiful woman, but she died some time ago." Surprised to have gotten this much out of him, she decided to press her luck. "Who was she? Tell me about her." She couldn't help but feel jealousy at hearing him call another woman beautiful.

"She was a Hungarian countess. Do you know where that is?" She shook her head no. "A very far away place. She was strong-willed, with an iron fist and a powerful ruler. Her people didn't really understand what she was. They knew she was different, but the concept of a woman needing to drink blood to stay alive was so far out of reach for them that she was able to hide her nature for a long time. As her servants, we knew fully well what she was, and I became her main donor. Before that, I was a simple keeper of the flames. I cleaned the many chimneys, scrubbing the hearth. I was young and hoped she'd make me her count. But then, she became hungrier, and took to daughters of the lesser nobility who had been sent to the castle to continue their education. And when their daughters never returned home, questions were asked. She didn't believe humans and vampires could coexist and she didn't want to, so she didn't stop when it became suspicious. She knew what would happen before it did, and when her people came to arrest her, she knew she'd be executed. She asked me if I wanted to be turned and continue her work. I accepted, and here we are."

"When was that?" she whispered. "December 1610."

"What happened then?"

"All the servants, peasants, and other influential families she had taken care of for years testified against her. And I never saw her again. But I made her a promise and I work every day at keeping it."

"To continue her work? What does that mean?"

"Vampires are the top predators and until we are recognized as such, I will not rest. I came to the Americas in 1620 looking to conquer another side of the world."

"So, there are others like us across the world," she whispered, tucking that information away for a later time. "But are we alone here?"

"Oh no, vampires are everywhere, and I have met a few on this side. But none that I could imagine forming an alliance with. They're all too submissive, too afraid of humans to stand up and meet their calling." He said this with an air of disgust and disappointment.

"What is it you want?"

"I foresee us spreading like wildfire. Reaching and controlling all corners of the earth."

"But what if I don't believe in that? And I do want to coexist with humans?"

"Don't be foolish! It'd be like asking a lion to live with a sheep. No, I will teach you how to reach your full potential. You'll be a true queen and ruler by my side."

"If you hate humans so much, why did you stay with me for so long before I asked you to turn me?" Confusion seeped into her voice.

"You were never an ordinary human. The way you reacted to me was unlike anything I'd ever experienced before. Besides, you kept me fed and physically satisfied. Where else would I have gone?"

Was that it, really? She closed her mouth,

feeling like he would shut down any arguments she made. Was she being foolish? Was it such an abstract idea to live peacefully side by side with your food? Only taking what was necessary when necessary? She wondered again why she was so different from him— was she an abnormality?

"Will you try finding others who share the same mindset as us?" She really meant *as you.*

"I have given up on that idea. Instead, I'll create my own clan of like-minded individuals." He tightened his hand around hers and kissed it. "We're going to create an exclusive family."

"What if I don't want to? What if I'm happy with it just being the two of us?" She raised her head, sitting up. "We could leave here and see the entire world." She spoke quickly and excitedly. "I want to experience everything that's out there."

He sighed deeply. "Listen to me, Alia, because I won't repeat myself." He lifted her chin with his fingers, forcing her to meet his eyes. "I have worked too hard and too long for anything or anyone to affect my plans. You'll be a good girl and do as I say." His fingers hurt her face.

"And if I leave you?" she said in a strangled voice.

He barked a laugh. "Leave me? You? A new vampire? And where would you possibly go? Do you have any idea how dangerous it is out there for a lone vampire? You are helpless throughout the day and a perfect target for anyone who may suspect anything. You want to leave me? Then go." He released her and left the bed. "I won't stop you, but you will not be welcomed back here when you realize how stupid that mistake was. You'll be on your own."

"You'd rid yourself of me that easily?" She felt the tears rise and clenched the sheets to her chest.

"You're either with me or against me. Make your decision carefully."

She'd stay. Of course she'd stay. She had no money, no property, and as he mentioned, nowhere to go. Better to be with a crazed man than alone at everyone else's mercy. She could become who he needed her to be.

I drifted in and out of consciousness, unable to move. My mind kept going back to past events, although some part of me acknowledged I was in real trouble. My skin burned and I felt my flesh begin to peel, but the drug hadn't run its course through my veins yet. I became somewhat aware of a man kneeling next to me, studying me, and I tried focusing on his face, even though my vision blurred.

"Ma'am, are you alright? You need to wake up." He shook my arm lightly, but I couldn't move. He looked around, standing up and putting a hand in his hair. It appeared as though he considered going about his day and minding his own business, but then changed his mind. Covering my body as much as he could with his shirt and sweater, he carried me to his car where he laid me down on the backseat.

"No hospitals," I struggled to say. I wasn't sure if he heard me, but I knew hospital workers were sometimes very prejudiced towards my kind, and I'd have better odds anywhere else. As much as I tried staying alert, the car lulled me to sleep, and I lost track of where we were headed.

My mind went into a coma in order to regenerate itself, but I was well aware of some agitation around me. Eventually I awoke and found myself in an unfamiliar bedroom. I was lying on a bed, wearing the same clothes. It took me a few minutes to realize I was fully exposed to the sun. I let out a frightful scream and jumped up, looking for cover.

When the man entered the room, I was sitting in a corner, panting and covering my eyes. I had never been exposed to the full afternoon sun for more than a couple of minutes, and my eyes now burned and watered. I heard his heartbeat; the beast in me raised its head. The man took a remote control out of his pocket and electric shutters rolled down over the windows. I relaxed a little and rubbed my eyes. He stared at me for a while before finally speaking.

"I'm sorry about the light; I didn't expect you to wake so soon." His voice was deep and pleasant to my ears.

"Where am I?" I kept my eyes closed.

"I found you by the bay burning up, quite literally." I could hear the smirk in his voice. "You're safe here in my home."

"How long have I been unconscious?"

"Two days."

I opened my eyes and gazed at him intently, trying to sense the truth behind the cover. He smiled at me, a large, genuine smile, and touched his forehead.

"Don't bother; I learned to block my mind from vampires."

"Why are there UV filters on the windows?"

"Well, for occasions like this one."

I didn't like this game. "Who are you?"

"Rafael Dominicci. And you are?"

I waited to see if that was a joke. "Alia Henry."

He didn't seem to recognize my name, and I didn't know whether to be impressed or offended that he hadn't heard of me.

My body was stiff, and my burns cracked as I tried getting up by holding on to the wall. My legs gave out. The hunger struck me hard and fast.

"Oh hey, easy," he said, rushing to my side.

"No, stay away." I put my hand up, stopping him in his tracks. "I need to feed," I explained. "I don't want to hurt you." My head was spinning, and I focused on breathing deeply.

He exited the room while I tried to control myself, and then returned with a jar containing a red liquid. "It's pig's blood—take it," he said as he handed it to me.

I jerked away, accidentally causing him to drop the jug; blood splattered all over his clothes. He knew this wasn't good and made for the door. I caught his hand and sank my teeth deep into his forearm as I pinned him to the ground. He cried out in pain and fought to get me off. He was strong, but not strong enough. *Please stop, please stop,* I kept telling the beast. I abruptly came to my senses and released my hold while he pushed me off him. I fell back to my knees, trembling and shaking my head.

"I'm so sorry," I stammered. "I usually have control." He sat with his back against the wall, putting pressure on his arm with the other hand. I couldn't help but lick his blood off my lips. "You're bleeding. Let me help you."

"No," he quickly answered, getting up. "It's only a flesh wound. I can take care of it."

Walking out of the room, he closed the door behind him. I sat on the bed and tried to recollect my memory. I couldn't exactly remember all that had happened at the club, but I knew Paul drugged me. I looked down at my legs and noticed my burns were now completely healed. It was amazing what a little human blood could do. My attention returned to the young human in the house.

I peeked through the now half-opened door and followed the commotion downstairs. This was a big house. There seemed to be four rooms upstairs and other than framed paint- ings, there were no pictures on the walls. I made my way down the staircase, willing my feet to be quiet on the wooden floor.

The man was sitting in the kitchen, his back to me, and like a cat on the prowl, I slowly and noiselessly walked closer.

"There's more blood in the refrigerator if you'd like it," he said, turning around to face me.

"How did you know I was there?"

"I'm just a human with acute senses."

"You always keep blood in your fridge?"

"Of course not, that'd just be strange. I went to my butcher after I found you." That actually made sense.

"Am I your prisoner?"

"Prisoner?" He laughed. "You are a guest in this house."

"Then I may leave right now?"

"I suggest you wait until the sun sets."

I sat on a barstool across the island from him and didn't hide the fact that I was curiously inspecting the room. I liked the classic white design of this kitchen. The backsplash ceramic tiles were a nice touch. Maybe I should renovate the manor's interior to be more modern.

"Why did you help me?"

"A family member of mine was turned to vampirism when I was young. Human or vampire, anyone in trouble and helpless, should be lucky enough to receive help."

He was attractive, even to me: an oval face with light brown eyes and thick eyebrows. I found myself entranced when his full lips separated into a large smile. His dark hair was longer on the top and gelled messily. He wore a dress shirt, his broad chest straining against the fabric, but only the right sleeve had been rolled up to his elbow. His right forearm harbored a stained bandage, and I now noticed the medical supplies on the counter. My fault.

I scratched my throat, finding my voice. "Do you shelter vampires often? How do you know I won't try to kill you?"

"I'm hoping there is enough humanity left in you at this moment to realize that I saved your life."

His expectations of my kind were impossibly high. He bet too much on mutual respect.

"You're not meant to figure me out right now," he said. "But if you spend the evening with me, I promise to answer all of your questions."

"Spend the evening?" I repeated, and I couldn't contain the skepticism in my voice.

"Yes, would you like to join me for dinner?" He laughed wholeheartedly at my expression, which was undoubtedly dumbfounded. "I promise, no tricks. I just want to spend some time talking to you. I haven't been around a vampire in a long time."

I considered his invitation. Why not? This definitely broke the monotony. I nodded in agreement.

"I can't go dressed like this," I said, motioning to the dirty dress I had been wearing for two days now. He took my hand, leading me to a downstairs bathroom. I hadn't noticed how soft his skin felt when my teeth pierced it. Against the interior door hung a long and beautiful cocktail dress.

"Whose is it?" I asked, rubbing the soft material.

"Yours. I was hoping you'd accept my offer, and I went ahead and bought it. I think it's your size."

"So where are we going?"

"To a very refined restaurant I hope you'll like."

He left me to change, and I had to take a moment for myself; I didn't really understand what I was feeling at the moment. He was only a simple human, yet I felt attracted to him. I looked at my reflection; the little bit of blood I'd ingested had already brought some color back to my face.

"What am I doing?" I whispered to myself. This couldn't possibly end well.

I took a quick shower, enjoying the scalding hot water. My hair had been a mess to detangle thanks to lying on the ground all night. The new dress hugged my slim body in an amazing way. It uncovered my back and showed a great deal of cleavage, while the dark color emphasized my creamy complexion. I brushed my wavy hair with a hairbrush I found in a cabinet. My heels and purse had been placed outside the door.

Rafael was waiting for me in the kitchen again, sipping on wine. He had changed into black pants and a white button-up shirt paired with a black tie.

"Here's an appetizer." I politely but reluctantly accepted the blood served in a wine glass. "Is something wrong?" he asked.

"No. I just am not very hungry at the moment," I said, blushing. We both knew I wasn't hungry because I had attacked him. "I'm sorry about your arm. Does it hurt a lot?"

"It's actually not that bad." He continued drinking his wine, almost nonchalantly, as though having a vampire in his house was no big deal. I observed him.

"How old are you, Rafael?"

"Twenty-nine, and yourself?"

"I was turned at the age of twenty-three, but I was turned 249 years ago."

He was surprised and even choked a little. "I didn't think there were still vampires as old as you out there," he said, still coughing.

"Why not?" Let's see the extent of his knowledge.

"Most elders were murdered or killed themselves out of depression. Am I correct?"

"You're right, I am the last one." I wasn't looking for a pity party from him, but we needed to get off this subject. Silence lingered for a few uncomfortable minutes until he finally scratched his throat.

"Before we leave," he said, "I think we need to add something to your outfit."

I followed him back up the stairs to a room: his bedroom. I liked the dark paneled wood furniture. He walked to a dresser, opened a drawer, and took a box from it. He slowly pulled out a set of pearl earrings and a pearl necklace. They were breathtakingly beautiful. He motioned for me to come near him and carefully placed the jewels on my skin.

"Whose are these?" I asked, touching the necklace.

"They were my mother's. She passed away eleven years ago."

"I'm sorry for your loss" would have been the right thing to say, but this world wasn't a fair place, and we all had lost someone too early. I couldn't bring myself to say anything. I felt like an awkward silence settled over us, but he then took my hand in his and twirled me, scrutinizing me. Pleased with the result, he led me out of the house.

While I waited for him to pull the car around, I looked at the gorgeous and enormous oak trees in his driveway. What beauties. Nature always fascinated me. Evidently, this was my first breath of fresh air in a few days, and I enjoyed the dry, cold air.

I guess I should have been more worried about my club, but I didn't care much, and I knew George or Lidia would be able to handle it. This unforeseen turn of events was taking me away from my dull life. I felt a vibration in my purse and dug for my cell phone. I had thirteen notifications from missed calls and text messages from George and Paul. I would deal with Paul at a later time. I sent a quick text to my driver just so he wouldn't worry anymore: *I'm OK, will be home soon.*

I never had an interest in cars. However, I had plenty of time in my life to learn what I liked and didn't like. He drove a gray Maybach 57S Cruisero with a very charming coupe body style. It had a powerful motor I definitely liked. We both remained silent throughout the ride, but I didn't feel uncomfortable.

"The stars are bright tonight," I whispered.

I laid my head back and watched the landscape fly by on the curvaceous road. He valet parked the car and led me to the restaurant's entrance. Al Dente's lobby was overcrowded with some couples standing, while others sat at the bar patiently waiting for the next available table. I began walking towards the host stand, but Rafael grabbed my hand and showed me inside.

"Did you call ahead?"

"No." He smiled, still walking on.

"So we are just going to skip all these people?"

"Why not? I own the place." He flashed me with a dazzling smile. I was surprised and impressed. Now that I thought about it, I had read about this restaurant in the tabloids, from the quality of food and wide wine list, to the elite and famous eating here regularly. I didn't eat out often; too many restaurants did not cater to my kind.

The decorations, paintings, and photographs let me know how old the restaurant was. It was absolutely charming. A slow Italian serenade played in the background. Our table was a bit secluded from the rest and I looked around, taking it all in. The candle's light seemed to darken Rafael's eyes. They hypnotized me.

Our waitress introduced herself as Heidi, her smile too big and seemingly frozen on her face. She seemed nervous to be serving her boss and I sympathized with her. She was about to feel even more nervous when I told her of my dietary restrictions. She handed us menus and took Rafael's drink order, bypassing the etiquette of requesting the lady's first. Her uniform of a white blouse, dark pants, and an apron was immaculate.

"What do you have to drink that is vampire friendly?" I asked, attempting my best to look sweet and nonthreatening.

Her smile faltered slightly as her eyes grew wide. She quickly glanced at Rafael before smiling again.

"Oh, well, we have moose, pig, or deer blood you can choose from. All is fresh and acquired daily."

"Great, I'll take a demi glass of your deer blood." I was impressed she even used the "b" word. Most humans shrank just at the mention of it. I saw a little smile forming on the corner of Rafael's mouth.

"It's only a demi glass and if you must know, I hate pig's blood. It's too fatty," I whispered, leaning across the table.

He laughed and raised his hands in an apologetic manner. "I didn't say anything! Also, she's new," Rafael informed me with a flick of his eyes towards Heidi, who was retrieving our drinks. "I have a really good relationship with the employees, but she hasn't gotten to know me yet."

"Ah, yes, that must be the only reason she's so nervous," I teased.

The menu looked phenomenal, and I chose a steak tartare I couldn't wait to get my hands on. While regular food didn't taste like much to me, the closer it came directly from the animal, the more I would enjoy it. We conversed politely about the restaurant's success, of my art, which he had seen, but these unimportant subjects bothered me.

"The dress, the jewels, dinner... it's all very nice, but the only reason I agreed to come here was to get answers out of you," I said curtly, dabbing at my lips with a dark cloth napkin, making sure I had no blood on them.

"Is that the only reason?"

"What other reason would there be?"

A faint smile appeared at the corner of his mouth, but he remained quiet. "Fine, what would you like to know?"

"Tell me about you. How are you so familiar with vampires?"

He sighed. "When I was eight years old, my mother was turned into one. After that, she took care of me for ten years to the best of her ability."

"She raised you after she changed?"

"Yes. She never hurt me, but I can only imagine how hard it must have been for her. She never drank my blood or touched me."

I became very interested in his life story and I saw contentment in his eyes. Our food arrived, forcing us to pause our conversation momentarily. "Do you know who sired her?"

"I looked for him, but never found anything. He changed her right in front of me, but I never saw his face." His eyes were far away, and I knew he was reliving the memory.

"That's really horrible. How did she die?" He looked down. "I'm sorry, I shouldn't have asked," I backtracked. I almost laughed at us eating scrumptious food while talking about such a serious and sad topic.

"She killed herself after I turned eighteen. She left me the family's restaurant, this restaurant, knowing I'd have more than enough money to accommodate myself. I had all the documentation necessary to prove I owned it and then I just took it over."

"It must have been hard growing up in that environment."

He took a deep breath. "I was a very lonely kid. I lived a lie for a very long time, lying about my parents and making up a fantasy world where my dad was in the army and my mom was a stewardess. He was on base and she was up in the sky. I didn't feel human, but knew I wasn't a vampire. I had a massive identity crisis. Couldn't find my place in the world."

I felt compassion for him because these were feelings that I fought every day.

"On a lighter note," he said, chuckling and trying to ease the atmosphere, "we should order dessert. I hear they have one hell of a chocolate mousse here."

I laughed. However good desert might be, it would have very little taste to me, and I had to politely decline the offer.

"Don't you have questions for me?" I asked.

"I can tell there is something different about you, but I can't put my finger on it."

"I'm not just a normal vampire. I'm also a witch. I was a witch before being turned. My powers as a vampire are hard to control and unpredictable... It's as though they want to escape me, and I constantly have to reel them back in."

"What do you practice?" The fact that he didn't laugh or make mocking comments was impressive.

"I mix a bit of different practices. My beliefs are that objects, places, events, and beings leave a spiritual essence behind, past what the mortal world shows us. I can access those memories, reading them like a book. I am a nature worshipper; Mother Earth is my only God. I can refuel my energy with a walk through nature and I can manipulate the energy around me. I also believe Mother Earth leaves signs and omens, should we know how to read them."

"Manipulate energy—what does that mean?"

Instead of explaining, I thought a demonstration would be easier. I glanced at the tables around us, making sure no one was looking our way, and held my hand over the small candle's fire. I slowed my breathing down, closing my eyes, and felt the warmth enter my skin. My fingertips tingled as I absorbed the fire's power until it sputtered out. Turning my palm over, a glowing energy rose from my skin, and I morphed it into a sphere.

"That's incredible," he whispered. He attempted to touch it and was met by resistance, as though it was hard.

"I could always absorb and release energy to some degree, even before becoming a vampire. Now, it's magnified and dependent on whether I feed or not." It took all my focus to keep it going and I began feeling sweat dripping down my back. I closed my hand, releasing the energy with a sigh, and took some deep breaths.

"So, no levitation for you."

I smiled thoughtfully. "No, no levitation for me. I dabble in other practices, like spells and using the elements, but it really isn't my forte. I'm an energy witch. I feel the energy around me, which also comes off people. If someone's emotions are running very high, it creates an energy that I can feel."

"Like empathy?"

"Sort of. It has to be a really strong emotion."

"Can you feel what I'm feeling now?"

"No, but I'm guessing... excitement?"

"That's a lucky guess. My mother was also a practicing Wiccan."

"Really?" My interest was once more raised.

"I don't exactly know how powerful she was, but I remember she practiced it. She lost her powers when she became a vampire though. How did you manage to keep yours?"

"I am not sure. My powers just never went away."

"She really taught me how superior vampires are. How beautiful and fascinating your race is."

I immediately stiffened. "Are you some sort of vampire fanatic? The type of guy who wants nothing more than to be turned? Is that what you are?" I didn't bother hiding the annoyance in my voice.

"Of course not, I value my life. I just think it must be great being able to control your own mind and body as much as you do, to experience and see so much as well. You must know so much, have met so many people."

"Yeah, I showed a lot of control back at your house," I said laughing, then I paused. "Being a vampire isn't all that great. It gets extremely lonely."

"You don't have anyone special at home?"

"It's hard to meet someone who's not intimidated by my age

and power."

"I'm not intimidated, and you look pretty good for an old lady." We laughed.

"Well, you're also not a vampire."

"Does that really matter to you?"

For a moment I thought he was joking with me. I didn't understand how genuinely honest his question was, and how confused it made me feel. Attraction? It couldn't be—he was human. I had not dated a human since being turned. Messed around some, yes, but you didn't get too attached to your food.

He was in the mood to go dancing, and remembering how things turned out the last time I was at a club, I didn't particularly like the idea. However, I agreed to go just to spend more time with him. Like any other club in the city, this one was packed. As he danced a few inches behind me, I wished there was no space between us. His scent was so delicious, it drove me mad. He had released the knot in his tie ans looked terribly good in his clothes. I could smell his cologne above all the sweating bodies surrounding us. Then, suddenly, I felt his warm hands on my hips and his touch sent my heart racing. As we joined each other in rhythm, I wanted nothing more than for things to stay this way forever. Still behind me, he gently held my right hip and removed my hair off my collarbone with his left; the feeling was indescribable. I nearly lost control, and as I turned around, I realized how close our mouths were. Not to take possession of his lips was utter torture. I couldn't be with him, shouldn't be near him thinking these thoughts.

I let him drive me back to his house, not wanting the night to end.

"Would you like to join me for a swim?"

"I don't have a swimsuit," I replied and quickly damned myself for setting this up to potentially become a skinny-dip offer.

But like a gentleman, he didn't go that route. "I'm sure I can find a T-shirt and shorts for you to wear."

I smiled thoughtfully. "Then yes, I would love to," I simply said.

He dug into his bedroom closet, handing me a large shirt and shorts. After changing, I met him by the pool. Mountains surrounded us and the scenery was gorgeous. For the first time, I was able to see his body uncovered, and I was not disappointed. I saw his developed back muscles tense up as he entered the cold pool, and goose bumps formed all over his olive, tan skin. He splashed some water along his chest, the droplets sliding down the curves of his strong arms. As he turned around, I saw the deep lines of his stomach that plunged down below his bathing suit. Attraction, it definitely was.

"Aren't you going to get in?"

The question took me by surprise; I hadn't noticed how long I was standing there at the edge, staring at him. Without an answer and without a shiver, I slowly entered the icy water until I was submerged by it. He cautiously pulled me back to the surface, holding me tightly in his arms. The wind had picked up, forcing the trees to dance around. *Let go of your inhibitions*, it whispered. I didn't want to, did not want to let myself fall for a human.

Aggressively and sort of unexpectedly, he kissed me, pushing his tongue inside my mouth. The aggression completely turned me on and as he held me tighter in his arms, I felt him grow thicker against my body. I moved my face away from his; I had to stop this. He deserved a better fate than anything I could possibly give him.

"I'm sorry," he whispered. "That was completely inappropriate of me."

"I think it's too late for me to call a cab; the sun will rise soon," I said. "Could I stay in your guest bedroom?" His taste was still in my mouth. He nodded. It was definitely not too late to call a cab, but I didn't want to go home yet and wanted to sort through these feelings. "If you'll excuse me, I think I'll retire now," I replied as I rushed out of the water and into the house.

I found a clean shirt in the spare bedroom's closet that I wore as pajamas with my underwear. I took a shower watched some of the sunrise through the UV filter windows. The brightness made my eyes water and burn; I struggled to keep them open, but it was so beautiful. I don't know why I hadn't made the decision to get these windows installed at the manor yet. They were a relatively new invention and I guess I hadn't fully trusted them to work, but clearly it was time to make the switch.

I sat on the bed, loneliness and shame slowly creeping in. Malcolm had done a number on me. Over 150 years of feeling unequivocally unworthy of the man I had loved. And for a while, I had felt as though sex was the answer, that it would fix everything that was wrong in my relationship... until it became clear there was no fixing it. I was free of that man, but the damage remained and would turn up as anxiety when I met someone new. For Christ's sake, how long would I let Malcolm ruin me? I took a deep breath, getting up and deciding to knock on Rafael's door.

He was lying on his bed, shirtless, watching the news.

"Do you mind if I lie next to you?" I could make baby steps.

"Not at all." He tapped the bed next to him.

He moved over and let me settle down. He put his arm across my waist and sighed. I quickly fell asleep, feeling comfortable and at peace. A sleep without nightmares and without visions.

The night had fallen once more by the time I awoke. Rafael was next to me.

"I like this," he said.

I looked at him and smiled. "I haven't slept this good and this much in a long time." We kept eye contact for a moment, knowing our time together was coming to an end; I had to return home.

"You seem guarded," he said. "You've probably heard it a million times before, but I wouldn't hurt you."

I didn't respond. I went back to the guest room and changed. I didn't give us a chance to have another meal together and I sensed his heart accelerating when I called a taxi immediately. I gathered my few belongings and we remained silent as we waited outside for the yellow vehicle to arrive. The air was filled with tension and nerves. When the cab finally arrived, I awarded Rafael a faint smile before stepping away. He walked me down his driveway, then held the car door open and handed me a piece of crumpled paper with his number.

"I would like it if you called me," he whispered in my ear, and I wondered how long he had been holding on to it. I wanted to kiss him again, feel his lips on mine once more, but I didn't.

"I think I can manage to call you," is all I said, and we both knew we'd see each other soon. Fate wouldn't have it any other way.

We texted about our days before going to bed, but weeks passed before I saw him again. In the meantime, I kept my eyes on the news as more bodies were discovered around town and other vicinities. I did not want to get involved. I wanted to let the police do their job, but what the heck was happening?

Rafael coincidentally happened to arrive at my club on a Friday night with a group of friends. I was standing in the DJ booth when I immediately smelled and saw him enter. Our gazes crossed and I climbed down to meet him.

"Fancy seeing you here," he shouted over the music.

"I was wondering when you'd finally come find me. I own the place, after all."

"You own this?" His turn to be surprised.

"You really have never heard of me before, huh?" I half teased; I was still kind of shocked by it.

He took my hand, guiding me back towards his friends, who seemed uncomfortable in making my acquaintance. I couldn't hide that I was a vampire. They followed me into the VIP area where I offered them bottles of our most expensive liquor, and that seemed to buy their friendships. Eventually, I was able to snatch Rafael away.

"Come with me," I whispered in his ear.

The very top floor was closed off to the public for the night due to restorations; we would be left in peace. The open rooftop let the breeze caress our burning skin. The lights were off, but our faces were alight with the glow from surrounding buildings. We slow danced to our own personal songs and talked for hours. I couldn't help but notice he left his mother out of the conversation, and of course I did the same with Malcolm. Our pain was too deep to share this early on in whatever our relationship was.

"I read online there's going to be a ceremony in your honor next year," he said.

"So, you have heard of me!"

He shrugged and laughed. "I may have looked you up after you left my house, but I promise, I did not know you owned this!"

I smiled, then took a deep breath, returning to his question. "I received a letter in the mail about it. The government wants to hold a ceremony at the Capitol to honor me for the help I provided in establishing vampire rights. A big ceremony to be televised or something. I don't know how I feel about it, to be quite honest."

"I would have thought you'd be happy."

"I just don't feel like I truly deserve it." He made a disbelieving sound and I elaborated. "I've lived a long, long time and it would be naive to think I've always been this committed to human-vampire equality. Quite the contrary, actually."

"From what the article said, you've led the way for vampire reformation. Who cares what you've done centuries ago? It's about what you're doing for the future of both our species." I didn't say anything. "I'm curious though, where else have you lived?" he asked to keep the conversation going.

"I have actually lived most of my life around here. I had my home built on my vampire birthplace. The symbolism was too big for me to pass up that opportunity." We were now sitting close in a semicircular booth, the leather squeaking underneath us as we leaned into each other. "I spent a long time in the South of France watching over my brother's family. I also spent a long time in Italy and Spain." I looked at the stars. "I've traveled a lot looking for beauty."

"What do you consider beautiful?"

"Nature: mountain tops, rivers, forests," I said while feeling some heat rise to my cheeks. "I'm very connected to nature."

"I think you're beautiful, the most beautiful girl I've ever seen." He gently kissed me on the lips, holding my chin, and I let him. "Have you ever been to Breckenridge?" I shook my head no. "I would really like to bring you if you'd let me. I spent some time there when I was a teenager—you would love it."

Eventually he had to meet back with his friends who were ready to leave; some seemed annoyed with him for ditching them. I didn't want him to go, but I also didn't want to appear clingy. As old as I was, I had kept mostly to myself, not allowing too many relationships to take my energy after Malcolm. This was new territory and it terrified me.

CHAPTER FIVE

1775

Alia knew Malcolm was testing her at every turn, and she was beginning to understand how to behave to avoid his anger. He had expected her guilt and humanity to progressively vanish over the years, as he assured her happened with most vampires, but three years after her transformation, that was far from being the case. If she hoped to avoid conflict between them, she had to lie. She had to pretend. She had to hide her feelings and emotions behind a stone wall.

Yet, she also wondered what was wrong with her and why she felt so differently from her creator. The cruelty he exercised was unlike anything she had ever witnessed from him when she was a mortal. She was also starting to wonder if she'd ever be enough for him. He spent five years with her as a mortal and he had made her, yet she felt as though she always fell short of his expectations. Would it have been better to die in that barn? Did he regret his decision and wish the same? So she kept her thoughts to herself and did as she was told. The killing. The torturing. The feeding. All of it, just to keep the peace while slowly shutting down a bit more each time.

The Revolutionary War had just kicked off and Malcolm was giddy with the idea of lives being lost on the daily.

"I've seen wars in my home country before. No one will pay attention to what we do and who disappears."

And she allowed him his whims, if only to not be on the receiving end of his disapproval. They traveled across the land, begging for shelter within good-natured family homes before moving on to the next town, their bellies full. Mothers, fathers, children—none escaped them. And she let him perform all these atrocities, joining in and losing herself a bit more each day.

The following week, I met Rafael at the airport very early in the morning and we flew to Colorado for a quick weekend. We landed first in Denver, then rented a car and drove the ninety miles to our next destination, about an hour and fifty minutes away. I offered to pay the extra fee for getting a car with darkened windows, but Rafael wouldn't allow it and put the charge on his credit card. He connected his cell phone to the car's Bluetooth and put on a playlist he had created on his Google music: a good mixture of classic and hard rock and songs ranging from the 60s to the 80s.

I read off the playlist's artists. "Journey, Def Leppard, Blackhearts, Guns N' Roses, Mötley Crüe, Bon Jovi, Lynyrd Skynyrd, AC/DC...How old are you again?" I teased.

"Hey now, they are classics."

"I know, I'm just kidding. I love classic rock. I approve of this playlist."

He exhaled loudly. "I was actually really anxious for you to judge my music. Music tells so much about a person, you know? And you've been around for all of it!"

I laughed, leaning back and singing softly. Known for its ski resorts, Breckenridge, Colorado was described all over the internet as "a beautiful mountain town surrounded by scenic beauty," and that was putting it lightly. It was the height of fall and the temperature was chilly, even cold, and it had the driest desert mountain air I had experienced in a long time. I rummaged through my purse for some chapstick and mentally patted myself on the back for having the foresight to bring a tube. I offered Rafael some, which he gladly accepted after drinking some water he had bought at a gas station. He had told me the sudden elevation change could be tough to handle and staying hydrated was important to not get sick; I didn't bother explaining the elevation wouldn't affect me at all. The sky was extremely overcast. Walking around was no issue for me with big, black sunglasses covering half of my face and a cute olive-green fedora protecting the rest of it.

We walked down the colorful main street, my arm linked through his, window shopping and enjoying each other's presence. I could hear live music being played from rooftops and it really set the evening's mood.

"How long did you live here?" I asked, checking out a shirt on display with a Sasquatch "we believe" slogan. I chuckled and put it down.

"We moved here when my dad died, but we never stayed too long in one place because of... what she was. We were here about a year. I remember it as being the best time of my childhood. Who wouldn't be happy in a place like this, you know? And for a while, I almost let myself believe we'd settle here for good."

We continued our visit by the Riverwalk, following alongside the river and enjoying the mountain views. We sat down for a moment, listening to the rushing water and breathing the dry but fresh air. He led me to a trailhead and assured me the surprise would be worth the short hike in my low ankle boots. It indeed was worth it and much more. I was introduced to Isak Heartstone, a fifteen-foot wooden troll sculpture, and I laughed at the randomness of this being here.

"This hadn't been sculpted yet when I lived here," he said, laughing at my delight. "It was constructed in 2018." I was grateful to experience this with him.

When night began to fall, we took the chair lift and we saw the town's lights click on one by one. I got to see the entire city from above. It was magically beautiful but too short of a ride.

"I have another surprise for you," he said kissing the top of my hand as we got off the lift and checking his watch.

He led me back to our parked car and drove us out into the

mountains, refusing to answer my questions. He only assured me I would love it. The light was fading rapidly, but everything was covered in white and reflected the rising moon. He brought us to a snowmobiling lodge. I had never been on a snowmobile before, and I was excited to experience something new with him. We entered the warm, wooden cabin where the staff received us as thought they were expecting us.

"Welcome, Mr. Dominicci and Ms. Henry. We are excited you could join us tonight," greeted a small woman behind the front desk.

I then realized this was after hours and they were still opened just for us.

"They normally only allow guided tours during the day, but I convinced them to let me rent one machine for the next hour, just the two of us," he whispered in my ear. I could only guess he had tipped them tremendously well.

The staff handed us insulated boots, ski goggles, ski suits, helmets, and a pair of mittens each. They walked us around back to where the dormant machines were lined up and gave Rafael the keys. They quickly went over driving instructions which he brushed off, saying riding a snowmobile was like riding a bike.

He swung his legs around the first machine he saw and I followed his lead, snuggling close behind him. Rafael gave it some gas; the engine woke with a loud revving sound, and we were off. The snowmobile accelerated much faster than I thought it could. This was exhilarating.

"Lean into the turns with me," he shouted over the noise.

We rode up the mountain and since I didn't have to keep my eyes on the trail, I was able to enjoy the breathtaking views of the peaks. Most of my face was covered by the goggles and the helmet, but I felt the wind whip the little bit of unprotected skin and I loved it.

We stopped atop a peak and looked down at the valley. We could see downtown Breckenridge in the distance with its tiny lights. And when I looked above at the sky, the stars were twinkling so brightly it took my breath away. What a rush! I felt so alive.

"Switch positions with me," he said. "It's my turn to hold you now."

My boots sunk slightly in the powder, and I loved the crunching noise my footsteps made.

I felt like a child and wanted to jump up and down, hearing the snow crunch again and again. But I didn't and settled between Rafael's legs. He rested his chin on my shoulder and breathed deeply.

"Do you love it?"

"I do. Best surprise yet." I leaned into his body, loving the pressure of his arms around my waist.

"I'm surprised you've never made your way here before," he said.

"I devoted so much of my time to helping vampires be known to the world that I didn't allow myself time for anything else really."

Now that the engine was off, I could hear the wind blowing through the trees, making them creak as though they wanted to share their secrets.

"I understand why you loved living here. I love it. Nature is a part of everything this town is," I whispered, leaning my head against his chest.

We took in the beauty of our surroundings in peaceful silence for a while, enjoying each other's company. He kissed my cheek sweetly. "Alright, we should head back. I think we've already gone over our time."

We returned to our original positions and headed back to the lodge. We decided on dinner and had somewhat of a good dining experience at a beautiful, progressive, cabin-like restaurant that accommodated vampires. It would have been a wonderful time but for our waitress being so enthralled by Rafael's charm that she completely ignored me, never speaking to me directly. The sheer disrespect was something I had a hard time waving off. While Rafael ate, I sipped a darkened glass of blood, thanking the moose's essence I was deeply appreciating. I thought it was especially smart of this establishment to have darkened glasses to keep liquids inconspicuous.

We drove to our resort but learned there had been a double booking and they did not have an available room for us. I felt I was getting to know Rafael on a deeper level by seeing how he responded to obstacles and how he dealt with people. He never seemed to get mad; he was an "accidents happen" kind of guy. With our flight being at eleven a.m. the next day, we decided to start heading back towards the airport and find lodging on the way.

We stayed in a small hotel room that desperately needed redecorating. The carpet was old and smelled awful. The walls should have long ago been repainted, and the one bed's sheets weren't to be trusted. The only secure room was the bathroom, and that wasn't saying much.

"Believe it or not, they described this online as a decent hotel," he apologized, and I nervously chuckled; this place was a dump.

The silver lining was a pretty nice wooden Jacuzzi that was conveniently available. I checked the water—it smelled and looked clean enough. I hadn't thought of bringing a swimsuit and found myself in my bra and Victoria's Secret cheeky panties. I definitely did not mind seeing him bare chested again. The Jacuzzi's water was lit from the inside with a blue light, making the jets and flowing water look like the ocean.

We sat on opposite ends of the tub, heads back, and looked at the sky.

"Come over here," he said affectionately, bringing my attention back to him.

And as much as I wanted to, as much as I knew it would be okay and he would treat me with respect, I couldn't get my body to obey. I looked down at the blue water and willed my body to move. He saw this and watched me inquisitively.

"Tell me what happened to cause this mental block."

"I..." I couldn't even get the words out. My breath was stuck in my throat; my heart began hammering against my chest. *I was horribly abused for years by the man I loved and should have left so long ago and I let it ruin me.* Why couldn't I just say those words?

"Okay," he quickly amended. "Tell me what feelings come over you when I want to get close to you."

I exhaled loudly. That I could answer. "Excitement. But then panic, anxiety, pressure, fear." I avoided looking directly at him.

"What if I said we didn't have to do anything at all? Actually, what if I told you I didn't want to do anything?" I half smiled. "I'm in no rush. You can set the pace. You can let me know when and if you are ready, and I won't try anything out of place without your permission until then. Does that sound good?"

I nodded, feeling relief wash over me.

"Do you want to come sit over here?"

I walked through the water and settled next to him, putting my head on his shoulder and feeling my body relax into his.

"Can I kiss you? Nothing more, I promise."

His lips were once again on mine, soft and gentle. His hand slid around my back, bringing me closer, and he rested his other across my cheek. It gave me butterflies. When he pulled away, he laid a kiss on my forehead and leaned his head against mine, sighing deeply.

"Have you ever been in love?" I asked after a moment of contented silence.

"Yes, once," he answered.

"What happened?"

"It was hard being with anyone when my mother had to remain a secret. Have you?"

"Yes, once."

"And what happened?"

"He ruined me mentally, physically, and emotionally for far too long."

Rafael closed his arms around me, holding me tight, and I breathed in his lovely scent.

"Have you ever been with a vampire?" I asked.

"No, but I can't imagine your needs are much different than a human woman's."

"Well, I can think of one..."

"I don't think that'll really be an issue. We can keep you nice and fed. I mean, humans also get hangry you know," he said, laughing.

Although we had already lain in a bed together, he insisted on being chivalrous and sleeping on the pull-out couch. It looked old, uncomfortable and made noises each time Rafael moved. During the night, I got up and gently shook him awake.

"What is it? What's wrong?" he asked, worried.

His hand was on my mine and it sent a jolt to my numb heart. I showed him to the bed where I cradled myself against him, following the shape of his body. He put his arm across my waist and nuzzled his face against my neck. I appreciated that he didn't pressure me into anything further and soon fell asleep.

The following morning, we got back on a plane and headed

home. He held my hand the whole way and I wondered if he even noticed the coldness of my skin. When he drove me home and stopped the car outside my mansion, I knew he wanted to come in, but I just wasn't ready to open up that much. His eyes pierced mine with longing, and then he softly placed a kiss on my cheek. I exited the vehicle and walked into my house, holding my breath for a moment.

I heard a chime from my cell phone, letting me know I had received a notification. I expected to see Rafael's name but was surprised to see Detective Thompson's. He had texted me a news article about multiple corpses having been found a few states over.

We just found a fresh victim in town yesterday. This vampire either moves fast, or there's more than one, he sent.

I stared at the message; my breath caught in my throat. My mind blanked and I stood frozen. My past came back in rapid memories. How was there more than one? Where had they been hiding? I blinked a few times, scratching my throat, and texted back. *Let me know how I can be of help.*

His answer came quickly: *We have multiple teams tracking it/them. But I wanted to keep you updated.*

I put my phone back in my purse, exhaling slowly, glad I still did not have to get involved.

Over the next few weeks, Rafael and I talked daily but didn't see each other a whole lot since our Colorado escapade. We were busy with our respective jobs and responsibilities and it seemed our schedules couldn't align. It was foolish to fall so fast for anyone, but I longed for him.

The weather forecast for the evening was cloudy with a chance of rain, so I called Rafael and asked him to stop by. I figured it would only be fair to show him a place dear to my heart. I met him at the property's gates, a rose in hand. It had been just over a week since I had last seen him, and I watched him get out of his car. He looked good in blue jeans and a simple white T-shirt. I was definitely excited to spend the evening with him.

He gave me a curious look. "We're not going in, are we?"

"Not today."

I began walking into the wilderness, knowing he was right behind me. While he was carefully avoiding thorns and branches, none of it bothered my skin, and I walked right through them.

"Where are we going?" he asked, slightly annoyed by the unpredictable hike into the woods.

"We're almost there," I assured him.

The thick trees around us slowly opened up to a field. Time had surely taken a toll on the barely visible grave, which stood in the middle. The engraved markings were no longer visible. Rafael hadn't noticed and looked around.

"Why are we stopping now?"

"We have arrived," I responded. "I really should take the time and order another headstone."

"Yes," he said slowly, noticing the one in the clearing. "This one seems old. Who's in there?"

"This is where I buried my father over two hundred years ago." I sat down in the grass and he followed my lead. "But as you can tell, I haven't been here in a long time." I brushed the growing plants off the stone and placed my rose there.

He took my hand in his. His eyes were soft and friendly.

"I wanted to show you perhaps the most influential place in my life."

He raised my hand to his lips and gently kissed it, letting me know he was here for me.

"Tell me more about your father," he said.

"It's been so long; the memories are faded. I don't exactly remember his face or the sound of his voice." I was submerged in melancholy. "He was a good man; he loved me and my brother infinitely. My mother died when I was very young and I don't remember her at all. But he would tell us stories to keep her spirit alive. No matter the day or time, he'd work the farm so we'd never go hungry. He wanted me to have a good life." I scoffed and traced the stone's faded markings. I often tried to remember the details of his face and the sound of his voice, but it had been centuries, and my memory faltered. My, how things should have been different. I scratched my throat. "We should go," I said. "It's about to pour."

We couldn't get back before the rain started falling and his grumpiness amused me. We laughed for a moment by the gates as we continued getting wet.

"Come have a cup of coffee with me," he said while playing with my hand.

"I don't drink coffee," I replied, wiping water out of my eyes.

"I know, but you could watch me drink it. Spend a bit more time together."

"Alright."

He opened the vehicle door for me to sit in, wet and all, and I briefly thought he was overdoing it. He took his shirt off before getting in and I was okay with that. Coffee at his house sitting on a couch by the fireplace was very cliché. Nonetheless, it was very nice and romantic.

He had given me a large shirt to change into as my clothes dried by the fireplace. We cuddled and played with each other's hands, hair, mouths. I felt an easiness around him I hadn't felt around a man in a long time. I wanted him. I wanted to plow through my emotional barriers and lead a normal life with no trauma. One thing led to another, and he tenderly kissed my lips while moving on top of me. Clothes hadn't been removed yet, but he rubbed himself against me and I could feel him grow thicker. He removed my shirt and panties, pinning my wrists above my head, watching me. I could have easily thrown him off but had no intentions of doing so, and I let him study me, although I felt a little self-conscious. Since I hadn't asked him to stop, he brought his mouth to my mouth, then my nipples, licking, teasing. He rubbed his hand over my stomach, slowly but surely making his way further down. He seemed to move gradually as though he expected my consent to stop at any second. I was enjoying his touch, the sensations I hadn't felt in too long. He then inserted a finger inside me. Small gasps escaped my lips as he gently moved in and out of me, stroking my clit simultaneously. I was close to orgasm but didn't want to come this way and I removed his outfit with quick movements. I took a moment to look at this beautiful man standing naked in front of me, his defined torso, muscled stomach, his excitement for me clear as day. I grabbed the length of him, moving my hand up and down his shaft and making him moan. His eyes searched my face for any sign that I was not alright going further. When he found none, he pushed me back on the couch, spreading my legs apart. He stood over me, giving me one more chance.

"Please," I said, almost begging.

"Are you sure?"

I nodded vigorously, and with a twirl of his hips, he inserted himself inside of me. I gasped and clawed at his back, leaving red marks on his skin. Both moaning and sweating, our bodies rocked into a systematic rhythm. As I felt the orgasm about to burst through me, I wrapped my legs tighter around his waist. Finally, with pleasure overwhelming me, I took possession of his mouth, exploring every corner of it, and nibbled on his lips. My breath came out in short gasps as he plunged deeper and faster. I held on to his back, scratching it. I hid my face against his neck to keep myself from screaming out. It felt so good it was almost unbearable. I could feel his pulse against my cheek and I tensed, feeling the blood drain from my face.

"What's wrong?" he asked.

"Your blood... it's torture."

He stopped moving for a moment, "Go ahead; drink me." I shook my head. "I trust you. Please, go ahead."

I opened my mouth and closed it on his chest, puncturing the skin as he resumed thrusting into me. I drank his essence for a few minutes, and he had no idea how close I was to killing him, how the beast in me didn't want me to stop. I raised my head with a gasp.

Unexpectedly and forcefully, he bit me right above my left breast, hard enough to break the skin, and sucked a very little amount of blood out. I lay underneath him, unable to move, half due to the pleasure and half due to the shock I was in. He had just finished the connection ritual as he released himself inside me. We shared our memories, visions flashing before our eyes of each other's lives. We were forever joined to one another. He kissed his way to my mouth as he slowly pulled himself out of me.

"What were these images?" he asked.

"My life," I murmured.

"I didn't think anything would happen if I tasted your blood. Am I...?"

"Going to turn into a vampire? No, you'd have to lose most of your blood and drink a lot more of mine. We are just linked now."

He frowned and I watched him. He did not understand what he had just done. He did not comprehend what he forced onto us, and like it was no big deal, he kissed me once more and went to the bathroom. I couldn't believe what had just happened. He had bound himself to me. He now belonged to me, his mind, body, and soul. I could control him like a puppet if I wished to. I began to get angry. I liked being independent, and now I had a human to worry about, to take care of. This was a lifetime commitment I wasn't ready for. What happened to asking for permission?

I couldn't deal with this at the moment and chose not to. I quickly put my clothes on and quietly left the house without a word to him. I walked a good amount of the way under the rain before calling George to pick me up, telling him which road I was on. My phone buzzed incessantly from Rafael's calls and texts and when I finally picked up, I was ready to blow up.

"What happened? Why did you just leave?" he asked with worry in his voice.

"Rafael, what you did, connecting yourself to me like that, is not okay. I am not okay with what happened. You said you wouldn't try anything out of place, but that was out of place. And I know I'm the first vampire you've been with, that no one explained to you how things work so you don't realize the implications, but I need time to process how I'm feeling with this. Please stop calling me."

"I'm so sorry..."

I turned my phone off and continued walking alongside the road until George retrieved me.

CHAPTER SIX

1779

Malcolm wanted her to be ruthless and view humans as lower creatures but truth be told, Alia did not like what she had become from the very beginning. They were nomads, had been traveling the land for a couple of years now and taking whatever pleased them along the way. He taught her to trust her animal instincts, but it seemed her humanity would not diminish. She almost wanted it to, just so she could match what was expected of her. He didn't share with her what he was searching for, and she had learned that asking him to open up about his plans would just upset him. So, she just followed along.

"You are a queen in this world," Malcolm said. "I will get you everything your heart desires." He gently kissed the top of her hand. "Are you hungry?" he asked.

"Famished."

"Good answer."

"Where are you leading me?"

He walked her deep into the forest. She had not bathed in some time, as Malcolm constantly had them moving from town to town; she currently was covered in mud and dried blood. She didn't look or feel like a queen. Alia didn't mind being dirty. She had never had the luxury of prestigious clothing or the privilege of bathing daily to begin with, but she was surprised Malcolm paid so little attention to his appearance. They marched until they reached a colonial mansion. The columns holding the roof up must have been thirty feet high, and the wooden front door was massive.

"Where are we?" she whispered.

"Our new home."

"But, my lord, the people inside…"

"Food, Alia. I'm getting tired of having to repeat myself on the subject. They are food and nothing more." His lips curled up in distaste.

She didn't dare state her mind; she knew how he'd react. He knocked on the front door, which was opened by an enslaved girl. He threw himself at her throat before Alia could even register it, then let her bleed out to the side and entered. Alia followed him inside, unsure whether to indulge or listen to her conscience. She let him have his fun and knowing he expected her to help kill, did so reluctantly. She was always surprised at how wonderful blood tasted, and in that moment, she couldn't conceive of refusing herself the pleasure.

She then looked through the house for the

Lady's bedroom, paying little attention to the screams and shouts. Was that a gunshot? She shook her head in disbelief. Humans always fought so hard. She didn't want to be a monster, but she didn't mind having the chance to obtain things she never had during her human life. She inspected the wardrobe, which was filled with corsets and dresses that fit her, although she would have to acquire new shoes.

She quickly washed herself and walked back downstairs wearing her new garments as Malcolm was finishing his last meal.

"Now you look like a true queen," he said.

All were slain, with the exception of the girl who had opened the door, who was now gasping on the floor. She held a hand to her neck, blood seeping through her fingers, while trying to crawl out of the door.

Malcolm approached her slowly, a small, condescending smile on his face. He grabbed her by the hair and dragged her back inside.

"I'll kill you!" she screamed, unafraid.

Alia liked her fire. She could tell this girl was a fighter and she could use a friend like her. Alia felt alone, in love with a power-hungry vampire. She wanted, no *needed*, a friend and a confidante. She wanted this girl to be like her.

She had never sired anyone before, and Malcolm reluctantly shared his secret. Teaching her things that could make her independent of him always seemed to bother him.

"You must exercise control and drink until they

are on the brink of death. You must never share your blood unless they have fully approved of the transition first." Something flashed across his eyes, a memory perhaps.

"How much of my blood is needed?"

"You'll know when it's enough. You'll feel it."

Elizabeth rose within twenty-four hours. Her skin was warm brown and as smooth as glass. Her dark hair curled down to her shoulders, and her almond-brown eyes pierced through the night. As afraid as she had been of them, Elizabeth quickly learned Alia was the lesser evil of the two, and they had better stick together to survive Malcolm's antics. Although both women were beautiful, they were complete opposites. They became closer than sisters, sharing thoughts and feelings. Malcolm, however, didn't particularly like Liz and was extremely cruel to her on more than one occasion. This was a side of Malcolm that Alia had never witnessed before.

He was the pack leader. He was cold, strong, and ruthless. He installed a strong sense of fear within the girls. Neither one of them could ever stand up to him. It had to be his way or no way at all; he could destroy them at any time. They had no free will; they were his.

I woke up with an excruciating migraine and groaned into my pillow. I hadn't been able to get a good night's sleep since I left Rafael's side. An irritating result of being bound to someone: you couldn't bear being separated. I knew he was feeling despair and was as restless as me. I missed his presence because he made me feel young and safe. I expected him to be home, but couldn't be sure of his whereabouts, and it made me nervous. I now had the urge to protect him as well. His soul wouldn't be at ease until he found me again, but I didn't care. Well, I did, but I didn't want to.

As I entered the kitchen, heading for the fridge, Lidia told me he stopped by the house while I slept, only to be turned away. He hadn't asked for my permission before joining himself to me and he would have to pay the price. I sat at the counter filling a plastic cup with blood, then put my head in my hands and groaned some more.

"You can't avoid him or turn him away forever, you know. This needs to be handled." Lidia smiled in her glass.

"I know, I just don't want to handle it *right now*."

I had to keep myself occupied so I wouldn't think of him. Suddenly, I remembered I needed to have a serious talk with my ex, Paul, and hopefully that would take up most of my day. I rehearsed what I would say to him about drugging me and leaving me to die, getting progressively madder. My whole current predicament was because of Paul and if I could take it out on him, I would.

I waited until the sun had completely set before heading over to his apartment. I ran up his building's staircase, taking two stairs at a time, then stopped abruptly. His front door was slightly opened, which was strange and unusual, and my senses flared up as I cautiously stepped inside.

"Paul?" I called out. "Are you here?"

The place was a complete mess: chairs were overturned, the dining table was crushed to the floor, and broken vases and other decorative items were scattered all over. I guessed a fight had broken out. The air was thick and putrid with the smell of death, and I could feel a presence watching me. I gasped, finding Paul's mutilated body on the kitchen floor, and put my hand to my mouth. He had clearly been bled dry by an Astaroth. I began to shake, my muscles tensing with the need to bolt. Still, I glanced around, looking for any indication of whether the creature was still here.

A low, hungry growl came from behind me. I slowly turned around, my heart beating frantically, and came face to face with an Astaroth vampire. Astaroths couldn't even be considered as part of our species. They were brutal, soulless creatures, vampires who had completely lost their humanities. They were what all vampires became over time once they let their inner demons win fully. The gray and decaying corpse that must once have been a man held an old shirt of mine in his claw, brought it to his face, and smelled it. It then charged me much faster than I anticipated, knocking me down. I held his claws away from my face while trying to get him off me. I felt his teeth penetrate my forearm and I cried out while my own blood dripped down on me. A fiery yet numbing feeling began to spread up my arm. I used the power in my legs to kick him in the chest and while he crashed to the floor, I ran out the door using all the speed a vampire had. Still running, I chanced a glance behind my back and as though I had imagined the whole thing, the Astaroth was no longer there. My arm was still bleeding freely and proof enough it had actually happened, but I had almost doubted it for a second.

My mind was so preoccupied I drove home like a maniac, slamming down on my horn and constantly checking the rearview mirror to see if I was being followed. The dual front door banged open as I ran inside the manor, a trail of blood following me, and I began rummaging through the kitchen for any first aid kit.

"What happened?" Lidia gasped, out of breath from running down the stairs. Maybe seeing this much blood was a bit shocking as well.

She sat me down on a wooden chair and began cleaning my wounds. "Someone had to have been behind this. Astaroths are barbaric beings; they can't think for themselves." My mind was reeling. "It's as though it was looking for me."

I called Detective Thompson, leaving him a voicemail about Paul's body being found and a possible rogue vampire on the loose. I did not want my name tied to this and hoped the Astaroth would be long gone, but I knew my blood was all over the scene. They'd just have to run it in their database.

This couldn't be happening again, not after what had happened to my clan, my family. What the hell was going on? I checked in with the police a few hours later and was informed Paul's body had been retrieved and any family would be contacted shortly.

Meanwhile, I could feel Rafael stirring. He was restless and I ached for him as well. I longed to touch him. I needed to be in his arms, and I missed his lips. Without him near me, I felt empty and sad. I was barely able to think of anything or anyone else. He was so close to me, yet so far away. For both our sanities, we had to be near each other. I was annoyed that while I should have been worried about the events that took place today, I was more concerned about Rafael.

CHAPTER SEVEN

2000

S now was falling heavily on the city of Manhattan for this holiday season. There had been a storm warning, and not a soul could be found outside. The light was dim inside an apartment as a mother laid her small boy to sleep while humming a tune. She had a creamy complexion, high and rosy cheekbones, deep brown eyes, and a long, black braid hung over her shoulder. She was very beautiful, although obviously tired.

"Rafael, you must go to sleep." She pulled the bed sheet up to a little boy's chin.

"When is Daddy coming back?"

"The day after tomorrow, very late, honey," she answered, tucking him in.

She read him a story called *The Little Prince* and he began drifting to sleep when a knock echoed on the front door. She didn't move, expecting the person to be knocking on the wrong door, but a minute later the knocking turned into banging. The woman apprehensively left her child, walking towards the entrance. The chain was in the lock, so she felt secure enough to open the door. A gasp escaped her lips.

"What are you doing here?"

"I wanted to see you," said a man.

"You can't be here; now's not the time."

"Now's the perfect time."

She closed the door and put her forehead on the wood. "Please, please go away," she begged.

He began pounding on the door; she knew it would soon break open. What was she going to do? How was she going to get away from him?

"Mommy?"

The little boy stood in the hallway. She rushed to grab him, then locked themselves in her bedroom. She considered running down the fire escape ladders but knew the man would catch up to them in a matter of seconds. She opened the closet and pushed the boy in, shoving him behind coats.

"Rafie, baby, you must stay in here and be completely still. Don't let him hear or see you." She wanted to sound so in control, but knew she was scaring her child regardless.

"I'm scared," he whined.

"I know, honey, but it will be okay." She hugged him tightly and closed the doors. "Hide, baby, hide," she sobbed.

The front door broke wide open and light foot-steps approached. She pushed her dresser in front of the bedroom door, hoping to slow him down, and began opening her window. She would at least attempt to lead her attacker away from the child. He walked in as easily as if there had been no obstacles.

"Don't do this," the woman openly cried.

"You said I could take you. You said if I helped you control your powers, I could take you whenever I wanted, and you'd join me."

"I was young; I didn't know what I was saying."

"You cannot annul this agreement."

She made to grab a baseball bat that was leaning against the wall and swing, but he was too fast. He bit her throat. A loud and painful scream came from her lips. Rafael's breath caught and his throat got tighter. He placed his hands over his ears, and he could hear his own heartbeat. Fear invaded him and he held his eyes tightly shut. When he opened them, the man was still holding her, but her eyes were glazed over. As he killed her, his gaze was fixed upon the closet. Panic overwhelmed the boy. The stranger's eyes of deep blue glowed in the dark. The man made the woman drink his blood, then she dropped to the floor and convulsed.

The murderer walked out of the room, but Rafael didn't budge. He stayed huddled in that closet for hours. Once certain he was alone, he crawled out of his hideout and lay next to the body. Her lips and face had turned blue, and she was cold to the touch. He wasn't strong enough to pull the limp body on the bed, although he tried. He put a pillow under her head and covered her body with a blanket. He lay next to her for the night.

The next day arrived, and she was still sleeping. The child began to realize she may never wake up. The day came and went as he watched television. He was getting very hungry but had never had to fend for himself before. He ate the only cookies and chips in the apartment. Somewhere inside him, he laughed at not getting caught. Suddenly, a sound emerged from her room.

What he saw stopped him in his tracks. His mother was awake; she sat on her bed looking dazed and confused.

"Mommy?"

Her eyes turned towards him very slowly and the look she gave him frightened him. Yet he stood his ground and remained where he was.

"What happened last night, Mommy?"

"I don't think I'm the same," she murmured, strangely looking at him. "I think he turned me."

Rafael was really scared now. This wasn't his mother; the look in her eyes didn't belong to her.

"Baby, come over here," she said.

"No, you're going to hurt me. You're not the same."

She seemed surprised. "I have not changed. I have evolved. I love you and I would never hurt you."

He didn't know how much he could trust her, but he took the risk of settling down next to her and she put an arm around his shoulders. "You're still cold. I put a blanket over you last night."

She looked down at her pale skin. "I suppose this is the way I'll always feel from now on. He didn't touch you, did he?" She quickly scanned his body.

"No. Who was that?" He wiggled his way out of her grasp that was too tight.

"A mistake from my past."

She complained about being hungry but wouldn't eat any food and stayed in her room, mumbling to herself. His father came home, happy and eager to see his family after a long trip. He was surprised to find the front door unhinged and his son watching cartoons at such a late hour.

"Honey?" he called out for his wife. No answer.

The boy ran into his arms, forgetting about the recent events. His dad was home; all was well again. But it was not well—far from it.

"What happened to the door and where's your mom?" the man asked.

"She's in the room, but you don't wanna go in there. She's not herself. She changed."

"Steven? Is that you?" she called out. "I need you. Please come in here."

The man was worried and scared of what he was about to find. "I'll be right out, little man. Stay here."

"Daddy, please don't go in there."

His father never came back. His own wife attacked him and drank him dry. Rafael and his mother moved soon after that day.

These weren't my memories I was dreaming about, but his. This meant he must have been seeing mine as well, and I was not thrilled at the idea of my entire being, secrets, and feelings being shared with someone else. I brought my attention back to the dream I just had. Rafael had only mentioned his father passing away, but not the how. My heart hurt at how traumatizing that must have been for him. And there was something else nagging at me. Those eyes looked so much like Malcolm's, but he had died long before that fateful night in New York. Hadn't he? Now I was no longer sure. I would know those eyes anywhere. How would he still be alive? I could, of course, have just called Rafael and had him meet me to discuss his memory, but I knew I would never let him leave my side if I saw him again. However, this couldn't be something I swept under the rug as I tended to do with most things; I had to get to the bottom of it.

I went searching online for any information concerning the murder of a Steven Dominicci. I remembered Rafael mentioning he was eight years old when his mother was turned, and I did the math to figure out what year it had been. Unfortunately, I couldn't find very much at all, just the simple facts. There were speculations that the wife was to blame but no proof had ever been brought forward, and the whole case had been closed. Vampires had not come out yet and it became one of those unsolved mysteries. I shut my laptop with a frustrated sigh.

Later that evening, Rafael found me at the club, and I berated myself for forgetting to let the bouncers know he was not to be let in. I felt it as soon as he entered the building and watched him inspect the first floor's rooms from a private balcony. I stood back in the shadows, making sure he wouldn't see me if he glanced up. He made his way through the crowd, shoving people out of his way, and refusing to dance with many. I felt relieved to see him and annoyed simultaneously. He seemed unaware of a female vampire closely following him. Which she must have taken personally, seeing that her face was plastered all over billboards, promoting her latest movie. He walked into a bathroom and so did the undead actress. I decided to intervene and when I stepped in, she had him pinned against a wall, struggling to break free.

"Get away from him. He's with me." My tone was firm.

She glanced back at me. "He doesn't seem to be with anyone. Get your own meal."

I let my power wash through her. Electricity could be felt in the air. She sucked in a breath and her pale face blanched even more when she realized who I was. She released Rafael gently and walked away, offering an apology under her breath. She was clearly offended and returned to the dance floor. I made a mental note to have her thrown out but had a more urgent matter to deal with at the moment. My body wanted to be held in his arms, but my mind was furious. He looked at me, rubbing his neck where she had grabbed him.

"I've been watching since you got here, Rafael. What do you want?"

"I've been looking for you. I've been trying to get a hold of you for days!"

"Well, I'm here now. What do you want?" I asked again with a hint of anger.

"I just can't stop thinking about you," he replied, brushing my hand with his.

I was having a hard time containing my anger. I took a step back. "You linked yourself to me. You forced this on both of us. You had no right, and you have no idea what you got yourself into."

His face fell and he locked me in a tight embrace. He traced his thumb along my jawline and his touch sent my heart racing. "Don't be mad at me. You're right, I didn't know what it meant or why you were so upset. I looked it up and I understand now what I got myself into. But I want to be with you."

"You don't know what being with me implies! What you are feeling was brought forth by my blood! Had you not drunk it, you wouldn't feel this way. Look at yourself—you are being ridiculous. For Christ's sake, you could have been hurt tonight!"

"You couldn't be more wrong." He furrowed his brow, looking the most serious I'd ever seen him. "I grew up in this environment; it doesn't scare me. So maybe our feelings for each other are enhanced, but they were there to begin with, and I know you feel the same way."

"Rafael! You are forgetting what I am! I am not like you, and I never will be. I died a long time ago!" My frustration was now boiling over, and I was nearly shouting.

"Then turn me into a vampire. I would become one to be with you."

How could he be so calm talking about his own death? "That is out of the question. What happened to you valuing your life?" I was dumbfounded and repulsed. "I would never do that to you."

I turned around, ending the discussion, when he grabbed me once more and pushed his lips on mine. I let him and enjoyed it. I hated my betraying heart.

"Tell me you don't feel anything for me." He cupped my face in his hands, forcing me to look up.

"I don't want you," I answered feebly.

"Can you sound like you mean it?" I felt the tears rising; he hugged me. "You don't have to turn me; I just want to be near you as a part of your life. What's the worst that can happen?"

"You could lose your life."

"And I'm okay with that, as long as I spend whatever time I have with you."

My stubbornness quickly faded away as my heart shattered and reason settled in. I was alone and miserable. The nights I spent with him had been some of the best I had experienced in decades. Yet I fought these thoughts. My head warned me to keep my distance. He was a human and would undeniably die long before I would. My heart, on the other hand, longed for nothing more than to love once again.

Unmistakably, the heart always won. I left the club early and took Rafael home with me. I showed him around the mansion, but he wasn't interested in all the antiques or paintings. He wanted me right there, right then. His hand cupped my face, titling it to his, and his mouth was over mine again. I was tired of fighting myself and completely surrendered to him. I brought him to my bedroom, rushing to flip Malcolm's frame down before he entered. Rafael took his time undressing me, touching me softly and leaving light kisses over my neck and shoulders as I stood in front of the bed. I shivered with desire for him. He dropped my dress around my ankles and laid me down gently. I tried to kick my heels off, but he stopped me.

"Leave them on," he said. "They're sexy."

He unbuttoned his dress shirt, keeping his eyes on mine. I raised myself, trying to help him, wanting to speed the process up. Again, he wouldn't allow me.

"I want it to be about you today. I want to make up for our first time together. So lie down and let me do the work."

Well, I wasn't going to argue. He kneeled in front of the bed and brought my hips closer to the edge where he began feasting on me. I grabbed at the sheets as I rocked my body into his mouth. He stopped right before the release came and crawled over me. I grabbed his face and kissed him, tasting myself on his tongue. I clawed at his back as he eased himself inside me, feeling the muscles tensing underneath my fingers.

"Tell me how you want it," he whispered, his voice deep and hoarse.

"Hard. I want it hard," I gasped.

He plunged inside me, again and again to his full length, and I wrapped my arms around his neck, holding on tight. And when the pressure in me finally released, I took possession of his mouth. He finished moments later and we lay in bed, limbs still tangled. I let him take my worries away, if just for one night. Tomorrow would be a different story.

Over the next few weeks, I couldn't deny I felt serene when he was around. I slept well, my nightmares had stopped, and I was more relaxed than I had been in years. This *felt* right, and it was more than the blood bond speaking. We were exactly where we were meant to be. I shared my experiences of the world with Rafael, my stories, my accomplishments, and my failures. I introduced him to my family through my paintings, in which he seemed to take real interest. I showed him the people I had sired who should still have been with us, had the Universe not had a funny sense of humor. We talked magic, literature, music, and movies. His smell fascinated me. He wasn't a regular human; he was growing to be so much more— my lover, my confidant, and maybe even my best friend. He brought me back to life and eased my aching soul. I needed to have him around. Inescapably, his humanity would become a problem, but as of right now, I was glad to be enjoying life again. I loved the way he touched me, the way he made me feel like I was the only important being in his life. When he looked at me, I knew he saw the real me. I loved how fast my heart raced when he said my name and the stupid smiles he put on my face. I loved how comfortable I felt in his arms and the butterflies that formed in my stomach when he looked at me. The respect and consideration he showed me was not something I had been used to in my last serious relationship—this was new and uncharted territory. I could imagine loving him and being his.

CHAPTER EIGHT

1852

Alia had countless dresses, which gave her the allure of aristocracy. She had the attitude to match the clothes, and no one questioned her authority. She and Liz walked the foggy streets and because of Liz's complexion, they had to be careful as to not draw too much negative attention to themselves. Many white folks looked at Liz suspiciously, judging the girls' uncommon friendship to be misplaced. Little did people know that Liz held more power over them than they had on her skin. Liz walked slightly behind Alia as to appear submissive to the White woman.

Alia's shoulders were exposed, which was scandalous enough, a tight corset embracing her waistline. Liz's hair was up in a chignon while Alia's was curled and loose down her back. Around the woman's neck was displayed a beautiful ruby, enticing men to look at her chest. Although the sun was covered, both ladies held umbrellas above their heads with long, gloved arms. Malcolm sent them hunting. He wanted a large family, a clan. He was the king, fearless and powerful. Alia and Liz were his queens, beautiful and cruel.

Their family had increased dramatically. It had just been Malcolm and Alia alone for a few years before Liz was made, but they had turned about thirty members, men and women, over the last eighty years. In retrospect, it didn't seem like much, but they had to be picky. Malcolm didn't want to spend eternity with someone he couldn't tolerate.

Alia and Liz walked the short distance into town and brought cattle home to lessen questions from the humans, keeping them blissfully ignorant about the disappearances around town. A small wall surrounded the property; the spiked gate creaked as they opened it. The vegetation was slightly overgrown. Large columns positioned around the house held the roof up. Inside sustained thirty rooms over four levels with an indoor fountain in the entrance hall. Alia had spent over sixty years decorating the residence. While burgundy draperies kept the rooms dark, chandeliers hung down the high-vaulted ceilings, reflecting light onto the marble floor. The walls supported paintings and mirrors in dark frames. The antique wooden furniture was exquisite: tables, wardrobes, and buffets. An immense semicircular staircase presented itself across the front door.

Alia always refused to watch the feasting; tricking people to their deaths was enough to make her stomach turn. She walked them to the house, locked the doors behind them, and quickly left before the screaming could start. She had made the decision to starve herself until it was absolutely necessary for her to feed. When she fed, she tried her hardest to not kill.

However, Malcolm quickly caught on, and on one specific night that would remain etched into her memory forever, he forced her to remain with her family for dinner. This barbaric act repulsed her. She braced herself in a corner, covering her mouth and nose, trying to block the smell of blood out. She was so hungry herself. Malcolm shouted for everyone to stop feeding, grabbed her hair, and forced her into a crimson pool.

"You are a vampire. Now feed," he ordered. "You brought them here—you are a part of this!" He pointed to all the other vampires. "They'll have to wait until you start."

He threw a small girl into her arms; she was young, perhaps eight or nine years old. She had been easy to attract to the house. She was poor, cold, hungry, and was promised a refuge. The girl was crying loudly; her eyes were wide with fear. A million possibilities ran through Alia's head, but there was no way out, and the girl's fear only increased the vampire's hunger.

Malcolm was testing her loyalty. The intensity

in his eyes sent a shiver down her spine. Everyone was watching her, hungry and wondering why she was defective. She gave in to herself and drank until there was no more. Alia was losing her soul. The feasting resumed for all.

I was so used to dreaming about my past and waking up with a headache, I didn't even think twice about it. I wished I could say I had more good memories than bad, but unfortunately that wasn't the case, and my rest never felt truly restful. The hunger had come back. I had already tasted Rafael's blood and being around him was becoming exceptionally hard for me. If I focused hard enough, I could hear the blood pumping through his veins, his heart thumping in his chest, and I found myself focusing on that too often. I craved his blood and thoughts of murder invaded me. Yet he still wanted to spend more time together, not understanding what kind of danger he put himself in. Not understanding the temptation he put me through and how much self-control I was constantly having to develop to not rip his throat out. I silenced the voices but still needed to feed from something alive. Cold, refrigerated blood wouldn't cut it right now.

I asked Rafael to wait for me and went for a walk. I strolled through the trees, taking my time, and touched their trunks, absorbing their energy. Eventually I sat on the soft grass and, closing my eyes, begged nature to offer me a sacrifice. A red fox lay down in front of me. I thanked it for its life and bled it dry quickly, trying to minimize its pain. I buried it and walked back to the manor, gratitude filling me.

I found Rafael in the kitchen and began helping him clean the dishes.

"You know..." he said, encircling my waist from behind with his arms, putting his head on my shoulder. "You could always nibble on me," he joked.

I didn't think his comment was funny, and if he knew my cravings, he wouldn't make such remarks. A low growl escaped my lips, and I dropped the plates I was holding into the sink. Leaning onto the counter, I breathed deeply, trying to calm myself. The boy was testing my will power. He slowly took my shaking hand and kissed it.

I snapped it away and turned to face him. "This is the last time you'll make comments like that. Do you understand me?"

He put his hands up in surrender. "I am just kidding when I say that."

"No, you're not. And you have no idea how hard it is for me to keep control around you and how tempting it is when you keep offering yourself to me. I would kill you, Rafael. So please refrain from 'joking.'"

"I apologize and I understand. It won't happen again. Come with me, I have a little something set up for us."

"And what could that be?" I asked suspiciously.

"Just come with me."

I reluctantly followed him outside into the darkness. He wouldn't answer my questions no matter how much I pressured him, as per usual. We must have been walking for five to ten minutes, and I was glad to have my sneakers on. As we arrived at our destination, my eyes focused on the surprise. He had prepared a romantic picnic underneath the stars.

"When did you have the time to set this up?"

"You kind of lose track of time when you head into the woods," he answered.

I lay on a velvet sheet as he lit a few candles. I let my head rest on the ground and looked up. Being so far away from the city lights gave me a clear view of the sky.

"It's just so beautiful out here," I murmured as he took his place by my side. "All this energy is rejuvenating. Do you feel it?"

"I feel your energy."

We remained silent for a moment. He had his head on my stomach and hugged my waist. I played with his hair but still, I was troubled, and he sensed it.

"What's wrong? Why are you so tense?"

I didn't know how to approach the subject. I expected he would close up the moment I asked about his mother. "I've been dreaming of your memories," I said, carefully choosing my words. "I saw your mom getting turned, and I think the vampire who killed her is the same one who transformed me. I could never forget his eyes. But I thought he died some thirty years before you were even born. I need to know as much as you can tell me about him." It was difficult keeping my voice from shaking. I wasn't sure if it was excitement, fear, or pain.

Rafael immediately stiffened and cleared his throat, coming to a seated position. "I don't know what to tell you. I was eight and you've apparently seen as much as I did of him. My mother never talked about him."

I kneeled in front of him, sitting back on my heels. "Rafael, she seemed like she knew him very well. She never mentioned anything about him? You don't know a single thing about him?" He had to be lying.

"I said I don't," he answered, raising his voice. "Why do you need to know so badly? I've seen your memories too, you know, and if it is the same person and he's alive, would you go back to him?"

I had to hold back my laugh—that was such a silly question. "Never. Don't think that way. If you saw some of my memories with this man, then you know most weren't good. I just need to know if he's alive."

"Do you really think my mother would have told me who he was? She knew better. He ruined my life; I would have tried to destroy him and gotten myself killed." His hatred was tangible. I had never seen this angry side of him before, and it surprised me. He saw the emotion on my face and scooted closer to me.

"I'm sorry," he said. "It's a touchy subject."

"He wasn't the only one who died," I whispered. "If he's alive, maybe some of the others are too. My family." And I surprised even myself with the hope I found in my voice, how much I was holding on to it since having that dream.

Understanding crossed his face and he seemed to calm down. "You're not looking for him, you're looking for them?" I nodded and he sighed, placing his forehead against mine.

"You'll run off before I leave you," I whispered.

"What are you talking about?" he looked at me, searching my gaze.

"It's all about acceptance," I answered slowly. "Every choice we make brings consequences. When I made the decision to date you, I accepted the fact that I may not be with you as long as I originally planned. But I'm okay with it—I've accepted it. If you found someone else, someone like you, I would be upset, but I'd understand because I have nothing to offer you."

"I wish you wouldn't say things like that," he said, holding me tightly in his arms. "I don't want anyone else."

We ate some food, or rather, he did, and I lay back, watching the stars. His phone rang, and I turned to my side, watching him with my head resting in my hand. He had such an appealing charisma. I focused on our surroundings, trying to not listen in on his conversation. He hung up the phone and sighed.

"John would like me to go to a music festival with the rest of my employees tomorrow night." He rubbed his forehead.

"Don't you want to go?"

"I do, but I was planning on spending the night with you..." he trailed off.

"But you don't want me to go because you're worried about them meeting me," I finished. He seemed uneasy. "You don't need my permission to hang out with your friends," I contin-

ued, turning my face away so he couldn't see the disappointment in my eyes.

I knew our differences would start getting in the way
sooner or later.

"It's not like that. I want you to go with me, but they have
never really interacted with vampires. I don't want you to feel
worse about yourself if they don't handle it well."

I looked back at him. "So, you don't care about your friends
being terrified of me, you just don't want me feeling bad
about it."

"Exactly." He chuckled. "It sounds silly now that you
say it."

I laughed loudly. "That's because it is." He was out of his
mind. "I'm old enough—I think I'll be able to handle myself."

I remained quiet as he ate some more and thought about
Malcolm. Now that Rafael brought it up, I wasn't sure how I
truly felt about it. Would I go back to him? There had to be a
reason I had survived my clan's massacre, because that is
exactly what it was. And if Malcolm had been alive all these
years, what did it mean?

CHAPTER NINE

2009

It was Rafael's birthday and for a seventeen-year-old boy, he seemed to be much more mature, both physically and mentally, than most in his age group. He had been forced into adulthood early on, keeping secrets and taking responsibilities most never experienced.

He and his mother lived in a luxurious home in Colorado that she had acquired herself. He didn't ask her how; he knew he wouldn't like the answer. After she murdered his father, they moved around very often. They had to keep moving to keep the trail of bodies from catching up to her. He spent his childhood mainly alone because she couldn't control herself around other humans, and people did not know about vampires yet. He had grown up as a strong and independent young man. But he was so lonely. He had been robbed of any meaningful relationships with other humans.

His girlfriend of six months had long, curly red hair, and her creamy skin was soft to the touch, emphasizing the darkness of her blue eyes. Chloe came from a rich and prominent family. She was the sweetest and most genuine person Rafael had ever met. She was a regular client at the coffee shop he worked at, and he suspected she really only drank so much coffee to be near him. As much as he did not want to involve anyone in his bizarre life, they fell hard and fast for each other. Her parents may not have liked it, but nothing could have stopped it.

Whenever his mother lost control over herself, he often spent days, nights, or weeks over at her house looking for love and comfort. She was the only one to ever see him cry, curled into a ball on the floor. Hugging him, she never asked questions, but merely let him weep.

They had been drinking to celebrate his birthday. It had been her idea. She thought he would have liked having drinks on his birthday as most teenagers would, but he knew better than to get intoxicated. He had too many secrets that needed to be hidden. She, on the other hand, was completely inebriated.

"How come you won't let me meet your mother?" she slurred.

"Not tonight, babe."

"Not tonight or any night, apparently! Am I not good enough?" She stumbled; he caught her in his arms.

"Nothing is wrong with you. I just want to have a peaceful night."

"Rafael Michael Dominicci, if you don't bring me to your house, this night is over."

"Then this night is over. I'm certainly not going to introduce you to my mom while you're drunk. I'll drive you home and walk to my house."

She began to sob and apologize for ruining his birthday, but he maintained he wanted to go home. He parked her car in her driveway, walked her to the door, and made sure she was alright. He then enjoyed a peaceful twenty-minute walk back to his own house. With his hands in his pockets, he thought about the catastrophe that just had been avoided. The house was dark except for the lit fireplace. His mother stood quietly, looking at the flames. She never spoke much; she seemed haunted by her personal demons.

"Hi, Mom," he whispered. No response—she had not even wished him a happy birthday.

"Hi, honey," she answered, after a moment.

As he kicked off his shoes, a knock was heard on the front door and his heart sank. Hoping the person would leave, Rafael and his mother remained silent, looking at each other.

"Rafael? I know you're in there." It was Chloe's voice.

"What are you doing here? You shouldn't have driven," he asked, slightly cracking open the door.

She had been crying. "I just... I just don't want to end the night like this. Please let me in."

He glanced back to see where his mother stood

and she nodded in agreement, bracing herself for the self-control she would have to demonstrate. He knew she didn't drink often and was pretty hungry most of the time. His hopes were crushed the moment he let Chloe walk inside. His mother snarled and growled like a starving beast. Rafael stood between his girlfriend and mother, trying to reason with the second and pushing the first out the door. Chloe began shrieking, which only added to the fire.

Her death was quick and painless. Too quick. Rafael was not sure what had happened. In the blink of an eye, his girlfriend lay inert on the ground with the vampire drinking her blood. Bellowing, he used all of his strength to get his mother off the corpse and knocked her into the wall. Chloe was dead, gone forever. He wasn't angry with his mom, but furious with himself. He should have known better. A stabbing pain festered within his chest and tears ran down his cheeks. Screams of agony escaped his lips. Was he supposed to be breathing? He held the body and cried. The one person he loved was dead, and this would always be his life.

He could see his mother remained where he had knocked her over, watching him. He held her gaze, wondering what could possibly be going through her mind. He would have never been able to guess how she felt, but years later, was able to connect the dots through a letter he found in her belongings.

She had imposed this upon him, and in that

moment, she gave herself a deadline: she would end it all in a year. When he turned eighteen and legally became an adult, he would be fine without her. He already didn't need her now and hadn't in a long time. She had been selfish to put him through the last ten years, and the guilt was too much for her to handle. They left Colorado after this incident, never to return.

I slowly opened my eyes. It wasn't time for me to wake yet. The memory I just had wasn't mine, and it left me with a sense of sorrow I was too accustomed to. I looked over to Rafael's handsome sleeping face and hugged his body. This beautiful man had endured so much as well.

"I'm so sorry," I whispered, morphing my body to his, and fell back to sleep breathing in his scent.

The day went on. Rafael and I were excited for the evening's plans. He told me about the friends we would be meeting at the event, their names, what they were like, funny anecdotes about each.

We had arrived at the music festival several hours ago. Rafael officially introduced me to his friends, who turned out to be more tolerant than I had anticipated. Maybe the drugs they had already ingested helped them become more understanding, I could feel their senses being dulled. Emilia was a young, short woman with thick, long, black hair. She must have been in her mid-twenties. Her green eyes pierced through the night to watch Rafael. She very obviously had a thing for him, but I wasn't jealous. Shane was a bit older, with short brown hair. He was as tall as Rafael but slender. Both had the beauty of an immortal. Rafael's other friends didn't catch my attention. They had been shocked to realize he was dating a vampire but held their composures well. I wore a beautiful white dress and had braided my hair. We danced to the music, laughed, and danced some more.

Around midnight, I got a throbbing headache and became uncomfortable. I was surrounded by thousands of people, and most of them were on drugs. This was so many more than what I usually came across at the club. I was struggling to block myself from feeling their unguarded emotions. I felt attacked, as though needles stabbed through my head. I tried to keep the sensations from flowing through me, but it was too much for me to bear. I collapsed into Rafael's friend's arms. Danny, I think his name was, dragged me away from the tent and helped me sit on the grass. I remained with my head between my knees; my stomach felt as if it were being ripped apart by some devious force.

"Do you want to get away from the music?" Rafael asked, crouching next to me and putting his warm hand on my neck.

"No, I'm fine. I want to stay here."

"Why? Are you sure? It would help you relax."

I nodded, and as I stood on shaking legs, he put a hand on my back. "I can carry you."

I wrapped my arms around his neck as he delicately lifted me off the ground. I embraced the softness of his skin and tangled my fingers into his hair. With his arm underneath my legs and his other hand securing my back, he paced across the field, taking me away from the insanity. My strength faded for a moment; my arms and head fell back, scaring my companion and pushing him to walk faster. He sat next to a tree and set me between his legs. Although he had given me his shirt, which showed off his apparent muscles, I was still shivering ferociously, but it was more due to the exhaustion I felt than the temperature. He circled my waist with his arms, turning his back to the wind.

"What are you doing?" Shane asked, sitting next to him.

"She's shaking, I'm blocking the wind."

I breathed heavily, with short gasps.

"Alia, you must regulate your breathing."

I rested my head on his shoulder and dozed off for a couple of seconds. His friends worried about me. Some wanted me to see a doctor right away, but Rafael shushed them. My condition was temporary. A few moments later, he helped me walk back to his pickup truck and drove me to the top of a hill where I could regain my full energy. The darkness and icy temperature surrounded us as we both lay in the bed of his truck while I looked at the stars. I rested on my back with his head on my stomach and his arms wrapped around my waist. His right hand caressed my side and massaged my stomach while I stroked his soft back.

"You're going to catch a cold," I said.

"Don't worry about me, I like the cold. Are you feeling better now? You had me scared for a minute."

"I'm much better. Nice first impression, huh?"

"Don't worry about them. They'll get over it."

Kinkily he bit my stomach, holding the skin and fabric tightly between his teeth; it sent chills down my spine.

"I love you," he said. "You don't have to say it back, but I want you to know that." He put his leg on top of mine and rested his head on my shoulder, closing his eyes, all while I played with his silky hair. That was a big step, saying "I love you." Did I feel the same? I spent so long being afraid of love. Could I allow myself to feel it? When replenished, we headed back to the manor. Home. Once assured I'd be fine, Rafael, exhausted, set out for bed. As for me, I decided to take a walk through the acres on my property.

I marched up to the highest hill, absorbing the full moon's energy. Once at the top, the air became increasingly colder, although it didn't bother me. With the unusual large moon facing me, my pale skin seemed to glow in the dark night. I turned my side to the source of light, letting the wind play with my white gown and hair. I closed my eyes, knowing I was losing a great deal of power. This connection with Rafael had me so scatterbrained and agitated. I often found myself in a fight or flight response, my heart beating wildly. At this point, not even nature could help me control these feelings. I didn't blame him, but he made me feel emotions I had long forgotten. He loved me, he said, and I had been incapable of saying it back. I felt very strongly for him, but was it love? I had thought I was in love before, but it had never felt like this. I was panicking a bit.

The demon in me awoke and asked to be fed, demanding a bloodbath. I opened my dark eyes, and everything looked much brighter, more vivid, a sign I was losing control. I heard voices calling my name and telling me to let go. I took a step towards the drop, hoping an adrenaline rush would be sufficient to silence the hunger, and threw myself backwards. Letting myself fall, I opened my arms and felt the darkness feed on this rush. A little way from the ground, I turned and twisted, landing on both of my feet with a small bounce. Putting my hands in my hair, I made sure the evil inside had calmed down and lay down on my back in the middle of the field, stretching my long figure like a feline. I knew I'd have to feed on warm blood soon. I could no longer deny this need. My senses becoming gradually more acute, I rubbed my legs against the soft grass, felt it grow underneath my body. I was inhaling the sweet aroma of fresh air when, suddenly, the thirst kicked in again, harder and stronger than before, and it knocked the air out of my lungs. I realized I would not regain control until I had fed. As I rolled onto my stomach, grasping the earth with my fingers, my eyes frantically looked around for prey. I became aware of an animal hopping around a few feet away from me, most likely a rabbit. The beast took over and made me dash after my victim with incredible speed. In my folly, I still felt sadness for taking a life and made sure it felt no pain.

My appetite satisfied for now, I buried the poor animal's body while licking my teeth. The thirst always won. It was such a relief letting the beast escape sometimes and letting it take over. It felt like I was allowing myself to truly be who I was. However, I knew with certainty if there had been a human— other than Rafael—in the vicinity, I would have attacked it, and

I was so grateful to live this far out. The sun would rise soon, and I felt Rafael stir in my mind.

I felt lighter on the walk home, the beast at bay. The house was completely silent when I entered. Lidia was away for the weekend and George must have been sleeping. I quietly walked up the grand staircase and snuck into the bedroom, where I found Rafael lying on the bed with his back to me, pretending to be asleep. He still wore his black jeans without a shirt. I heard the rhythm of his heart accelerating once I entered the room. The grass had wet my gown, making it transparent. Rafael turned around and set his eyes on my delicate silhouette.

"Long night?" he asked, raising an eyebrow.

I smiled thoughtfully and stroked the chimney embers, adding another log to the dying fire. I stripped off my useless piece of clothing and sat onto the stone chimney's border. Bringing my knees to my chest, I hoped the fire would bring warmth to my permanently cold skin. My lover came to my side, putting a warm and gentle hand on my shoulder while crouching down to my level. The fire made beautiful shadows on his face, and as he leaned in for a kiss, I jerked away.

"You don't want to do that," I whispered. "I just fed."

He gave me a simple, innocent look, letting me know it was all right. I stood up, my back to him, massaging my neck with my long fingers. He circled my waist with his arms firmly from behind, letting my head rest on his shoulder.

"The demon demands more and more fresh blood," I murmured. "I used to go so much longer in between feedings."

"Why do you think that is?" He kissed my neck.

"I think my powers are growing some more. It's getting harder to control myself and the demon is taking advantage."

"Would it be so bad to hunt daily?" He said, then laughed. "I guess I should say nightly, huh?"

"Yes, no, maybe." I exhaled through my nose, exasperated.

"I don't know. I've never let myself go full vampire as much as I wanted to, because the more I feed, the more I want. It's a neverending need."

"And you're afraid you'll lose all control?"

"I'm afraid I'll lose myself. Isn't that the end all vampires meet? Why the eldest were killed off? I've worked so hard at keeping a semblance of humanity. I don't want to become a bigger monster, feeling nothing but bloodlust. Especially not around you."

He turned me around and cupped my face in his hands. "I don't think you give yourself enough credit, and I don't think you'd go crazy. Now, please go take a shower, you smell like a barn animal. And let's go to bed." I laughed and pushed him away from me. I was definitely in love. When would I be ready to admit it?

CHAPTER TEN

1863

The American Civil War had been underway for a couple of years now. So many wounded every single day—over five hundred cots per hospital—and this thrilled Malcolm because no one would look twice if an injured soldier died in the middle of the night.

He had sent Alia and a few other women to pass as nurses at the general hospital, which was, in fact, a barn in the middle of Pennsylvania. It was a horrible place, full of disease and suffering. It was their job to harvest the soldiers' blood before sickness settled in.

Alia walked in between the makeshift beds, holding a handkerchief to her nose, repulsed by the fetid smell. There were thirty rows of seventeen beds, all occupied, and it was not enough room. There were more soldiers lying outside on the lawn. Agonizing screams were heard all around. From limbs that had been amputated to amputations that were currently taking place, nurses and doctors had their hands full going from patient to patient. They did not have the time to notice a few nurses aimlessly walking around. It was hard for Alia to keep her head on right and not let her beast take over. There was so much blood everywhere. So much pain.

She passed by a bed and felt a hand wrap around hers. When she looked down, she met a pair of beautiful hazel eyes.

"Excuse me, miss," the soldier gasped. "Can I get some water please?"

"Of course." She smiled sweetly. "I'll be right back."

She went to one of the many water stations, filled a glass, and returned to him. He couldn't sit up easily, so she sat on the side of his bed, placed a hand behind his head, and titled the glass to his lips. He drank deeply and sighed in satisfaction. She could hear the blood rushing through his body in an abnormal cadence. He was classically beautiful for a man, with well-defined features, high cheekbones, a straight nose, full lips, and dark eyebrows.

"What is your name?" she asked.

"Lord William Johnson III."

"Lord? Why are you here?"

He sighed, more from the pain he was in than at the question. "Silly me had to prove to my father I was something more than a drunk who enjoyed all his liquor." He chuckled and grunted in discomfort. "In retrospect, I should have stayed in his cellar, don't you think?"

"What happened?" She scanned his body. "Where are you hurt?"

"A mine went off far enough away that I still have all my limbs, but close enough to have thrown me against a tree. The doctors said I have internal stomach bleeding. It'll be some time before I die but die from it I will."

She made to stand up, but he caught her wrist. "Please stay with me. I know it's selfish, but I don't want to be alone right now."

She looked around for her family—the ladies would not be happy to see her sitting around—but they were busying themselves on the other side of the building.

"As you wish." What was she supposed to say to a dying man? "Is there anything you'd like to discuss? Any regrets you'd like to relieve yourself from?"

"Are you asking to take my confession? You might be the prettiest priest I've ever met," he laughed painfully, and she blushed. "I guess my biggest regret is not having met a nice young woman to cherish. I would have liked to have a family of my own if I hadn't struggled with my love of alcohol so much. I would have taken her around the country, and we could have experienced the world together. I always thought I had more potential than just following in my father's footsteps and continuing *his* legacy. I always thought I'd achieve more. Maybe if I had been someone else."

She hadn't felt the need or want to change anyone after Liz, but she could see this man being part of their trio. She could feel the potential he was talking about, his untapped power. All additions to the clan had to be approved by Malcolm first, but she didn't have the time to argue her case with him. Surely she could make one decision on her own, couldn't she?

"Will you miss your life?"

"When I'm dead? I'll be in the arms of God then."

Alia didn't answer and averted her eyes.

"You're not a God-fearing woman," William said. "That's okay, I never believed in all that either. I'll miss alcohol, I suppose."

"What if I said I could save your life, but you could never go back to your old one?"

The screaming resumed, louder, closer to them. Someone getting a leg amputated. William closed his eyes tightly, then said, "If it means I don't have to stay here any longer, then I accept."

"Alright, I will be back in an hour when most of these men are asleep." She closed her hand around his. "Don't die before then."

"I'll try my best," he responded.

When she pushed through the barn doors just over an hour later, the screaming had subsided. The only men not sleeping were the ones whimpering in too much pain, or those whispering their prayers to God. William's face had turned feverish, and he had begun vomiting dark blood next to his bed.

"There you are, my dark angel," he said, propping himself on his elbows with pain as a stomach spasm took him over. "I thought you might have been a dream."

She sat next to him and gently pushed him back down. "Are you ready?"

He nodded and she closed her lips on his neck, drinking him, not really caring who saw them at this point.

"What—" he began, but she placed her hand on his mouth to shush him.

His blood had already started turning poisonous and she did everything she could to stop the gag that was coming up her throat. He didn't fight, he barely moved, but his eyes were wide with fear. When she rushed her blood down his throat, she had to push her wrist tighter onto his mouth to stop him from moving his face side to side.

His human body died, and the doctors placed him on the carriage that went out once a day with all the other fallen soldiers to be buried in a mass grave. If anyone noticed the teeth mark on his neck, none mentioned it. She intercepted the carriage under the pretense of being a family member and wanting to bury the body in her family graveyard. She placed William on her own horse and led him back to her house where he would rest peacefully until his awakening.

Malcolm was less than thrilled. "Tell me again," he said, pinching the bridge of his nose, "what made you think you could make this decision on your own?"

"I don't see why it would only be yours to make. You keep repeating I'm your queen, I'm your queen. Well, I made a choice."

She began to walk away but he grabbed her arm, twisting it behind her back. "I'm the king, and I make the decisions for this clan." He circled her throat with his free hand and applied pressure. She began choking. "You better hope he finds himself useful to us, or I will destroy him and punish you for taking liberties. You will always consult me before making additions that will affect the clan," he whispered in her ear before pushing her away.

She massaged her neck, coughing. "You're a lunatic, you know that?" He took a step towards her and she flinched.

She wished she could wipe the smirk off his pompous face. "That's what I thought," he said. She watched him walk away and hated that she had shown fear in front of him.

While William struggled for some time with his new lifestyle, he did prove to be quite useful after all. Not long after being turned, he began developing psychic abilities. His visions were sporadic, confusing, and sometimes unreliable, but his power grew year after year, and Malcolm reveled in the ability to stay a step ahead of other clans forming around them. He couldn't allow anyone else to grow larger than their family. And due to William's usefulness, Malcolm went out of his way to make William comfortable, allowing him liberties that the girls never had.

It was quite obvious to Alia that after Will met Liz, it would take no time for the two to become fast friends. Liz and Will, even quicker than Alia had anticipated, became inseparable lovers and hunters. He treated her with the upmost respect and complete adoration, making Liz feel safe and cared for. She deserved the absolute best and that was all Alia wanted for her friend. He became a brother to Alia, one who often stepped in to block Malcolm's abuses, physical or mental, and if Malcolm was threatened by William's many interceptions, he never let on. But he also never removed him, which led Alia to suspect he either relied on these visions heavily or he had another use for William. She began seeing a pattern develop within their family. She didn't know how Malcolm knew to target them, but most members had some sort of magical ability. Some stronger than others, but present nonetheless. She wondered what Liz's was and when questioned, her friend didn't seem to have an answer.

T he wind picked up and the air felt cold. The weather didn't bother me, but I instinctively tightened the scarf around my neck and huddled closer to Rafael, holding his arm. It was a trick I had learned that made me look more human. My boots rung on the frozen floor with every step, adding to the stores' echoing Christmas music. The city center was decorated with all sorts of flashing lights and Christmas trees, but snow was missing from the festivities. Rafael and I slowly walked down the pavement and window shopped, his hands deeply buried in his jacket pockets. The joy emerging from people during this season was palpable and I felt good. Rafael and I were enjoying a simple night out being a normal couple, laughing and smiling. I should have sensed danger brewing, but I was soaking in happiness.

"Walk into the alley," a voice said behind us.

Rafael stiffened, holding my hand tighter, and I saw a gun pointed to his back.

"Alia, don't," he warned while leading us into the alley. Why were these streets suddenly so empty?

The man pushed me against the wall, and I fell on my knees. Mechanically, Rafael stepped forward to help me, but I shook my head no at him. The robber stood between us, still pointing his gun at my boyfriend. I wanted to destroy our aggressor for ruining such a beautiful night but calmed myself. I would give Rafael a chance to deal with this in a human manner.

"Empty your pockets."

"Listen, you are making a big mistake," Rafael explained with his hands up. "You don't want to do this."

I kept my eyes fixated on him, waiting for a signal to end this ridiculous waste of time. The man's trembling hand raised the gun higher to Rafael's head. "I don't think you're in a position to tell me what I want and don't want. What I want right now is your fucking wallet."

"Honey…" This was making me very nervous.

"Babe, please don't. Sir, put the gun down."

I put my hands up and slowly raised myself off the ground, ready to pounce at any minute.

"Empty your pockets now, or I'll shoot her!" The gun turned to me, and a menacing calm descended on me before I let the beast take over.

I could not tolerate this absurd situation any longer, and I hastily grabbed the hand holding the gun, bending it backwards until the bones broke. He screeched, and I wanted nothing more than to plunge my teeth into his flesh. His pulse beat against his neck, and I was suddenly so hungry.

"Alia, please let him go!"

"He meant to hurt us." Was that my voice? It sounded strangely far away.

I found myself in a semitrance fighting my demons. Rafael was struggling to break my hold on the thief. Finally, I dropped the man to the floor and was led away. Rafael held my hand, walking with long steps, almost dragging me and forcing me into a trot behind him. He was mad. I could feel his increasing anger and it became contagious.

"Let go of me! I am not a child!" I jerked my hand out of his.

He looked around as we stood in the middle of the road. A few people watched us with inquisitive looks. Giving me a dark glare, he resumed his walk back to the car. I brushed my hair behind my ear, crossed my arms, and took my time following him.

The car was already on when I entered it and buckled my seat belt. He remained quiet, silently fuming.

"Are we going to talk about what's upsetting you so much?"

Silence. I sighed and looked out the window, then back at him. He stared straight ahead. Was he at least going to drive?

"Listen, I know what you saw was pretty disturbing—"

"I don't care about that," he cut me off.

"Then are you going to tell me why you're huffing and puffing?" My voice rose.

"I need to be the man in this relationship."

"Excuse me? You are way out of line right now. I clearly lack a certain something to be the 'man' in this relationship."

"I have a need to protect you, not the other way around."

"You are being absolutely ridiculous! Would you have preferred I let you get shot?!"

"You didn't give me a chance!"

"I did give you a chance! And it was already taking too long! These are not situations to test your chance with."

"You make me feel weak."

"I do not have the power to make you feel any way. That is your insecurity speaking." I could see him clenching his jaw. "You know what? Next time, I'll let you get shot. I'll let our next robber put a bullet through your head, but I refuse to let myself get hurt. I may not be able to die but it still hurts like hell. So excuse me for stepping in. I saved my ass as much as yours. I'm sorry I am different from you."

"It's not about being different! It's about feeling like an insignificant fly! I was scared and unable to protect you." He slammed his fist on the steering wheel.

I looked at him, incredulous. "I don't try to make you feel inferior, but this needs to stop. I am not putting up with a superiority complex. News flash: I am a vampire, and you are human! We are not equally as strong! Where is this coming from? Did you forget what you signed up for?" I was met with more silence. "Get me home."

I was angry and my ego was hurt, so I remained quiet

throughout the ride. I didn't want him staying over, and it seemed to be a mutual feeling.

A quick and rather cold peck on the lips, and I was out of the car, walking into my home. I found myself falling back into old patterns of feeling numb and shutting my emotions off. These fights, these differences coming in the way, were beginning to take their toll on me. I was frustrated with myself for being near tears and considered packing my bags, running away from feeling like this. What was happening to us and why couldn't I stop it? I had spent centuries feeling cold detachment and I did not expect to be feeling this way now with Rafael. It didn't feel good. I kept hoping to receive a text from him, maybe even an apology, but my phone remained quietly by my side, and I felt my heart shatter some more.

Then, finally, a *ding* as I was headed to bed, a simple text message: *Good night. I'm sorry*—but my emotions were turned off at the moment. I felt no pleasure or anger from his text. I felt absolutely nothing. The world could end right now, and I wouldn't care at all. I was back to square one with my feelings. I threw my phone across the room, damning him.

CHAPTER ELEVEN

1921

He had the most beautiful light eyes she'd ever seen, truly comparable to Malcolm's, but his were neither cold nor cruel, and she found it easy to drown in them. Tall and well built, he had a very charming smile. What attracted Alia more was his personality and his respect for women; at twenty-three years old, he still waited for the right girl to share a night with and while most men would feel bashful, he openly talked about it. It gave her a taste of what she'd never have: someone who cared about her well-being as much as theirs.

He didn't know she was a vampire—that part she had kept to herself—but knew she was involved in an abusive relationship, and he didn't mind taking care of her, giving her a bed to sleep in from time to time while he took the couch. He trusted her entirely and yet she had to take him. Malcolm had his eyes set on him, had sent her here to begin with; it amused him to turn good people into monsters. But mostly, it amused him to break Alia again and again, forcing her to commit atrocities that he knew would haunt her. She was well aware of what the consequences of refusing his orders were and she just didn't have the strength to endure them. She had to do this.

She didn't have to try very hard to and get this good man into bed; he had long ago fallen for her. The moment she arrived at his apartment, he could tell something in her demeanor had changed. She kissed him aggressively, fumbling with his clothes, and as she let him lay her down on his bed, she despised herself for what she came here to do. As if taking his innocence wasn't enough, she also had to take his life. He began working his way down, kissing and sucking on her breasts, her navel…

Her mind was reeling. She didn't love him, only cared because of the attention he gave her. She craved sweetness and gentleness so much that she would have cared for anybody that gave it to her. She couldn't do this after all. "Wait," she gasped. "You don't want to do this with me."

"Yes, I do." He kissed her neck.

"No, you really don't," she said as she pushed him off her and scrambled to pick her belongings off the floor. "You don't want to waste this experience on me. I don't really care about you." She cupped his face in her hands. "You are one of the few good ones and I don't deserve you. I will never leave him for you; he'll kill me if I do."

"We could go to the police, find a way to be together."

"You don't understand what he is like. No, this is over."

He tried stopping her from leaving but in vain. She hesitated in going back to Malcolm, and with good motives. He was infuriated. It wasn't the first time she defied him, and this was the last straw. He was deranged and beat her with ferocious cruelty. He meant to belittle her in front of their family. Her bones broke, her blood spilled, but he didn't falter. She was so hurt; she couldn't beg him to stop anymore. As Malcolm was about to cast his final blow, William held him back, making Malcolm snarl and growl like a wild animal, but it also gave Liz enough time to grab Alia. She dragged her out of reach, and cradled her friend's head in her lap. Alia, unable to move, was attacked by a series of bloody coughs. Finally, Malcolm threw William off him.

"Get these two out of my sight before I kill them!" he bellowed.

Alia was carried to her room and taken care of by Liz. She remained by her friend's side. Alia's wounds would have healed instantly, but she hadn't fed in a very long time.

"He's completely lost it," Alia whispered, afraid of listening ears.

"Honey, I don't think he ever had it," her friend replied, dabbing at her wounds with a wet towel.

"He's going to kill me someday. I have to get away, leave before it's too late."

Liz thought for a moment. "You mean *we* have to get away. If you're leaving, William and I will follow."

"I can't ask you to do that."

"We've only stayed for you. We don't want to be here any more than you do, but I couldn't live with myself if we just left you behind. We can leave once you're healed." She hesitated. "You know, blood would help speed the process."

"No, I won't give Malcolm the satisfaction."

Liz sighed, exasperated. "You can be just as stubborn as him." She shrugged. "Then we wait. I'll plan everything. Just stay out of his way."

No matter how badly Malcolm hurt her, he expected Alia to sleep in his bed, and as she lay there awake, her wounds finally healed after a couple of days, she felt a sense of excitement she hadn't experienced in a long time. Tomorrow was it. Tomorrow, William, Liz, and Alia would escape. Malcolm was asleep next to her, and as she watched his chest rising and falling in a slow but steady pace, she couldn't help her lips from curling in disgust and felt nothing for him other than hatred. What would happen if she just ended his life right there and then? Would the rest of the clan applaud her or turn against her? It seemed all but Liz and William earnestly viewed him as the pack leader. She wondered if she actually had the guts or even the strength to kill her own maker. She could cut his neck and watch him bleed into oblivion—giving her just enough time to stab him through the heart and cut it out of his chest before he healed. It would ensure their safe travels but if she missed, he'd be on her in a heartbeat. She could imagine it so well that she almost tasted the victory. No, leaving quietly was the best solution.

She silently left the room when night began to fall and met Liz and William down the hallway. None said a word, not wanting anyone overhearing their plan and giving them away. They acted casually, although Alia kept looking over her shoulder, and left the property's grounds and headed into town. They hopped on a train, hiding in a wagon, and watched the landscape roll past in darkness. Alia felt far from safe but dared to hope for the first time in a century. Malcolm didn't know they were gone yet and wouldn't know until morning when she didn't return to bed. They had made sure to spread their scent all over town so he wouldn't notice their departure until the sun was coming up, much too late to stop them. It would give them a head start.

They did not have a destination. They would try putting as much distance between themselves and Malcolm as possible, crossing the country and continuously moving. They did not expect he would let them go without a chase. They went underground during the day, sleeping in abandoned stores, metro stations, and even sewers as a last resort, and recommenced their travels by night.

They temporarily settled in a small town while coming up with a new, solid plan, living in an old, single-story abandoned house. The wooden flooring was caving in, the wallpaper was peeling off, rat droppings were everywhere, and there was a serious mold issue. It was perfectly imperfect and would hopefully hide their scent.

They enjoyed their first taste of freedom by heading to the movies, attending a theater piece, going out dancing, and seeing a side of the world that wasn't centered around death and violence, but enjoyment. She worried about Malcolm finding them, seeing his face on passersby, only to blink and realize they were, in fact, strangers. Her anxiety grew with each passing day. It had been too easy to escape him, and she knew he was too controlling to let them go. Weeks passed, a month rolled by, and still no trace of him. Could he have chosen to let them go? Liz and William didn't seem to worry about it, but they should have.

Following a hunting outing, Alia arrived home one night and immediately sensed something was wrong. He had found her; she could recognize his smell from anyone else's. She stood outside the dark house, considering whether to go in or not. She could turn on her heels and leave, but also needed to know if Liz and William were safe because she couldn't smell them. If she left now, she could still have a chance at her freedom, but couldn't leave the only two people she cared about behind. She stepped inside the small kitchen and a man was sitting in the dark, his back to her. She froze and backed away, hoping he hadn't heard her.

"If you run, I'll kill your friends."

"Where are they?" She walked around his chair to face him.

"On their way back to the mansion, where they will be severely punished."

"Why are you doing this?" she whispered in defeat.

He moved faster than her eyes could perceive, smacking her into the wall where she crumbled to the floor. She had no fight in her.

"Because you belong to me," he whispered in her ear as he knelt. "You are mine. Whether you want it or not, you are my queen, and you will begin acting as my queen. I will no longer be embarrassed or made a fool of by your actions. Next time you disobey me, I will kill someone you care about. I hope you enjoyed your little vacation because I will *never* let that happen again."

He half pulled, half carried her to a car parked in the street and shoved her into the passenger seat. They both sat in a mostly empty train on their way back home. She hated him with a burning fire and couldn't stand to look at him. She cried quietly, but the tears rushed down her pale cheeks one after the other in a repeating sequence, and she didn't care to hide them. He forcefully dragged her back into the mansion where he left her in the entrance hall. Everyone stared at her with curious looks. She avoided their eyes, put her bag on her shoulder, and walked up the staircase to her bedroom. She put her belongings on her bed and looked around. She hated this place so much. The darkness of the walls, the outdated furniture.

Uncontrollable tears invaded her eyes once more. She wondered about Liz and William, but they weren't in their room, and their scents were long gone. She stood by their open door.

"Where are they?" she asked.

"They are being disciplined."

Malcolm had tried to creep up behind her, but she had smelled him. It was a familiar scent that now made her stomach turn with hatred. He began rubbing and kissing her neck. He had to be kidding.

"I missed you," he murmured.

"I'm sure you didn't. With all these whores you're accustomed to, I'm sure you barely noticed my leave."

He slowly moved her into the room, but Alia was rigid. She didn't want to be intimate with him. Never again. Her body was no longer for him to toy with.

"Don't," she snarled between closed teeth.

"Don't refuse me, Alia, it could become gruesome." He tightened his grip on her arm, and it hurt. "I always get what I want, one way or the other."

She expected he wouldn't take well to her refusal but couldn't hide the shock from her face. "You disgust me."

He pushed her on the bed, ripping at her clothes like an animal. She saw this for what it was: she had defied him, and he was now asserting his dominance over her. She should have killed him when she had the chance and she had missed so many opportunities. She tried to fight him off, punching and kicking as hard as she could while he tried to pin her down. Her struggle didn't bother him a bit; if anything, it excited him more. She desperately looked around and noticed a small knife on the desk that seemed close enough to reach. She extended her arm, twisting on her belly, struggling to touch it. Her fingertips were almost to it as Malcolm dragged her back. She felt the weight of his body on hers as he straddled her legs. She let out a small laugh in relief as her hand enclosed around the handle and aimed it towards Malcolm. He stopped moving for a moment, then stood.

"Again with this? How is that going to help you?"

She angled the blade at her own throat. "I swear if you ever touch me again, I will kill myself and then I will be free of you regardless." Her voice broke and she began sobbing hard. "I can't do this anymore. Do you hear me?" she shouted.

He watched her closely and whether he cared that she lived or not, he stood up and walked to the door. "Fine. You and I are done. But you are not allowed to leave, and if you do, I will always bring you back. You are part of this household forever."

The rest of the clan did not interact much with Alia. She was certain Malcolm had given them orders to alienate her. Eventually Liz and William reappeared, and Alia would never learn what truly happened to them. They kept their lips sealed on what had taken place. William remained the same, if not a little guarded, but Elizabeth had changed. She was cold, distant, and wanted nothing more to do with Alia who had tried to talk with her many times. Liz would bluntly walk in the opposite direction, or leave the room when Alia entered. Malcolm's plan was working. His queen was being isolated from those she loved. She was alone, his to toy with.

She didn't view it as an ending friendship. She viewed it as a true betrayal, and Liz's betrayal was like a knife carving Alia's heart out. Not only had Liz given up hope, her promises and her love, but she had given up all together on Alia. This hurt her worse than anything else could ever have. Alia tried to block these feelings out, but the pain still flowed. How could she let go so easily? They had been together in this for so long. She longed for her sister, her friend, like a part of herself was missing. How could she survive Malcolm's tantrums alone? She stood no chance.

These were memories that always depressed me. How could things have gone so terribly wrong? Playing the piano was always comforting, so I played it for most of the day. I was taught by the best, Mr. Ludwig Van Beethoven himself when he was younger, and I particularly enjoyed his music. "Moonlight Sonata" and "Fur Elise" were by far my favorite pieces. We met in Vienna in 1787, and he fell head over heels for me. That was one thing Malcolm encouraged in his constant search of new additions to the family: travel. I strongly considered turning the musician, if only to listen to his music forever, but Malcolm didn't allow it. His disappearance would have raised too many questions. It would never be unraveled, but the long love letter titled "Immortal Beloved" referred to me.

My Bösendorfer 290, the largest piano model, was in the entrance hall underneath the chandelier, the light reflecting off its polished black wood. I had returned to Vienna to visit the Bösendorfer salon and to select my own handcrafted instrument, paying a small fortune to have it custom made. I was still playing when Rafael let himself in. He was in an unusually cheerful mood, as though the previous night never happened, which quickly annoyed me. He wore workout shorts, and he had sweated through his shirt. He dropped his gym bag next to the piano and bent down to give me a kiss.

"I'm really sorry about last night. You don't make me feel weak. I was just really scared and unable to protect you."

I answered him with a noncommittal shrug.

"I didn't know you played so well," he exclaimed.

"There are still a lot of things you don't know about me," I answered bitterly.

He wasn't taken aback by my hostility. He simply sat next to me on the bench and listened to me play. My eyes were closed; no expression crossed my face. I was giving myself to the music. It was beautiful, slow, and terribly sad. It brought emotions out of Rafael he didn't know still existed. Sadness gripped his stomach and tears began to well up. His surroundings disappeared—only the music remained. It was a powerful feeling. All the years he had been alone, depressed and misunderstood, submerged in the dark. I could sense what he was feeling from our connection, but I would have guessed at his emotional state regardless, for the music made me feel the same. His throat tightened; he shook his head and cleared his throat. He saw his mother's face, beautiful and smiling, as radiant as he remembered her. The pain he had learned to live with engulfed his being. She had abandoned him and left him to fend for himself. Adjusting and surviving had been so hard. I love you, I hate you, I miss you, he thought. The feeling wouldn't leave; he jumped up and walked a few feet, breathing heavily. I slowly stopped playing, opening my eyes and watching him. He turned his flushed face to me, a hand in his hair.

"Did you feel that? What the hell was that?" he asked, gasping.

"Magic. I'm a witch, remember?" I answered with a smile.

He seemed worn out. For the first time I saw the deep purple bags underneath his eyes. When had this happened? Had I ignored his well-being?

"When was the last time you had a full night of sleep, Rafael?"

"A couple of nights ago. I just... can't sleep very well without you."

"That's not healthy. Why don't you go upstairs and take a nap?"

"Because I don't want to miss a second of being with you." He circled my waist from behind.

"When was the last time you ate?" I kept questioning.

"What's with all these questions?" He was getting annoyed.

"You look terrible, Rafael! Just because I don't eat food and don't need much sleep doesn't mean you must follow my lifestyle. Get something to eat and rest."

"Okay, but come lie with me." He walked towards the kitchen.

I could always feel his mind being active during his waking hours or inactive during his sleep, but I felt something new—his mind, going blank as though someone turned the power switch off. A slight panic surged through me. I ran to catch him as he collapsed. I slid on the floor and caught his head in my lap before it hit the ground. I called his name, but he wouldn't wake. Was he breathing? I put my ear to his mouth, feeling his breath. What was I to do? Call an ambulance? I scrambled to my feet, grabbed my cell phone out of my purse to dial 911, but then stopped. I lived about thirty minutes from the closest hospital. By the time an ambulance got him there, an hour would have passed.

"George? George!" I screeched.

He came running down the hallway and stopped short, seeing Rafael on the floor.

"Is he..."

"He just fainted, but he's not waking up. We need to get him to the hospital." I had a suspicious feeling he may have thought I bit him.

George nodded, ran to grab the car keys from his room, and met me again. He grabbed Rafael's feet and I grabbed under his arms, and together we carried him to the car.

"Alia, the sun..." George grunted. Rafael was not a small man.

"I'll be fine, keep going," I answered as we passed the front door.

The afternoon sun hit me, and I gritted my teeth. God, it hurt. My skin started smoking. Blisters were already forming and soon they'd burst—me with them. Thanks to George's help, we quickly got my partner in the back of the car. I dropped into the front seat, and we sped towards the city. I kept looking back, hoping to see him waking up, but his skin had turned a clammy yellow. His face was covered in sweat.

After what felt like an eternity, the car came to a screeching halt in the parking lot and I ran inside the lobby. "I need help! Someone help me, please! My boyfriend is unresponsive in the car." I must have looked like a mess, frantically screaming. A couple of male nurses ran out with a stretcher, and I finally let myself take a long, hard breath.

I was not allowed to follow Rafael through the double doors. They had asked me for my identification, which clearly labeled me as a vampire, if the burns didn't make it obvious enough, and the doctors didn't trust me around their patients. I waited impatiently in the waiting room, a million thoughts running through my head. The other people in the room had given me a wide berth and I sat alone in a corner. In a matter of seconds, I had been reminded how feeble human lives were. What could possibly be taking them so long? For the first time in what seemed ages, I was scared. Scared I was about to lose him, and it was my fault for not taking care of him. A nurse met with me.

"How is he?" I asked, hugging myself tightly.

"He will be alright. Exhaustion and severe dehydration. Nothing too serious, but we want to keep him overnight so we can check on him. His heart rate dropped dangerously low." She hesitated before continuing. "Would you please head to the cafeteria and drink something? Your wounds are not healing and you're scaring everybody."

"Oh, yeah, I'm so sorry about that." I looked down at myself. "It didn't even occur to me."

My mind was blank while riding the elevator down, and now that I sat at a table, cupping a microwaved mug of whatever kind of blood this was, I was beginning to get angry with the situation. Who had I been trying to fool? Rafael had connected himself to me, and I was the last person who should be responsible for a human's life.

It took a long time to convince the nurses to let me see him. The room was white with no paintings, no plants, and nothing to bring color. The blinds had been pulled so I could walk in. A strong smell of rubbing alcohol floated in the air. Rafael lay asleep in a hospital bed. I swiftly lay next to him and intertwined my fingers with his. I put my head on his chest and listened to his heartbeat. It was regular. It pleased me.

He had gotten sick, and it was my fault. I should have known better. He was trying to keep up with me. I would end up killing him. I had been rather selfish and should have stayed away from him like I had originally planned. In that moment, I made a new choice.

How could I be doing the right thing when it hurt so much? For the first time my heart and mind agreed—I would not be okay. I had to leave the love of my life in order for him to stay alive. Sacrificing his health to be with him was not fair. I'd hurt, I'd cry, and hopefully, I'd get over it. Thinking about life without him brought tears to my eyes. A feeling of shame, emptiness, and disgust filled my heart. I held myself tightly, hoping to ease the pain. Every time I thought of our broken future, or what could have been, the familiar feeling pierced my heart. Despair.

He woke up the same evening, and I was still listening to his heart. He groaned and moaned at the sight of the needle stuck in his arm.

"What the hell is this for?"

"To hydrate and feed you. Something you're apparently incapable of doing for yourself."

He groaned again. "Can we please not do this right now?"

I paced around the room. Worried, he watched me quietly. "I just can't put you or myself through this anymore. It was an unreasonable delusion."

"What are you talking about?" he painfully raised himself higher.

"Us. You don't fit in my world, and you never will. I am spending more time as a mother than a girlfriend. I don't need to take care of anyone else but myself."

"You don't mean that. I know what you're doing, babe. This is nothing. It was a mistake on my part. It won't happen again."

A mistake that would have much worse consequences the next time. I needed to untie myself from him for his own sake.

"It's over, Rafael. I have nothing to offer you. I can never have children. I can never be a girl for you to protect—we're just too different. You need to forget about us. This never happened." I turned my back and made for the door.

"You know I can't do that."

I looked over my shoulder and replied, "I'll make sure you will."

I felt his heart rip apart as I walked out. I didn't want to look back, ever. It hurt me, so much more than I thought it would. I had asked George to return home when I received Rafael's diagnostic and was surprised to see him still waiting in the parking lot. I felt so grateful for this amazing human in my life.

"I had nowhere else to be," he said with a shrug, opening the back passenger door for me. I sat down, trying to hold myself together as much as possible.

Quickly the tears blinded my sight, and the road became a

blur. I asked him to pull over as I began sobbing, unable to breathe. I stepped out of the car. Putting my hands on my hips, I gasped for air. I watched the rain drip as I listened to its rhythm and its music; I felt a wave of comfort wash through me. I was terribly cold, but the rain soothed me. It was calming. A light breeze picked up, sending a shiver down my spine. I knew what I had to do.

I returned to my property and waited for the moon to rise to prepare myself for a spell. My blood ran through Rafael's veins and our bond was strong. Only heavy magic could obliterate it. I gathered a red candle for strength, a white candle for healing, a blue candle for change, my dagger, and a picture of us. We had taken it in Colorado months and months ago and we looked so happy. I headed to the roof where the stars would be my guide. I cast my magical circle, stepped in, and sat down. I cleared my mind and became one with myself. I was unsure if I really wanted to erase both our minds, which made meditating and focusing on the task at hand a bit more difficult than it should have been. I first lit the red candle, chanting and begging the spirits for the strength I'd need. I raised my arms above my head.

"Friendly spirits hear my plea! Come down upon me and obey these words of power! Give me strength! Give me your will! Give me control!"

I was so focused that I hadn't noticed the wind picking up. A storm was approaching and the air was filled with electricity when a lightning bolt hit me, its energy being diffused to me. I was power and force. It was seductive, and I found myself in a state of euphoria. The spirits were granting my wish. As much as I wanted to take my time and enjoy this feeling, I knew I had to hurry and complete the spell before it wore off. I lit the white candle and began chanting. Although the weather was becoming rough, my magical circle protected the flames.

"White to heal and hope. White to return peace and innocence. Starry Goddess full of might, help me tonight."

I lit the blue candle and cut my index finger over the flame.
A few drops trickled over it and I drew the rune for romance
over the picture and burned it, destroying the romantic connection we had built.

"I burn you, Rafael, out of my sight, out of my mind and
memory. I burn myself, Alia, out of your sight, out of your mind
and memory. The moonlight shines over me as I banish these
memories," I yelled. We had been together less than a year, but
I couldn't deny we had spent good times together. He had made
me feel more alive than I had in centuries, and that was important to me.

The spell was nearly over with. All that remained was
blowing out the candles in reverse order, and our memories and
feelings would be whipped out. The need for strength came
into play at this moment. Could I finish this? I uncertainly blew
out the blue candle. Did I want to finish it? My heart ached and
I felt the tears drip down my cheeks onto my lap. I loved him, I
knew I did, and I had to remind myself I was doing this for his
safety— wasn't I? With the white candle in hand, I forced the
sobs back but did not blow it out. I placed it back down. I was
so afraid to let him in, to let him see the ugliness inside me
because if I did, how could he ever love the demon in me? I did
not feel I was worthy of his love. The walls around my heart
were fueled by every excuse I could find to push him away, but
I couldn't deny myself love any longer. It was selfish in a way
and if we didn't find a way to coexist, he would certainly get
hurt again. But I would fight for love. I was not going to finish
the spell. I knew I had reached the right decision when relief
flooded me.

I carefully erased the protection circle, eliminating the
magic, and tried calling Rafael. Once, twice, thrice. I called the

hospital and a nurse informed me Rafael demanded to be released early. His vital signs had risen back to normal levels and they had let him go. I quickly packed an overnight bag and drove to his house. Luckily for me, the roads were pretty empty at this hour, especially with this amount of rain coming down. I pushed my car faster than I probably should have, making it there within twenty-one minutes. His truck was out front, and the house was dark but for his bedroom window. I was drenched from my short run from the driveway to the front porch and banged on the door.

He looked surprised to see me standing there. "Alia? What are you doing here?"

The thunder broke right over our heads, making me jump. "I am so sorry for what I said earlier. Can I please come in? I just want to talk." I made to walk in, but he blocked the door with his arm.

"There is really not much to talk about. You're right, it's over. We're terrible for each other."

"Wait, what? You can't mean that. I don't even believe that." My heart was racing. I began feeling panic.

"Don't you?" I could hear the tremble in his voice, the way his heart was breaking speaking these words. "You never even told me you loved me. This," he said, pointing at us, "never meant anything to you or you wouldn't continuously try to break things off every time we have a fight."

"I know I took this a bit far, but I was really scared for you. I've been alone for so long, and it's really hard for me to let anyone in. I just didn't want to see you get hurt again."

He shook his head and began closing the door on me. "Do us both a favor and make right on your promise. Make me forget you."

"I couldn't do it," I cried as I crumpled to the floor. I shook my head. "I love you too much to end it. I love you, I do."

He stood on the doorstep, looking down at me, and I couldn't meet his eyes, I just continued sobbing. He knelt down, grabbed my chin, and forced me to make eye contact.

"You love me?" he asked, with a mixture of hope and doubt.

"I do, so much." I put my arms around his neck and wrapped my legs around his waist as he lifted me off the floor, kissing me passionately.

We never made it to the bedroom. Kissing and tasting each other as though it was the first time, we ripped at each other's clothes. I knelt in front of him, unbuttoning his pants and taking him all into my mouth while he placed his hands on the back of my head. I felt him shudder as he was getting close to releasing and he lifted me off the ground, taking possession of my mouth once more, laying me on the stairs. They dug painfully into my back, but I didn't mind as he pulled my jeans off and returned the favor until all I wanted was him buried deep inside of me. When I got my wish, he rode me right there on the staircase, ass up, and pulled on my hair. It was animalistic. It felt natural, as though my world was back on its axis. He was mine and I was his. I never wanted us apart again.

CHAPTER TWELVE

1925

The house was buzzing with activity. They were expecting hundreds of guests and Alia had charged everyone within the house with different responsibilities to help prepare for this party. A large group was charged with cleaning the mansion, while smaller ones were to set up the thirty-two round banquet tables and chairs in the ballroom. Each table, decorated with vibrant flower bouquets, had to have its own tablecloth and tableware. In the meantime, she worked on the seating chart, all the while monitoring the set up. Looking around, she then realized two people were missing, and annoyance flooded her. No surprise there. She had had little interaction with Liz and William over the years. There had been no coming back from their falling out but she was still in charge and expected them to fall in line. She put her chart down with a sigh and went searching for them. Walking through the house, she was pleased to see the party coming together nicely. At least everyone else was doing as she asked.

She heard their voices shouting from inside their closed bedroom and felt no shame in eavesdropping.

"You must leave! You are in danger!" William begged.

"And you are mad! The party is in a couple of days. I am not going anywhere," Liz answered, laughing.

"Don't make me force you."

"And don't threaten me, William."

"Please! Why won't you ever listen to me? Something terrible is going to happen!"

"Stop it! I've told you before, I refuse to live my life by your visions! I make my choices and I decide what happens in *my* life!"

Alia had never heard William so indisputably afraid and although Liz had not seemed to take the warning seriously, it had found a spot in the back of Alia's mind. She walked away, not revealing herself, and tried talking to William about it later in the day. He had been upset about her listening in and he pretended she heard him wrong.

Now, two days later, she sat rigidly by Malcolm's side. She was looking down at the hundreds of vampires dancing in the large ball room. Their clan and disciples in her castle. The women wore long, beautiful evening gowns while the men wore tuxedos. All danced in rhythm, as if rehearsed, to the classical orchestra. Alia was by far the most beautiful. Her purple-and-silver gown went past her feet, the sleeves tightly attached to her shoulders, gradually becoming larger and looser by her wrists. Her eyes illuminated her face, and she wore no makeup. Her hair was up in a tight braid and decorated with a golden tiara. She and Malcolm sat on their thrones as if they were royalty. Everyone was at their feet.

Liz was on the dance floor and seemed to be having fun, switching partners vigorously. She didn't appear bothered by William's absence. Where was he? He had been acting extremely strange, and it wasn't like him to miss a party of this size. She felt it in her gut—something was not right.

"What have you done to William?" she asked in a low voice and continued watching her people.

"I don't know what you're talking about, dear." Malcolm's voice was not as deep and calm as it normally was. It held an edge of anxiety. Another red flag.

"If you've hurt him, you will pay for it."

"I assure you, I don't know where your friend is. Besides, you sired him. If he were hurt, you would feel it." He looked worried and somewhat stressed.

Suddenly, a crash resounded from the other side of the room, loud enough that the music and dancers stopped. A body had been thrown into a glass door, sending shards every which way. The corpse was a husk, entirely drained of blood and muscle mass. Alia and Malcolm raised off their thrones to get a better look, but they were so far away and so many people were in the way that she couldn't see much. Then, low, guttural growls could be heard all around the room, letting all attendees know they were surrounded.

"Malcolm, what is happening?" she asked, but didn't get to hear his answer.

Abruptly, a breed of monsters she had never encountered before entered the room and began a massacre faster than Alia could understand. Blood sprayed on the tablecloths and the guests began screaming in utter fear, attempting to find exits that were blocked off by more monsters. She found herself surrounded by screams, pleadings, and blood. She and Malcolm ran down the dais and were soon separated. Vampires were running around her, knocking into her, trying to escape. But each one fell, demons ripping them to shreds. She was breathing hard, unable to think of what to do, how to help her family. Where was Liz? She had to find her. She began walking forward on unsteady feet, her heart pounding in her ears, while more bodies fell around her.

Malcolm saved her, took her in his arms, and carried her away. Because the creatures seemed to be congregated in the ballroom, he took her to the kitchen.

"We have to save them," she mumbled, shell-shocked.

"Alia, listen to me, you must hide here or they will kill you."

"What are they? How do we kill them?"

"They're called Astaroths, and we don't. *Stay here* until I come back for you. Do you understand me? Stay here. It's an order."

He cared about her after all. She lay low on the ground, behind an overturned banquet table, hoping to become invisible. She grabbed a butcher knife that had fallen and held it tight to her chest, feeling as though it gave her the smallest chance of survival. Her breath came out in gasps as she heard voices but couldn't make out actual words or see who they belonged to. Danger surrounded her. Her senses screamed for her to leave this place and she knew she should listen to her instincts. But Malcolm and Liz were still in there. She raised her body and scrutinized the darkness. Finally, she saw shadows walking by very slowly as if looking for someone—her, perhaps. She flattened herself back onto the floor, holding her breath, chocking back a sob, and praying they wouldn't discover her. The stench of blood was overwhelming. Why was Malcolm taking so long? Had it been an hour, two, or more? She took short, anxious breaths, and her head spun. He had told her to wait here, but she now realized he may not come back after all. She sobbed silently, slowly drifting into madness, tears dripping down her cheeks onto her dress. She slipped into a state of mind between dreams and reality.

The sun would rise soon; she could feel it. She had waited for hours and hours, but she was alone. She saw an opportunity open and ran back to the gruesome scene. The Astaroths seemed to have left, although she couldn't be sure. Her friends, her family were all ravaged and mutilated. She walked from room to room, looking at the unseeing faces. She found Elizabeth's body, held it tightly and cried, screaming her distress. Alia's skin started warming up. Soon, all these bodies would return to ashes. The shadow had left long ago, and now was her turn.

After a few weeks of us going back and forth between each other's houses, Rafael officially moved in with me. I took care of making sure he ate and allowing us to sleep more. Since our schedule was different from the other people living in the house, Lidia cooked for him every day, leaving meals on a plate in the microwave for when we woke. On the days we happened to be awake, we sat with Lidia and George around the dinner table, sharing a meal, as a normal family would. I would have prepared Rafael's food myself, but it didn't have much taste to me, which made cooking practically impossible.

It was unusual for me to feel this nurturing towards another being, but I accepted the task. However, he seemed different. More reserved. Even slightly aloof, and I knew why. He felt I may change my mind again and the uncertainty was eating him alive. He didn't actually verbalize this to me, but I could sense his emotions as though they were mine.

He needed to get out of the house, and I booked us a stay-cation to the most peaceful place I knew. The beach held many secrets at night. The sun had just set, and the light was turning a pale shade of blue. The water was chilly under my feet as we walked along the surf, hand in hand. I inspected the sand for any shark teeth and other cute shells, but mostly found dead crabs and jellyfish. I sat on a blanket between Rafael's knees. I wore jeans and a light white, flowy tank top and I felt the wetness of the sand seep through the blanket. The strong wind, salty and sandy, was chafing my skin lightly. The raging waves crashed onto the shore, mesmerizing me into deep thoughts. The ocean seemed so empty yet wasn't. It only appeared to be that way on the surface. Deep within, a countless number of adventures awaited. The water was beautiful and cruel. It could be angry and calm at the same time. It brought fear and awe, much like me. Yet unlike me, the water followed no rules. It took whomever it pleased and had no one to answer to. The ocean was free, and I felt a pinch of jealousy.

"What are you thinking about?" Rafael murmured.

"The freedom the ocean has."

We lay back on the blanket and watched the electric stars. He seemed to loosen up a bit and laid his head on my chest, circling my waist with his arms. There was the warmth I missed. I could feel his heartbeat, strong and steady. Calm.

Some strange feeling came over me. Was it hunger? No, I was being watched. I sat up and looked around. It seemed no one was there but I knew a pair of eyes were on me. Uncomfortable and uneasy, I felt the hair on the back of my neck stand up. Rafael noticed the change in my demeanor and sat up as well.

"What's going on?"

"We're being watched."

"Okay. So what if we are? Let them watch," he replied, trying to push me back down.

My anxiety spiked and goose bumps rose on my skin. "We need to leave right now."

"Are you serious?" I was already up and packing, not minding Rafael's protests.

I was used to living with this constant warning in my mind, but suddenly, it grew stronger, causing me to stop in my tracks and look around for possible danger. I found myself breathing heavily.

"What is it?" Rafael was beginning to worry.

"I'm not sure. Something is happening. Babe, listen to me, please go to the car and wait for me. I'll be there soon."

I left no room for debating and reluctantly, he did as he was told, walking slowly towards the parking lot. I remained still, listening attentively to my surroundings.

"Hello, darling." It came from behind me. I knew who it

was without needing to look. That voice had been imprinted in my mind forever.

A chill ran down my spine. An old flame which had been extinguished soon came to existence again. I spun around, and my breath was caught in my throat. Malcolm. There, looking at me as though we had never spent a day apart.

"You're alive," I whispered. "All this time I spent mourning you, and you're still alive." He seemed amused. "All these years you led me to believe I was alone. Why? How could you?" Unable to contain my composure, I let myself shake from head to toe.

"Alia, you never truly believed I was dead. You just tried to fool yourself. Otherwise, how would you have been able to feel my presence?"

So much pain resurfaced that I barely listened to his words. "But why?" I breathed out.

"Do you honestly have no idea?" he replied.

A warning had been lingering in my mind for some time and I now realized my senses had been cautioning me about him, but I decided to suppress the feeling a little longer. The emotions which transpired from him told me a story I didn't know. I needed to hear the truth.

"How did you survive the attack? Did you have anything to do with it?" He remained silent but wore a crooked smile, looking at the ocean. "You did. The attack on our home was you; you planned it all. Didn't you?"

He faced me, his head tilted to the side, and his eyes pierced my soul. He knew what effect he was having on me. I remembered why I had fallen for him to begin with. Those blue eyes, piercing through my body and checking every inch of my skin, caused my knees to nearly buckle.

"You have always been nothing but a pawn in my game. From the moment I met you when you were a mere witch, I knew how powerful you'd become as a vampire. I told you when we first met, I am attracted to power. All I had to do was turn you and watch the years fly by as those powers grew within you," he said and paused for a moment. "When I bleed you, they will be transferred to me." He smiled.

I took a step back and he moved closer. "What was the point of killing the clan?" He paced slowly.

"They were all weak. I knew it was only a matter of time before they revolted against me, so I had to get rid of them. I paid for the Astaroths' allegiance by offering them a buffet. You weren't meant to die by their hand that night; I wanted you to the side for myself."

Anger was boiling my blood. "Then why didn't you ever come back and kill me?"

"Oh, I would have. I tried to come back, but Elizabeth somehow knew what was going on and tried to save you. It was a sweet attempt, but senseless. I really enjoyed killing that bitch. By the time I was done with her, the sun was rising."

The figurative knife he held in my heart turned and opened a larger wound. Liz. The guilt and longing I felt seemed to tear my whole being apart. I wondered if she had known how much I loved her. I wished I could tell her how sorry I was for resenting her all these years. She had tried to save me, costing her own life.

"But I'm glad that girl stopped me because I never would have guessed you'd survive this long on your own and how much your power would grow. As untrained as it still is."

I thought about Malcolm's intention to bleed me and something dawned on me. "So the Astaroth that attacked me a couple months ago followed your orders?"

He seemed pleased with himself. "It was only meant to bring you to me."

"I'm not going to let you kill me," I said in a shaky voice. I felt embarrassed for seeming so weak in front of him. I felt once again as powerless as when he and I were together.

We had been talking for quite a while when Rafael decided to come see what was taking me so long. I heard him approach and as much as I wanted to shout at him to stay back, I knew better than to take my eyes off Malcolm and make a scene. He slowly walked to my side, and I became rigid.

"What's going on here?" he asked, looking at Malcolm. He had to have recognized him but remained in control of himself. He glanced at me, and I knew I looked scared.

"Ah, the boyfriend." Malcolm clapped. "This is about to get very exciting." He apparently had been keeping tabs on me. "Does he know who I am?"

"It doesn't matter; it's not important. Leave him out of this."

Malcolm sniffed the air. "Your scent is all over him. What are you doing dating a human? It's disgusting. If you care about him, I suggest you turn him before I get my hands on him."

"Leave him out of this! It has nothing to do with him. This is between you and me."

I didn't know whether telling Rafael to leave would do any good. Malcolm's attention was already focused on my boyfriend. I took a few steps back, forcing Rafael to follow me, holding his arm tightly.

"You're not leaving here tonight, Alia."

He launched himself at me, tackling me to the floor, hitting me like a boulder, and I felt my bones crack. I screamed out in pain while my vision blurred. Yet all I could think about was Rafael and the danger he was in. His first instinct was to come to my aid, grabbing Malcolm and raising him off me. I watched the scene in a frozen terror. Malcolm turned around, still held against his will, and plunged his teeth into the man's throat. Rafael's screams broke me free from my stupor. Using all my speed, I raised myself off the ground, spun Malcolm around, and broke his nose—possibly his jaw as well—with a quick blow. While he collapsed, I examined Rafael. He was gasping for air and kept his hands firmly attached to his bleeding neck.

"Rafael, please let me see, I have to see how bad it is."

The gravity of the situation became very clear to me. Malcolm had ripped Rafael's throat apart, leaving pieces of flesh hanging. He was bleeding in my arms, and his pulse was growing gradually fainter.

"You're going into hemorrhagic shock. I have to stop the bleeding."

We only had moments before Malcolm would get up. I wrapped my sweater tightly around the wound, but it rapidly became drenched. Unless I did something, he would be dead within the next few minutes. Smelling his blood made me hungry. It was painful. Malcolm groaned and rolled over, his injury healing.

"Kill him," Rafael struggled to say.

"I have to take care of you first."

He had nearly become dead weight, but I pulled him up. I put my arms around his waist and walked him to the car where he slumped into the passenger seat. I raced the car far away from Malcolm. Forget our belongings back at the hotel—they didn't matter. A battle soon emerged within me. I cared too much for Rafael to let him die, but he didn't have much blood left in him and I doubted I'd be able to stop myself from drinking him to death. But I needed to have some of it in my system to make the transition. Looking over, I noticed he was white as a sheet and losing consciousness.

"Rafael, stay awake! Listen to me. Do you want to become a vampire? Answer me! You must agree to it!"

After hearing his faint "yes," I bit his wrist and drank almost all that was left of his blood. *You must stop. You have to stop.* His taste was intoxicating and succulent but if I didn't pull away now, I would kill him. I loved him and he was a good person. I knew I didn't want to hurt him, and so I found the strength to stop. I bit my own wrist and rushed my blood into his mouth. The taste of it disgusted him and he tried to squirm away, but I forced him to continue drinking. While Rafael fell into a deep slumber, I reached my property's gates. Rain poured against the windshield and my vision blurred. I was becoming weaker due to the blood loss. If somehow Malcolm was to launch an attack right this second, I would be in no shape to fight back. When I reached the manor, tires screeching to a halt, I used the last bit of my strength dragging Rafael inside and I collapsed to my knees. It took a few seconds to refocus my mind on what was at stake and a few minutes more to rebuild my energy.

Lidia and George hurried to our sides, helping me up. I escaped their grips. "You must leave the property immediately. I don't have time to explain, but please pack your belongings, hide, and don't tell me where you're going."

"Whatever is happening, we can help."

"No, you can't! You will get yourselves killed and I cannot have this on my conscience too. You can help by being safe far away from here."

I pulled Rafael inside the basement and attempted to prepare him for a comfortable awakening. I wasn't sure whether coming back here had been a good idea. I was alone and trapped within this big house. The Astaroths would come for me. *He'd come.* I drank as much blood as I could get my hands on, changed into more appropriate clothing, braided my hair—hoping it'd stay out of my face—and waited for their arrival.

Finally, there was a thud on the rooftop, then another, and another. My heart raced. I couldn't doubt myself. This was my house, and I knew every corner better than anyone else. Unless he had been watching me. No, no negative thoughts. Windows shattered. I positioned myself on the veranda where I had a view of the whole house and paced back and forth, giving myself a pep talk. My weapons of choice were two Glock 19s loaded with wooden bullets. I once again verified that my magazines were firmly attached to my belt.

The first round of Astaroths rushed in like a flood and they immediately fell as I landed my shots to their heads and chests. Black blood splattered in every direction. To my surprise, more arrived. For an endangered species, there sure seemed to be too many left. I shot steadily, my aim never missing. After the bullets were all gone, I was left with a sword. I dove into battle. Slicing left and right, heads rolled. Yet I couldn't see the end of them.

I ran upstairs in the hope of having a moment to rest. My arms were becoming tired, the weight of the sword starting to make my muscles ache. I hid behind a colossal and antique marble sculpture from the Italian Renaissance era I had gotten imported, wiping the sweat off my face. I tried to catch my breath. With a pinch to my heart and an ounce of shame, I struggled to push the statue down the stairs, squashing a good number of my enemies who didn't have the time to get out of the way. I had to get them out of the house and into the almost rising sun. I sliced my hand, smearing my blood on my clothes so the smell would travel, and dashed out of an open window into the woods.

The commotion behind me assured me they were following. I glanced at my cell phone: 6:15 a.m. The sun would rise within six minutes and these beasts were dumb enough to not realize that. My skin already burned and stung. I led the monsters deep within the forest and with the sun literally chasing me, most of them burned to death. The light had almost caught up with me when I slid into a cavern and huddled myself there. Most of the Astaroths had died following me, I knew it. I hoped Rafael was alright. My eyes burned and watered but I saw a form advance towards the cavern slowly. Malcolm was wearing a white hoodie, keeping his hands concealed within the pockets. I should have been scared, but I wasn't. Instead, I stood in awe. He had always had such charisma, and I had almost forgotten. His handsomeness appealed to me still. *What's wrong with me? He's trying to kill me.*

He was in the shade now. "That was an impressive show," he said, getting closer to me. I could smell him. Such a delightful smell, one that was so familiar.

"Why are you doing this, Malcolm? What is it you want?"

"I'm proud of all you've done for our kind. I really am. But it isn't enough, and I cannot allow your little ceremony to happen. We are not equal with humans, and we will always be superior. We need to be recognized as being at the top of the food chain."

"But why are you torturing me? Why have you always done this to *me*?" It was almost a whimper. "Why couldn't we have just been happy?"

"Because you were supposed to be my queen! You were so pure, like a rose, and I looked forward to you becoming a corrupted vampire with me. You were supposed to be mine! Instead, you just became a thorn in my side, a goody two-shoes I resented. I've been dropping in on you from time to time and watching you, decade after decade, thriving and pushing vampires to coexist with our food. I can't allow this to continue. I'm ready to play and you're not going to refuse me that privilege, are you?"

"I thought you wanted to kill me?"

"Oh, but you know how much I love playing with my food."

He slightly pushed me against a wall and touched a strand

of my hair. His erection was hard through his jeans, and he pressed himself against me. His other hand moved up my leg, rubbing up my pants.

"Stop it," I gasped.

His mouth was at the corner of mine. I wanted him, right there and then. I wanted to feel him buried inside of me. My animal instincts were trying to take over and the beast in me wanted him. I had to remember the fact that, on top of the immense abuse he had put me through, he still wanted me dead. Wouldn't that just make it more exciting? He was kissing my neck and rubbing my body. A face flashed before my eyes. Rafael. The man I loved now, the man I had just transformed into a vampire.

"Stop it," I repeated louder, frowning. "I am not the scared little girl I used to be."

He tried pinning me tighter to the wall and I slapped him across the face. He took a few staggering steps back, putting a finger to his bleeding lip. His eyes flashed pure hatred, and I was taken aback by their intensity. The weather changed dramatically. The wind howled, the sky became a dark shade of gray, and a thick layer of cold water began to pour.

"How are you doing that?" I asked, wide-eyed.

"I'm too powerful for you, Alia. With this much power, I can even control the elements." Again, he came closer to me, putting his mouth near my ear. "Do you think it was intelligent to leave your boyfriend in what is now a pile of ash?"

I turned my head, and in the distance, I could see a thick layer of smoke rising in the sky. How did I not smell it before? Rafael. My heart sped with panic and my breathing quickened.

"Oh, did I forget to mention? He's not in there. He's already long gone. As I said, it's all a game to me. I'll even place the wages on the table. I want you, Alia. You can offer yourself to me, body and soul, let me drink you, and your boyfriend goes free. Or you can refuse me. You can try to rescue him on your own and you both may end up dying. But let me assure you, there is no scenario where you don't die eventually."

He came closer again, tilting his head to the side as if I would just offer him my neck. I scoffed and pushed him back. "That's your offer? Go fuck yourself."

"I've waited this long; I can wait some more. You're the last remaining rose of our clan and I am curious to see what you're capable of. Trust me when I say it's only begun. By the end of this, you will beg me to finish you off." He abruptly grabbed my shoulders, bringing my face closer to his, and planted a closed lip kiss on mine. Then he pushed me back against the rock, my head hitting it hard. I crumpled to the floor, seeing stars and feeling blood dripping from my skull. I felt nauseous from the certain concussion.

He wandered into the rain, and I attempted to follow him, although it took me a moment to heal. I tracked him like an animal but the water covered any imprints and I soon lost him and his scent. The rain had stopped the flames from completely burning my house down, but nonetheless, I had nowhere to go. I quickly walked through the remains, making sure Rafael was indeed not underground. My history, my past, my memories—all gone. Maybe it was for the best. After this I would have to start anew.

The wind and rain fought hard against me, but I ran to the nearest town. After about twenty minutes, I entered a small psychic shop, drenched to the bone and shivering. The cashier, a small, chubby lady, looked at me above her round glasses.

"Where did this storm come from?" Her very short, curly hair amplified her swollen face.

"I have no idea," I lied. I looked around the store for a few specific items.

"Can I help you find something?" the elderly woman asked.

"Yes, I am looking for a small, clear quartz necklace and a map. I need to scry for someone."

All was ready by the time I walked back to the register. "Your total is $17.95."

I always had money pushed deep within my pockets, a bad habit Lidia hated on laundry day, and I was now struggling to get it out. I pulled bills out with quick, nervous movements.

"Dear, are you alright?"

"Not really." I laughed. A dry, hysterical laugh. "But we all have our sob stories, don't we?"

I extended my hand, holding a twenty-dollar bill. The lady extended her right index finger and lightly touched my wrist. Feeling my pulse, she sent me a thought. *You will succeed in vanquishing him.* I was caught off guard.

"You're a witch too?"

"Yes, and the only true psychic in town, if you must know."

Her power reached for me, calming me. "I don't have the power of foresight. Can you read my lines?" I extended my hand.

The woman focused hard on my palm, holding it tightly in her hands. "You are going to be faced with a hard decision. You will be forced to face your past life and demand help. You will succeed but not without loss."

"Will we live?"

"Every step and decision you take changes the future. I cannot tell you whether you will live or die because something like this is never certain. But I can see a war is coming and it will take a long time to end. I see pain, lots of it, and anger. I see your success, but not without loss," she repeated.

I didn't know what to say.

"Maybe you ought to rest for a bit. You look exhausted. There is a room behind this curtain. You will be safe," she continued.

"There is no time."

"You have nothing but time. They won't hurt him. He's waiting to see how long it takes for you to crack."

Once again, I was caught off guard. "You seem to know more than I do. I suppose you're right."

I walked alongside the psychic, passing shelves garnished with candles, incense, and talismans. She showed me to a room and left me to wind down a bit. I sat on the bed and let myself feel all that I had been avoiding since being on survival mode. The pain of Malcolm's betrayal, the fear, the anger. All of my worst memories with him came flooding back and I felt my throat tighten, my anxiety rising, and I was unable to stop the sobs escaping my lips.

CHAPTER THIRTEEN

1984

Alia was go-go dancing on stage to a Madonna song. She twisted her stomach, hips, and arms sensually. The sway of her hips, her fingers tracing along her thighs, her style— it was always very sexual, her mid-thigh skirt riding danger-ously high. She was putting on a great show for the many women watching because this bar secretly only catered to them. Malcolm had always sent her hunting; she had never been to a club or bar for the fun of it. Until now. She had also never gotten to truly learn about her sexuality, experiencing the different possibilities within herself. Until now. All she knew was that she couldn't possibly imagine being intimate with a man after all Malcolm had put her through. She may feel different in the future, but as of right now, this club felt safe.

Alia was being watched by many. She made a gesture meaning she needed help getting down.

Her hands were instantly met by a powerful grip. She had seen this woman here before, many times, but they had never made a move towards each other. Jennifer was around twenty-eight years old. She was about a half foot taller than Alia and lean, yet underneath her white T-shirt was some hidden muscles. Her black hair was about chin length and combed over to the side of her face. Her dark eyes were surrounded by long, fake eyelashes. She was beautiful.

As expected, she offered to buy Alia a drink. They headed to a corner, hand in hand, drinks in their others to talk more privately.

"I'm glad you've finally approached me tonight," Alia shouted to be heard over the music and took a sip of her Long Island iced tea. Her shudder amused her new friend.

"You don't drink much, do you?"

"Not really, no," Alia answered.

Leaning into her and whispering in her ear, Jenn asked her to head back to her place where they could actually hear themselves talk. When Alia agreed, Jenn took her hand, bringing it to her lips, and kissed it softly. She then led Alia outside where they waited for a cab to drive by to hail it. In the meantime, Jenn gently pushed Alia against a parked car and placed a shy kiss on her lips. Her gaze seemed to ask if this was okay, and when Alia returned it earnestly, it then turned hungry. Alia had been with the same man for 153 years, and it had stopped being exciting long before he died. This... she didn't know what this was. Only that it was a new experience and the fact that it was with a woman took a lot of anxiety away.

Homosexuality was not accepted. The taxi driver watching them in the rearview mirror frowned at their proximity until they sat as far apart as they could.

Jenn lived in a crappy one-bedroom apartment with a small bathroom and even smaller kitchen. She seemed to love her little place though.

"Are you thirsty?" she asked.

"More than you know."

"I have some red wine."

"I suppose that'll do for now."

She quickly scanned the room. No family pictures, no letters, not even a pet. They drank and conversed for a few more hours, mostly talking about their experiences with the city.

"Tell me about you," Alia requested, sitting cross-legged on the sofa.

Jenn stood by the window, looking out at the city lights. "Well," she said, "I was born and raised in Wisconsin and when I didn't fit the mold of the perfect little girl, I left my town and family behind with the first chance I got. Now I'm here." She took a sip of her wine. "How about you? I don't quite get a gay feeling from you."

Alia turned her eyes away, thinking carefully on how to respond. "I recently got out of a very abusive relationship with a man and I'm trying to figure myself out."

"Hmm, I always find the non-gay ones who just want to experiment." Jenn laughed bitterly. "Well,

I don't discriminate. Men, women—sex is sex, and I don't mind showing you what this side is about."

She walked across the room and placed her hands on the couch on either side of Alia. They were face-to-face now. She smelled good, like the tropics, mangoes, and salt water.

"I don't want you to feel used. I don't know if I can feel something real," Alia whispered, her eyes locking on Jenn's lips.

"Who said anything about feelings? Besides, I can handle myself."

Their lips met, hot and furious. Jenn leaned her back, straddling Alia's hips and massaging her breasts. Alia's breath came out in little gasps; she had never imagined being so turned on by another woman.

Jenn introduced her to bisexuality and Alia viewed the beauty in enjoying what men and women both had to offer. Jenn and Alia were involved for a little less than a year, understanding that they were not in a relationship nor were they monogamous. Alia didn't mind not being tied down and although they didn't meet often, when they did, late at night after Jenn's bartending shifts, it was a moment full of passion and eroticism. And although Jenn was a very spiritual and open-minded person, Alia never had to tell her of her true nature.

One early evening, Alia's landline rang. "Hello?" she answered while drinking a glass of chilled pigeon's blood. It was gross, but it would have to do.

"Hey, it's me."

"Hey Jenn, what's up? Shouldn't you be at work?" She glanced at the ticking clock on her kitchen wall.

"I, um..." she cleared her throat. "I called out. I need to speak with you. Can I come over?" she said with urgency.

"Sure, what time?" Something was going on and Alia's heart felt fear for the first time in a long while.

"I'll be there in thirty."

This gave Alia just enough time to clean up the apartment, put away the blood, and make it look like a regular human lived there. Then a knock came and Alia's worry doubled upon seeing Jenn's face. She looked ragged, unkept, and like she hadn't slept in a few days.

"What is going on?" she asked, letting her friend in.

"Sit down with me." She led Alia to the couch and grabbed her hands in hers, their knees touching.

Jenn took a deep breath. "Have you heard about this new disease that's killing gays?"

Alia hadn't expected to hear that and stuttered slightly. "Ye-yeah, a little."

Jenn's eyes were fixated on the floor. "I've got it. They don't really understand it and they don't know how to cure it."

Alia stifled a gasp with her hand; she couldn't hide the shock in her eyes. "Are you sure? Without a doubt?"

"I'm positive. I went and got tested. I've had headaches and this cough for a few weeks and now these rashes. I'm telling you because you may contract it too. Because of me."

"Oh, I don't think I have it. You don't need to worry about me." Alia's mind was reeling.

Jenn furrowed her brow. "Everyone believes it only happens to others, but I'm proof it doesn't. You need to get tested too."

Alia grabbed her in a tight embrace and Jenn's tough demeanor crumbled as she sobbed into her friend's arms. "I'm so sorry. I just hope you never contract it."

Alia kept her hands on her friend's shoulders and looked deep into her eyes. "I haven't been fully honest with you about what I am."

Jenn's tear-streaked face became confused. "What you are?"

Alia stood and headed to the kitchen, then turned around. "I'm going to show you something and I need you to keep an open mind. Don't freak out. Alright?" Jenn nodded and Alia returned from the kitchen with a sharp knife and a cup. Jenn couldn't see what was in the cup, but she was more focused on the knife anyway.

"Alia, what are you—"

"Just watch." She sliced her forearm from elbow to wrist, unable to hold back a little grunt of pain.

"What the hell are you doing?" Jenn jumped up, rushing towards her friend.

"Jenn! Just watch!" She downed the liquid

inside the cup in one shot and within a minute, Jenn watched the wound heal up. She looked as though her mind couldn't process what she had just witnessed, couldn't formulate thoughts.

"The virus can't get to me, Jenn, because I'm not human." She let her friend inspect her arm with disbelief. "I'm a vampire."

Her lover remained quiet and walked back to the couch where she just let herself drop down. "That's impossible," she murmured. "I must be hallucinating."

Alia kneeled in front of her. "You're not. We never met in the daylight, did we?" She could see Jenn thinking back to their time together.

"I can save you. I can make you like me. You don't have to die from this."

Jenn seemed in complete disbelief. "Who are you?"

And so, for the next few hours, Alia opened her heart, telling her story. They started sitting on opposite ends of the couch, and eventually moved to the bedroom just to lay more comfortably with Jenn's head on Alia's chest. She told her about Malcolm, about Liz and William, about the places she had seen. Alia was hopeful she would agree to it, but Jenn just shook her head a few times.

"I just don't think this is for me, you know? Eternal life sounds interesting enough, but I believe there is *something* after this life and I want to see where it takes me."

Alia rested her forehead against Jenn's. "I understand," she said. "I will miss you."

One month later, Jenn was gone, the disease having ravaged her body. And as sad as it made her to have lost yet another important person in her life, Alia was immensely grateful to have crossed her path and for all the lessons Jenn had had the time to teach her about love and freedom. Still, she couldn't help but feel as if this was how things would always be for her: she loved someone and they died. She put herself out there only to have her heart ripped to shreds. Everyone she loved died in terrible ways.

I woke up in an unfamiliar room; the walls were painted dark red and a few candles were lit. I lay on a pillow-covered bed. I was hearing echoing wind chimes although I could not see them. The room had a very peaceful feel to it. The room was filled with magic, as though sounds were muffled, and the air stood still. I was comfortable and at ease. It took me a moment to remember where I was and why. I reached for my crystal and map, then began to scry. I held the necklace above the map and focused on Rafael. The jewel turned in a circle over the city and stopped on a street name: Harrison Street. Downtown. The only place remotely relevant to vampires was a blood bank on the corner of Harrison and Essex, near Chinatown. I sighed heavily, furrowing my brow. Malcolm was toying with me.

Before performing any spell, I needed to meditate. I sat cross-legged in front of a golden mirror, deeply breathing in and out. I focused on controlling my emotions and reaching my happy place. I wasn't sure if it was an imaginary place within my mind as much as astral projecting, but I wasn't in the room anymore and found myself walking upon ice-cold sand dunes. There were no city lights; darkness surrounded me but for the bright moon shining down on me and reflecting off the sand. I continued breathing deeply, letting the pure air enter my lungs, and my boots sunk slightly into the sand as I walked around. A black scorpion desperately trying to escape the arriving sand-storm crawled up the hill. I watched it and studied it. I sensed its worry and its need to take cover. I squatted down and played with it. The animal wasn't afraid of me and wouldn't sting me, yet I wanted it to, so I lifted it by the tail and held it in the palm of my hand. I raised my eyes and observed the storm's progress. A dark and enormous cloud was approaching with a fright-ening roar. The animal became increasingly agitated, and I let it go. I kneeled down on the sand, closing my eyes, and felt the wind whipping my face deliciously. It made my long hair dance and I focused on centering myself. I felt alone and confused. Rafael needed my help. He was weak—I could feel it. If Malcolm wanted a war, he would get one, but he had better be ready for my fury.

Once I opened my eyes, I was staring back at my reflection, and I began to think. I could not fight Malcolm as a regular vampire and win. He was infinitely stronger than I was, but I could raise the stakes with a little magic. I feared if I were to fight many vampires on my own, I would need a lot more luck. I searched the shop area, which was dark and seemingly empty, for a few different colored candles, being careful not to make a mess. Then, I returned to the room.

I kneeled behind a small coffee table—my improvised altar —and lit a white candle to represent myself. "This is me, under the Goddess." Followed by a black one. "This is all the negativity, troubles, and fears. These leave me now." Then a gray one. "Bad luck and danger will vanish." I held an orange candle, which I lit after saying, "Friendly spirits accompany me on this journey and increase my chances."

I sat quietly and imagined the negativity vanishing from my life and dissolving into empty space. I pictured the good energy and good luck flowing through me. With a pinch of salt over the flames in order to represent the earth, the blaze crackled, and with a drop of my blood to bind the spell to me, I knew it was working.

I stepped out of the room, looking to thank my host, but she was nowhere to be found. I saw a cordless phone on the wall and made a few calls before leaving the store. One to Lidia to let her know what was happening and see if they needed anything from me financially. Who knew when we'd be reunited? But she assured me they were safe and well with distant family. I didn't ask about their whereabouts and she didn't offer the information. The second call I placed was to someone I hadn't seen in years who owed me a favor still. I would need all the help I could get.

I peeked outside the store through the curtains and saw that the sun was heavily covered still. I imagined it would remain this way as long as Malcolm was nearby. I decided to travel underground, dropping into the sewers with an air of déjà vu. I was sure Malcolm would have people on the look-out for me, but he didn't know the sewer system like I did.

CHAPTER FOURTEEN

1925

Her shoes were deep in the water, and the bottoms of her breeches were soaked. It had felt strange heading upstairs after the massacre as though nothing had happened, and changing into more comfortable clothing, but she couldn't very well travel in her regular flapper outfits. She barely remembered the walk through the forest back into town where she lifted a manhole and dropped into the tunnels.

The smell made her nauseous, and rodents crawled all around her. She was disgusted to have been reduced to such living arrangements. The sewers were not a place she liked to attend, but what other choices did she have? She was completely alone now and she had to hide. She had not seen Malcolm's body, but he would have never let her get away had he been alive. This was proof enough of his passing. Other clans would hear about the attack, and she doubted they would accept her. She'd be viewed as Malcolm's leftovers. Although she should have been scared, she wasn't. She didn't feel anything anymore. She had become completely numb and aimlessly roamed the tunnels. Shock prevented her from getting her thoughts together and forming a solid plan of action. How could they all be gone? She hadn't been close to a lot of them, but she had lived with some of these vampires for over 140 years. They were her family. And now they were all gone. Why had she survived? All dead. All but one. William was still alive; she felt it like a tiny spark within her chest. Suddenly, her new goal was to find him and be reunited with her brother.

She searched the whole world, quite literally, for William. She had become quite a tracker, but he always remained a step ahead. She couldn't wrap her head around his many different loca-tions. What was he doing? Egypt was the farthest he'd gone and where she lost his scent. It was as though he had evaporated. Alia was in Tennessee, heading to a familiar place, when she smelled him again, and she knew exactly where he was hiding. She was being watched, followed. She wasn't afraid; she knew it was William. Why wouldn't he come out? His smell was the strongest at the cavern's entrance. Alia followed the way down to the darkness, unsure of what she would say to her old friend. There were so many questions and so much anger, pain, and remorse. She wondered which emotion would take her over first. She set eyes on the castle as she had done various times, but a dark feeling sent shivers down her spine. He awaited her arrival on his throne. It used to be Liz's. His beautiful face was slim, tired, ghostly, and she read the shameful expression all over his face.

"I'm sorry, Alia, I'm so sorry I ran."

Anger was the first reaction. She was so close to him now, she slapped him hard, and her fury only intensified. She seized him by the collar and threw him off the throne. He crashed onto the ground where he remained motionless. "How dare you sit there?" Alia shrieked. "You are no king. You are a miserable, pathetic coward!" She was trying to hold herself together, but loud sobs escaped her lips. "How could you leave us unwarned?"

"You were warned. You heard us, and I knew you would survive."

"Me?! What about the others? What about Liz? You could have told us exactly what would happen!"

"I tried to warn her! I did what I could! She wouldn't leave with me!" He was crying as well, completely still on the floor. "I went around the world looking for a witch and a spell that could bring her back, but it doesn't exist."

Her head was spinning, and she thought she would vomit. "What could possibly be so important in the future that you'd let your soul mate die?"

"What I saw needs to happen, for everyone's sake. My pain doesn't matter in the grand scheme of things. My shame, my guilt. None of it matters."

She dropped to the floor next to him, putting her head between her knees and into her hands. She had been through so much, with her only goal to find him, and now it all came out. She continued crying. "You living in the future cost us everything," she whimpered.

They lingered on the floor, quiet for a very long time. "Is anyone we love still alive?" Her voice was a whisper. She had cried for too long and a numbness invaded her body and mind.

He took a while to answer. "No," he finally said.

The tears kept coming, but she wasn't aware she was crying anymore. William was lost, and she tried helping him find himself for several years while losing herself in her own depression.

I shook my head. I had to snap out of it. Now was not the time for painful memories and this walk, which wouldn't be short, would take twice as long if I let my mind linger in the past. Luckily or not, depending on how you viewed it, I spent so many months living in sewers in my life that I knew exactly how to navigate them and get from point A to point B. They were all set up in the exact same manner. Turning down junction, after junction, I knew I was under the blood bank.

I pushed the manhole open and slowly eased my way out, making sure no one was around. The tall building dressed in white seemed almost impossible to enter without being spotted. Almost. The body heat scanners would be set up at the entrance and back door, a precaution all blood banks had to employ to prevent vampires from robbing them. I could easily go in, killing everyone in my way, but I didn't want the police and media tracking me. I saw no cameras dangling off the building and recording the street, so I casually walked around looking for a way in that didn't involve the front door. I broke a side window and snuck in through the basement in order to avoid the heat scanners. So far, so good.

Using my vampire abilities, I moved faster than cameras could detect. I searched the rooms, trying to stay invisible to the world, but it proved harder than I thought. Most rooms were locked, and I pressed my ear to the doors, listening in. No sound—Rafael wasn't there. A couple of heads turned in my direction thinking they caught some agitation in their peripheral vision. Malcolm was nowhere to be found. It would be an easy in and out. The first floor was not a success, but the next level promised some result. Every corner became heavily guarded with humans or vampires.

I caught his scent and found the room they kept him in,

breaking the locked handle as quietly as I could. Inside was all white with no windows and no furniture, and I felt as though I were in an insane asylum. A regular human guard, dressed in black, was stationed inside. He drew his weapon and was easily shoved to the side. Rafael was heavily chained to the wall and unconscious. His transformation was complete, and I felt his thirst. I advanced towards him carefully, for this much need to drink would drive anyone crazy.

"Rafael? Babe?" I touched his burning forehead.

The cold feeling of my fingertips woke him up with a gasp. "Alia? What's happening to me?"

"I changed you. You were dying; I had to. But Malcolm kidnapped you. I have to get you out of here."

I leaned in, trying to break the chains, stretching my neck. The beast in Rafael took over and he plunged his teeth in me. I cried out in pain and I couldn't get him to unlatch without hurting him.

"Rafael, stop it! You'll kill me!"

He couldn't. He drank more and more. I finally was able to pry his face away and watched him, horrified. He became an animal, snarling and growling. He attempted to come after me, struggling against the chains. Finally, when they broke, he launched himself after me. We tumbled to the floor, rolling around. He was nowhere near as strong as I was, but I had lost a lot of blood and felt feeble. I struggled to reach for the human's gun, then held it tightly. He growled and groaned but I was straddling him and held him in a position from which he could not break away. I cocked the gun and waited for a moment. He looked calm now and almost serene. I, on the other hand, must have looked absolutely terrified, as if I were the one about to get shot.

"Rafael? Are you back?"

"I'm so sorry. I couldn't stop."

My neck was bleeding still. I knew we had definitely made too much noise and three soldiers came rushing in, ready to shoot. Three humans. I suddenly understood what kind of test this was: would I kill them or let them live? I rose and broke the first one's neck in a fraction of a second, grabbed the second one, and threw him towards my boyfriend. "Drink!" I screamed.

"But—"

"No but, just drink him now."

I sank my teeth into the third one before he could start shooting. I felt my wound close up, the invigorating rejuvenation flowing through me. My skin tingled. My powers felt more charged than they had in a long time. I had passed Malcolm's test and failed my own. I hadn't killed a human in years, and he was already getting me to behave against my morals. I watched Rafael as he embraced his new vampire senses and wondered if he felt the same kind of guilt I always did, or if he would be a regular vampire that lost his humanity little by little. I grabbed the three guards' guns on the way out, placing one in my waistband and holding the other two. We stayed close to the walls, checking every corner as we made our way down the hallways.

Then all hell broke loose. We were being shot at and I was doing my best, returning fire and driving them back. Then, I felt him. Malcolm must have just entered the building and was headed towards us. Fast. I didn't know how many bullets I had left, but we were at an impasse. I made a fast decision, shooting at the nearest window, although it was across from us. Our backs would be completely exposed.

"We're going to have to jump."

"Out of a second story window?"

"It's the only way. You're a vampire now. You'll be fine."

"Alia, wait a moment..." Rafael objected.

"No time. He's here. You go first and I'll cover you."

We counted to three and I poked my head around the corner, shooting again while Rafael made his escape. My last gun clicked empty. Shit. I ran towards the window and jumped out, feeling a bullet graze my thigh. It burned fiercely, but thankfully it was only grazed and with the amount of blood I drank, it would only take moments to heal. I landed swiftly on my feet, rolling to absorb the shock, and looked back at the window. Malcolm watched me. I smirked and flipped him the bird before taking off running, Rafael following suit. I began filling him in on what he had missed.

"We can't go home—Malcolm burned it down."

"The manor was burned down?" Rafael looked around, seeing everything more vividly than before.

"Yes, keep running, or we will miss it."

"Miss what?"

"Our plane."

"Plane to where?"

"You'll know in time. Just keep running."

The streets were blissfully almost completely empty, most people being at work, but the few humans walking about watched us with suspicion, crossing the street or changing directions as to not be in our way. Then I remembered we were covered in blood. I led the way, teaching him how to use his new vampire speed. "You must envision yourself a few steps ahead of where you are at the moment and continue to see farther and farther away before you get there."

I was amazed to find my cell phone still in my back pocket, although the screen was cracked. I needed to talk to Detective Thompson and let him know what was happening. The line rang until I got his voicemail. I began wondering if the Detective was still alive. He had been tracking Astaroths, and unknowingly, Malcolm too. I chose to not ponder this anymore as we entered the subway and waited anxiously on a platform. We were on our own. I knew where Malcolm was, and I no longer cared if he had people keeping tabs on us. Nonetheless, I kept an eye on anyone looking a little too much in our direction throughout our ride. Rafael seemed to doze off.

We soon emerged from the station. We walked into a forested area and arrived at a small, hidden airport. A personal jet was carefully being prepared.

"Whose plane is this?"

I smiled. "Mine. Trust me, Rafael, I've lived a long life. I know many and own much. Malcolm may have burned down the house, but he hasn't cut off any of my resources. Yet." I was actually surprised he didn't. "Get in; we have a long day ahead of us. Nicholas here will fly us to our next destination while we rest."

The pilot nodded in agreement, handing me the duffle bag of necessities I had requested he bring us. Once I settled into one of the six seats, I changed my shirt and handed a fresh one to Rafael. We used wet napkins to clean the blood off our faces and hands. I then fell asleep quickly, leaning against the plane's tiny window. My belly was full and my blood felt like it was boiling with power. When I awoke, I looked down and noticed we had reached our destination.

Tight rows of trees entirely surrounded a large island we were circling over. Two large overgrown and dead trunks revealed the entrance. The land mass had a somber, furtive look to it. The pilot expertly landed in the very small space between the two trees and took off within minutes of dropping us off. Rafael shouldered the duffle bag, and we began our walk.

Little bright dots shined on and off throughout the whole forest. Thousands of fireflies lit up to show us the way. The bugs led us deep within the trees so high it seemed they reached the stars, and the air became thicker.

"Who lives here?" he asked.

"My oldest friend and my brother, William."

"Why does he stay in a place like this, so far away from everything?"

"It fits his personality. This island doesn't get many visitors."

"I can believe that."

A simple walk became a great hike. For many hours the fireflies still led the way up and down the mountain, and the smell of pine trees surrounded us. We walked until the sun was minutes from rising. Strings of light began to pierce through the trees. I wanted to keep going.

"Alia," Rafael groaned. "I can't walk anymore; it burns too much. I'm not used to it like you are." He was frustrated.

"Alright. We're close to a cavern. We can continue our walk in it, just bear it for a few more minutes."

I quickly found the entrance, and Rafael sunk to his knees in pain. I looked away in shame.

"I'm sorry, honey. I shouldn't have pushed you this hard. The blisters will disappear soon if you rest. I'll find you something to eat."

I knew my way around this cavern like the back of my hand. I had spent a very long time in here. I found his meal and it gave its life up without a fight. When I walked back carrying a rabbit, he eyed it disapprovingly. He didn't like the taste of animal blood, but understood the need for it, and once he fed, the blisters began to heal. I gave him some time to gather his strength. After all, the change still occurred even after the new birth and the body needed time to adapt.

"This cavern will take us to a passageway leading straight to the castle. It'll take about three hours to get there." I sat down in the dirt next to him and wrapped my fingers through his.

"Won't he be upset to see us barge in?"

"I think it's safe to say he already knows we're coming."

I guided our way down the path of darkness. Hundred-year-old stalactites hung low, forcing us to be very careful. The longer we walked, the colder the temperature became. The frigid weather didn't bother me, but it started to take a toll on Rafael.

"Is it always this cold in here?" he shuddered.

"The temperature remains a constant thirty-two degrees throughout the whole year."

"How do you not feel cold?"

"Mind over matter. You'll learn to use your mind to its full potential very quickly. Your body is already getting used to your surrounding and your mind will soon follow. Your senses will only grow stronger with time."

We stepped into utter darkness, barely able to see a foot ahead of us. We held hands and slowly advanced. A human would have certainly lost his mind in such a place.

"Alia..."

I could hear the panic brewing in his voice. "It's okay, love. I'm here with you."

"I don't like this. It isn't safe. We could be surrounded and not know it."

"We aren't. I would hear them or feel them. Don't let the dark play with your head. Be in control of your own mind. That is the first and most important lesson: control your thoughts."

"How do you even know that your friend is alive? Or that he's on our side? Malcolm could have gotten to him first."

"I know he's alive. As for the rest, I sired him. If I can't get in touch with him, neither can Malcolm. Besides, Malcolm thinks this place is long gone."

I could hear a waterfall in the distance, finally giving me some hint as to where we were. Of course, the water was freezing, but I eagerly washed my hands and dampened my face, encouraging Rafael to do the same. We were very close to our destination.

We resumed our walk. Still in complete darkness, we struggled to follow the path leading upward. When the floor became flat once more, the darkness became a bit lighter; we had arrived. We stood gasping from our ascension and looked at the ancient wooden doors barring the entrance.

"What is this place?"

"The castle belonged to my best friend Liz, offered to her by William. We'd come here when Malcolm became too much to handle. It gave us a bit of vacation. At that point he knew we'd always come back."

These doors were once opened by servants, and it was now our turn. There was no pulley or mechanism on the outside and they must have weighed nearly a ton.

"Help me," I said, grunting.

We pulled and shoved. Even with our vampire strength, we barely managed to creak them open, the gap just wide enough for us to slip in. We stepped into another world, a somber, antique castle. I could tell the torches had just been lit because I could still smell the fuel.

"At least we know someone has to be here."

The fortress was deathly quiet and empty of life. Visions of my past haunted me as we walked through the corridors, the black marble flooring reflecting our faces. There was barely any furniture left. The high-vaulted ceiling was far above our heads and painted with ancient war scenes. Rafael didn't feel at ease here.

"Why isn't he coming to greet us?"

"He's an intriguing individual. Follow me; I know where he's waiting for us."

We paced through the long, dark hallways, passing a lit fireplace. I stopped and stared at the antique stone mantle. My chest tightened. I ran my fingers through the crevices and was met by Liz's ghost: a memory. I saw us sitting on this floor together and remembered the conversations we shared in this place. The apparition held my stare, offering a sad smile, and I began to reach out for it.

"What is it, babe?"

"Nothing." I cleared my throat. "I spent a long time in here." His hand squeezed mine, and I forced my gaze away, resuming our walk.

We passed countless empty rooms. It felt like a tragedy to have let this place fall apart. What would Liz think of this? We stopped in front of a large wooden door. "Control yourself in there," I said. "William doesn't like newcomers. He will try and read your thoughts."

We pushed the creaking door open and entered. No torches were in the room, but somehow it was filled with a gray luminosity. A shadow appeared in Rafael's mind while a warning settled in mine. Placed against the opposite wall was a wooden throne raised on a platform and sitting on it was a man. The power and electricity that emerged from him made it hard to focus. He sat with the composure of a king. His face was expressionless, not angry, but certainly not happy to see an old friend. His eyes starred past us. Then, as if he awoke, he met Rafael's gaze, and Rafael dropped to his knees and bowed his head. He grunted with effort as he tried fighting the force that had taken over his body.

"William, stop it! Stop yourself!" I growled, letting every ounce of my power meet his. The castle shook.

"Why have you brought someone new here? This was her

refuge; this isn't a hotel." His voice was raspy and slow as though he hadn't spoken in a long time.

"I said stop it *now!*"

He let Rafael up, who let out a deep angry growl. "Alia, why are you disrupting my solitude?" William's tone was weary.

"We need your help. Malcolm—"

"Is alive. I know. I've always known." He sounded bored.

I stood with fear and anger gripping my sides. "You knew?" I whispered, appalled.

"Yes. I knew of his plans before they happened."

"And you didn't see fit to warn me? Why?" Just when I thought the rug couldn't possibly be pulled from under me any more than it already had.

"Everything happens for a reason. You taught me that. The course of events must go on."

It sounded rehearsed and I remained silent.

"Have you sided with him, then?" Rafael asked, speaking for the first time.

William's eyes flashed. I sensed his outrage at being spoken to by a newcomer. "If he knew I was alive, he'd rip my throat out and bathe in my blood," he answered, looking at me and not acknowledging Rafael's presence.

"Will you help us?" I implored.

"I do not wish to get involved. This is not my fight."

"There was a time we were ready to help each other and fight for each other no matter life or death. Why can't it be that way again? Malcolm ruined both our lives!"

"These times are no longer. You are welcome to stay here as long as you need, but I will not aid you."

Anger was seeping through me now. "Once he kills me, he'll know you're here. He'll come for you. What will you do then?"

"I will accept my fate. It's about time you do the same. Don't you think you've lived long enough?"

"No, I don't."

Rafael was listening attentively to the conversation. I held his hand and moved him closer to me, bringing William's attention to him.

"This is Rafael. He brought me back to life the day I met him. William, I wish you could feel what it's like to be in love again. If you're right and my time has come, I want to give him a chance at survival."

"You healed from Malcolm's presumed 'death' because he was not your soul mate. I lost mine! He's already doomed," he said, pointing at Rafael. "Malcolm will want the little power you've transferred to him."

"Then help us! Stop hiding behind your stone walls and do something with your miserable life!"

William was perceptibly provoked. "You call this a life? Losing everyone I've ever known?! Aging but not dying? This is not a life. This is hell! He may be happy now, experimenting with his new senses, but he'll learn. He'll know better," he roared, nodding towards my boyfriend, spit escaping his lips.

"If you're so bored with your life, if you're so unhappy, die helping me!"

He slammed his fists on the throne's arms and shot upward. "Enough! I have heard enough of this. You are welcome to stay here, but do not pursue my help and test my hospitality. Now leave me!"

I recognized the madness in his eyes. It didn't belong to my friend, but to a trapped animal. William was caged inside himself and inside his pain. "As you wish."

Closely behind me, Rafael followed out of the room. "He is completely mad," he exclaimed.

"A lot happened to push him over the edge. After losing his

soul mate and spending decades alone in this place—a constant reminder of her—his depression has ruined his mind. I will get through to him though."

The castle held many rooms. They had not seen any visitors over the years, and a thick layer of dust covered the beds and what remained of the furniture. I chose the biggest room, the one I used to sleep in another lifetime ago, and let Rafael rest. I was tired but restless. I walked out of the room, quietly closing the door behind me, and wandered the halls, feeling the smoothness of the floor under my bare feet. It was so eerily quiet, when years ago this castle used to be full of clamorous music and exploding laughter. I made my way onto the dining room's terrace. Trees bent over the balcony, letting no light pass through their leaves. This evening had not gone according to plan but at least we were safe for the moment. Mental exhaustion began to take a toll on my body and I leaned my forearms on the balustrade. I rubbed my watering eyes and let out a heavy sigh. I felt William's presence. He slowly approached and stood next to me. His skin seemed to glow in the darkness, he looked tired, worn-out, and old.

"You have always fought the most ridiculous causes imaginable. Do you still refuse to drink blood on a daily basis?" he spoke, looking out into the dark distance.

"Yep. You're one to talk. What do you do out here for food?"

"Beggars can't be choosers; animals satisfy me enough. Sometimes I find a lost kayaker or campers in the woods though." I scoffed at that. "Will you make him starve himself, then?" he asked.

"No, he will drink, but he will not kill in vain."

"Do you believe you will defeat Malcolm?"

"You tell me—you're the medium. I certainly am not ready to die just yet... and not by him."

I hoped William would hear the despair in my voice. He continued looking in the distance, lost in his thoughts. He looked so different from the man I sired. He looked small and fragile.

"Do you miss her?" he murmured, sounding like his former self. Talking about Liz brought him out of his madness.

"That is a topic I think we should avoid today."

"Do you miss her?" he repeated, his voice trembling.

I put my hand above his. "There is not one day I don't think of her and miss her. Sometimes the guilt I feel is unbearable to me too."

"I knew it'd happen. I foresaw it, and yet I didn't prevent it. I've been living in hell ever since, Alia. Isn't that what hell is? A place of utter despair, unable to repent of your actions? I could have stopped it; I should have stopped it. I was afraid and I have hated myself every single day since."

"I don't know. But don't you think you've blamed yourself enough, William? It won't bring her back."

"No, it won't. I've missed your presence. I've been so lonely." I put a hand on his shoulder. "You left me alone here in my misery for decades and only return when you need something from me," he continued, and I now understood his aggression.

"I'm sorry, Will. I had to leave. You know I had to. I saw what this place was doing to the both of us. It reminded me too much of everything we lost. I wish you would have followed me; there is so much to see out there. So much we had never been allowed to experience. So much love from unexpected walks of life."

He held tightly onto the ledge as if he would crumble. I took him in my arms, embracing him firmly, and stroked his hair. I felt and knew it was a matter of time before he perished.

"Stay with me? Just for a little while," he begged.

"You know I will."

He had returned to his former self, lonely and insecure. We stayed on the balcony, silently but enjoying each other's company. I eventually joined Rafael in a deep slumber. He was on his side, as always, fast asleep. I curled up next to his body and put my arms across his waist. His hair smelled good and comforted me. I didn't know if we were soul mates. Malcolm and I certainly hadn't been, but I knew losing Rafael would be unbearable to me.

CHAPTER FIFTEEN

1903

Watching Liz discover new places was like watching a child on Christmas Day. She was so full of curiosity and good-natured joy. "Where have you brought me, William?" She visited the empty rooms with a singular interest while Alia walked into the entrance behind her two friends. "Who does this belong to?" Liz continued.

He spun her around into his arms, her dress flowing around her, and kissed her neck. "This is your castle, a gift from me to you."

"What? This must have cost you a fortune!"

"I didn't pay for it," he answered with a devilish smile.

She laughed. "That doesn't surprise me." She gazed around with new interest. "So this is all mine. This place is going to be our refuge." She glanced at Alia, who nodded in approval. "He won't know about it. We can escape here and have our lives back!" Liz laughed again.

"And I shall gift you a throne, for this is your castle and you are my queen," he said, landing a passionate kiss on her lips.

Alia wondered what Malcolm would do if he learned of this place. Probably destroy it to teach them happiness was only a myth. She felt envy towards the love her friends had and wished it could have been this way for her as well. Malcolm would call her his queen, but he never showed her much affection. She was glad to have Liz and William's love at the very least.

During their occasional allowed "leave of absence," as the girls would call it, they often spent weeks at a time away from home and in their refuge. Liz had furniture imported from all over the world and hired the best artists to paint frescoes on her ceilings while sculptors and carvers worked upon multiple chimneys. The hired help's blood was as rich as their work and none of them left the castle unharmed. Liz just did not share Alia's humanity.

The girls would often sit by the chimney's fire and talk. And often Alia would break down. Liz would cradle her friend's head in her lap and listen while stroking her hair. She was too accustomed to Alia's loss of control over her emotions.

"I don't want to live like this any longer," she cried so hard she could hardly breathe. "How can you love someone, but hate him so much at the same time? I've become everything he wanted me to be, but still he abuses me constantly. I keep hoping he will magically return to be the man I once knew, but with each stab of deception, I die a little bit more." She paused for a long moment. "I can't do this anymore. I just can't. I need to end it." Her voice was calm and slow, toneless. She stared into emptiness.

Alia had never dared verbally admit her feelings and she knew it would worry Liz, but she had to get it off her chest.

"If you plan on digging your own grave, then you should dig two. For if you leave me alone in this world, you shall take my life as well." With her fingers under Alia's chin, Liz raised her friend's face from her lap. "I cannot survive this alone. Don't you *dare* do this to me. You may not have Malcolm's love, but you have mine. You are my sister and I need you. You are my other half, my better half. You're my rock and if you leave me, I don't know how I'll face the world."

Alia cried some more. "I'll stay for you, sister." She replaced her head into her friend's lap and let herself be rocked into peacefulness.

I woke up and cried. I now knew she hadn't deserted me, left me to die. She had been by my side until the very last hour, and I missed her terribly. I turned over and realized the other side of the bed was empty. I got up, washed my face in the bathroom basin—rainwater leaked into it continuously—and went looking for Rafael. The castle was strangely quiet, and I hoped William hadn't done anything stupid. I found them meditating in the former ballroom. I heard laughter and saw a couple dancing in my peripheral vision. More ghosts coming from my mind, and I was almost tempted to follow them, let them show me what they wanted me to see.

"Why don't you join us, Alia?" William whispered, keeping his eyes closed.

I sat down next to Rafael, crossed my legs, and sighed. I began thinking of Malcolm. Were we going to die? How could we possibly escape him? There was no way out; death was imminent. Panic settled in, gripped my guts, and tore them apart. Soon, Malcolm and how much I feared him was all I could think about. I was hyperventilating, and it was as though my thoughts wouldn't let me go. I was trapped within my own horror, and I imagined all the terrible things he would do to us.

Someone grabbed me by the shoulders and shook me violently. William. The second I opened my eyes and our gazes met, we both froze and remained immobile like statues. Somehow, something that had never happened before took place. He unwillingly transferred a vision to me, and I saw Rafael's inert body at my feet, blood pooling darkly around him. I felt my heart shatter, heard my scream for help although I knew none would come. I turned around in time to see the spike, thrown by Malcolm's hand, flying through the air and entering my chest, puncturing my heart. A fiery pain erupted throughout my whole body. The vision ended. We blinked and stared at each other. Tears began to well up in my eyes, and William looked away in shame.

"You weren't supposed to see that."

"You weren't going to tell me?" I whispered in disbelief.

"I..."

"You weren't going to tell me?" I shouted, rising to my feet.

"I couldn't."

"Tell you what?" Rafael questioned, looking back and forth between William and myself.

"How can you know and not want to help? Do I mean so little to you?" I was very close to hurting my brother.

"Know what?" Rafael asked once more.

"We're not going to make it!" I yelled, infuriated. I probably shouldn't have told Rafael that, but I was not myself.

"Please calm down." Rafael put his hand on my shoulder. I brushed it off.

"Don't tell me to calm down. You don't know what I just saw!"

"I can't control my power. These visions won't stop coming to me!" William yelled, grabbing his head and shaking it violently. "I have lived over a century seeing awful things happening and being unable to stop any of them! Do you have any idea what that's like?" He stopped moving, letting his hands fall by his side. "What would you have me do?" he asked calmly with an air of acceptance.

My eyes turned back on him. I couldn't hide the surprise. "If you're not willing to fight with us, then let me have your essence. Let me have your power." I found myself almost begging.

His eyes were shut; he already knew what I was going to say, yet he still flinched at the sound of it. "You know what that implies," he whispered.

"I know exactly what I'm asking you to do." Did I though?

Understanding and peacefulness crossed his now-opened eyes. He nodded slightly and turned his back to me, leaving the room. "Give me until morning, and then come to my chambers."

And in that moment, I felt so alone. I hadn't seen William in decades, but I loved him. He was my oldest friend, my brother. He knew me, the real me. I walked away from Rafael, needing to be alone.

The day went on rapidly and I felt like my memories were attempting to suffocate me. Laying on my bed, I blankly stared at the ceiling and I thought of Malcolm again and again. I mentally prepared myself for what I had to do when the sun rose. The morning was arriving too soon. I saw the first ray of light coming through the skylight and reluctantly got up. My heart was breaking with every step I took.

The castle was gloomier than usual and felt colder to my bare feet. I breathed heavily. I was so terribly desolate. His door wasn't locked. I expected he hadn't slept either. I turned the knob and entered the room. He sat by the dormant chimney looking at a picture of Liz. He had been miserable for so long. However, at this moment, he seemed happier than ever.

"I will see her again soon," he said radiantly.

"Yes, very soon." My voice was choked. "What did Malcolm do to the both of you after we tried escaping him?" I had to know.

"He threatened to kill us, but that had little leverage. But then, and I'll spare you the details, he threatened to hurt you more and more each day until your spirit completely broke if we didn't distance ourselves from you. If we didn't keep this to ourselves. You have to know it wasn't easy, but we did it to save you."

I couldn't contain the sob that escaped my lips. "We could have found a way... Why didn't you tell me he was still alive?"

"I didn't lie to you. You didn't ask the right question and what I saw must come to pass. What's done is done, Alia." He dismissed it with a wave of his hand. "Let's get this over with. I believe she's been waiting on my arrival for long enough."

He stood up. I advanced towards him, and we were face-to-face. My tears almost completely blurred my vision. He closed his eyes and raised his chin, exposing his neck. I put my hands on his shoulders, stabilizing myself, and enclosed my mouth on his flesh. I immediately felt his pulse underneath my tongue. A voice shouted within me. *No, don't do this to him, he's your brother. The last of your family!*

"There is no other way; it must be done," I answered it. I punctured the soft skin and tasted his blood as it rushed out of him, more and more. It was exquisite. I wanted more, wanted all of it, and despised myself at the very same time. As he became frail and collapsed, I held him and slowly lowered us to the ground while still attached to his neck. He was getting weaker, and I was getting more powerful with each drop of his blood. I had never felt anything like this. I understood why Malcolm wanted me. One more suction, and it would be over.

"Isn't it funny how you created and destroyed me? Yet this is exactly how I wanted it to end." He was barely audible.

"I'm sorry, I'm so sorry," I whined.

Visions of his former self appeared before my eyes. Happier times with Liz. The last bit of power rushed through me, and he was no more. I sobbed as I held the limp body and rocked it back and forth. "I'm sorry, I'm sorry," I repeated until Rafael found me and tore me away from my deceased friend, forcing me to let go of the body. He gave me some time to gather my thoughts and regain my composure.

With his help, I laid William on his bed and placed a picture frame within his hands on his chest. Liz and William. I remembered the day that picture was taken. It was in 1920 and although biracial relationships were not accepted, Liz and William walked down the Manhattan streets towards the cameraman, their arms linked without a care in the world, pointedly ignoring blatant stares. She wore a cloche hat that tightly covered her bobbed haircut. Her loose-fitting, knee-length dress had been captured, flowing with movement, and she held a hand clutched to her chest. Her adoring gaze was on William, who looked straight at the camera, grinning widely. His fedora was slightly lopsided and he held a hand to his pinstripe suit that was left unbuttoned. Even though there were other people in the background, the photograph's primary focus was showing the love that Liz and William shared.

I hoped they had found each other and were now reunited. It felt as though the door on my previous life was being shut. Only one person remained, keeping me tied to the past. I barely remembered the walk back to our room to gather our few belongings. My body was set on autopilot while my mind tried to work through what just happened. I sat down on the side of the bed while Rafael stuffed the duffel bag with our clothes. I hadn't realized he was standing in front of me when he asked, "What now?"

"I don't know," I answered in a frail voice. I let myself slip off the bed and sat on the floor, appreciating the bedpost supporting my back.

"What do you mean you don't know?" He grabbed my shoulders and shook me. "Alia, snap out of it. We need to come up with a plan!"

I pushed him off. "I don't have a plan! What do you think? That I know the answers to everything? I don't know what to do!"

He sat down next to me and put his arms around my shoulders. "I'm sorry about you friend's death, but he sacrificed himself for you. Don't let it go to waste."

"You're right. I'm just completely overwhelmed right now." I rubbed my hands over my face. "I don't know what to do. This is never going to end." I seemed to shrink.

"We can't stay here forever. Malcolm will find this place. We have to get back to the mainland. Do you know of a way?"

My memory was foggy. I rubbed my eyes and temples. "There is a tunnel that'll get us back to the shore."

He nodded. "Let's get going."

I forged all the castle's details to my memory one last time and as we made our way out, I knew I would never return here. I hadn't been through these tunnels in so long that I barely remembered the way. I had to search within William's memories and therefore it took us longer to escape the darkness.

"How do you feel?" Rafael asked, worried.

"All this power is hard to control. It's so much. I understand why Malcolm is addicted to it, but I, unlike him, have more willpower."

"That's what I like to hear."

Fresh air appeased our aching lungs as we walked out of the caverns into a forest and then into a town. It was misting slightly and very windy; we were getting wet slowly but surely. The town seemed deserted. We walked, looking around, and I picked a full purse off the ground. I looked through the wallet; credit cards and cash were still in there. Times were rough and I hadn't been able to get my bank cards from the mansion before it was set on fire. I pocketed the cash, finding it weird no one else had.

"Where is everybody?" I asked.

"Hiding from the rain I'd imagine."

"No way. These cars are in the middle of the streets. This one's doors are wide open."

We came across a small neighborhood store and I instructed Rafael to gather some essentials as I did the same for myself.

The automatic doors slid open, welcoming us in, but although the lights were on, it appeared we were the only people in there. I filled my basket with toothbrushes and toothpaste, deodorant, more sanitary wipes, hair ties, socks, some sunscreen, and a phone charger since my phone had long since died. We waited by the register in case a cashier would appear, then just left when no one ever came. Was it stealing if the town was empty? We looked for a car with keys still in the ignition and as we were about to take off, I saw a house's front door swing shut.

"Rafael, wait. Someone is in that house," I said, putting a hand on his arm.

He put the vehicle back in park. "Do you think it's safe?"

"I think we should check it out."

He left the car running and we slowly walked towards the two-story house, carefully surveying our surroundings. From our position outside on the front lawn, it didn't look occupied, and it was ominous to say the least.

"You're sure you saw the door close?"

"Yep." I shifted my weight from side to side, biting my bottom lip nervously.

"It could have been the wind."

"The door opens inward. Someone had to have closed it."

I slowly made my way up the steps to the front porch and Rafael reached for my arm, pulling me back. "Babe, I have a really bad feeling about this. I don't think it's a good idea. We should mind our own business and just leave."

"What if someone needs our help? I'm just going to look."

I took the last few steps to the door, the rotting wood under my feet creaking loudly, and I froze, listening for any sign of movement. Nothing. I let out the breath I had been holding and pushed the door open. Inside the house was dark but for the light coming from the windows. To my immediate left was a straight staircase leading to the second floor, and on my right was a living room. Further down the hall was a kitchen. I thrusted my chin forward, motioning for Rafael to check out the bottom floor while I made my way upstairs quietly. The carpet was old and could have used a good cleaning. Framed old black-and-white family pictures decorated the wall along the staircase. As I stepped on the last step, I saw one bedroom directly in front of me that was empty of life and although old, the furniture didn't seem out of place. I moved to the second bedroom on the top floor, the master bedroom, and didn't see anything abnormal either. But when I pushed the bathroom door open, I came upon two bodies. An older man and woman, perhaps in their seventies. I didn't hear their heartbeats and there was a faint smell of rot in the air. When the man's hand twitched, I closed the door rapidly and ran down the stairs, looking for Rafael, who was going through the kitchen.

"We need to go right now. There are two bodies transitioning to vampirism upstairs," I whispered furiously.

But the door was blocked by a small vampire child. "What are you doing in my papa's house?" Her dress was soaked through with what must have been her grandparents' blood.

"Nothing, love, we were just leaving." I had my arm out in front of Rafael and we slowly walked back towards the kitchen, which I had noticed had a back door. I kept my eyes on the child, ready to kill her should she attack. "Who did this to you?" The girl looked hungry, animalistic. I threw my hands up, channeling a barrier between her and us.

She looked down, frowning. "He said you would come. Malcolm." My blood froze in my veins. "He said to tell you that he's leaving you little gifts all over. He's waiting for you, and the longer you take, the more people will die." Then she began to cackle and that was enough for me.

"Rafael, go!" He ran out the back door and I followed closely behind.

"How could Malcolm have anything to do with this?" Rafael sat in the driver's seat of the running car. "How did he know we would be here?

"He knew I'd go see William. He must have known about the castle when he killed Liz. He's just toying with me." I looked in the back and saw a car seat. My heart felt a pinch of sadness for I knew this family was no longer alive.

I was glad Rafael took control of the situation. I slumped into the passenger seat where I found another woman's purse. It contained a few useful items like a hairbrush, perfume, and baby wipes. We continued driving for weeks. More and more cities were found deserted or left with corpses. All looked abandoned, as though the people had just vanished abruptly from them. Cars were left wide open, and shoes and bags were in the streets. Sometimes, pools of blood but no bodies were found. While most cities were empty, some now roamed with brand new vampires, all looking to relay the same message to me: "He's waiting for you."

It was easy to follow Malcolm; he left us a trail to pursue. I knew what he was doing with these missing people, and it made me sick to my stomach. Obviously, we weren't the only ones noticing all these events and the humans quickly caught on, the vampire-human treaty soon shattered to pieces. Self-proclaimed vigilantes erupted, hunting and killing all vampires they could get their hands on, and vampires were killing humans as self-defense. It was chaos. Blood being spilled almost on the daily. A lot of vampires either went back into hiding or joined Malcolm's side out of fear and anger. And while everyone's energy was spent on hating the other side, more disappearances happened each and every single day.

We drove continuously day and night, switching back and

forth so we could rest, and listened to the radio for news updates on the growing civil war. "We ask you once again to stay inside your homes as much as possible. During the day, if overcast, but especially at night. Do not attempt anything to put yourself at risk. Let the government take care of the situation," announced the radio host.

I turned the station off and wrapped my arms around myself. How much more was this going to escalate? We didn't even stop to feed, afraid of what we'd find or of how we would be received, but we were ravenous. The closer we were on Malcolm's tail, the stormier the weather seemed to get. We drove until the storm became so tough and violent, bright lightning zigzagging across the sky, that we had no other choice but to stop. We brought the car to a halt outside a lit restaurant.

"Keep the car running. I'm going to check out if there's any blood available," I said.

The wind howled garbage cans out of its way and the rain, which poured hard, stung my body like needles. In a matter of seconds, the sky turned from gray to pitch black. The stars were covered by a heavy fog. It seemed the world was coming to an end. I walked into the restaurant and the place was completely quiet. There were cars outside, but no one inside. Thunder exploded louder than I had ever heard it, shattering the windows and allowing rain to fly through the building. I walked around on my guard, looking for any signs of life. Not only were my clothes soaked and sticking to my body, but this whole establishment was beyond freezing. I could withstand rough temperatures, whether hot or cold, but this was just unbearable.

I approached the kitchen slowly and carefully. I rubbed my hands together; a clear mist escaped my mouth each time I exhaled. The air was putrid; the smell of death almost made me choke. I began to get very worried. I walked farther into the kitchen and froze in terror. I found the employees mutilated and dead. The freezing temperature kept the bodies from decaying too quickly. The lights went out, and I held my breath. I heard a noise coming from inside the walk-in refrigerator and felt my heart rate increase. I approached the glass window and quickly backed away, bumping into pots. Six Astaroth vampires were feeding on a body, and they had heard the noise. I slowly and quietly stepped away, keeping my eyes on the door. Were there more hidden throughout the restaurant? Suddenly, a hand grabbed my shoulder, and it took every bit of self-control to not shriek. As I spun around attacking, my rounded kick was blocked by a man. Rafael. Relief washed through me.

"What's going on?" he spoke softly.

"Shhh! Astaroths. We have to go."

A loud crash erupted. The door was flung open, followed by guttural growls. Rafael and I immediately broke into a run. As he passed the entrance door, one of the monsters jumped in between us. "Keep going, Rafael! Get out of here!"

He accorded me one last look and ran out into the rain. He was far too new at this and far too weak to battle an Astaroth. I was faster, but I knew I was in big trouble. I sprinted across the floor, losing the vampire behind me. I crawled underneath a table and huddled myself there. I tried to regulate my breathing and placed my hands on my mouth when a shadow passed by. What the hell was going on with me? I hadn't been this afraid in a long time. They may be more powerful, but I was infinitely smarter. If pushed to my limit, I'd be victorious.

I crawled out from under the table and hastened towards the bar. I grabbed the biggest knife I could find and looked for my adversaries. My heart pounded so hard against my chest it hurt. A claw came at me, only I had seen it in my peripheral vision and dodged it. I punched, kicked, and sliced at an incredible speed. I was pushing my body to the extreme, and finally got to the end of the monster by snapping its head off. One down, five to go. Forget it. I was beyond exhausted. I wobbled outside where more rain met me. I was blind. Where was Rafael? Another claw sliced my back. I fell to the floor with a gasp. I turned around to face my assailant, creating a protection barrier around me, but even I could see how weak it looked. In that moment, I desperately tried to gather energy from the storm, but I couldn't keep my focus going as the monster continued attacking. It launched at me but collided with the spell. It shook its head and slid a clawed hand down the length of my shield, webbing cracks forming all over. A little more force and it would reach me. I knew I wouldn't survive this. My breath hitched and I braced myself for whatever came next, unable to control my body from shaking. All of the sudden a car hit it from the side and it rolled, crashing in a shrill of pain.

"Get in!" Rafael screamed, opening the door.

I collapsed onto the seat once more and let the screeching tires take me away. I began crying, releasing the tension I had just held and unable to control the sobs escaping my lips. He grabbed my hand and kissed the back of it.

"I'm not going to let anything happen to you, Alia."

I had almost given up. I would have let that Astaroth rip me to shreds and I didn't recognize this side of me.

"What the hell is going on?" he asked.

"Malcolm is raising an army and they need to eat," I whispered. I felt woozy and closed my eyes.

"An army for what?"

"To take over the world. Become the higher species. Enslave humankind." I waved my hand around. "Blah, blah, blah. It's always the same thing with him." My head was spinning. I didn't know where we were heading, but we had to stop and feed now. "Rafael, I need blood."

Scruples had to be forgotten; blood was necessary. I wasn't

healing. We drove far out of the city where the rain lessened to a drizzle. He parked the vehicle near a forest and with a kiss, promised to be back soon. I attempted to get comfortable, feeling my back bleed freely.

I watched his hunt in my mind's eye. Another benefit from him having linked himself to me as a human. The wind made it difficult for the first timer, and he quickly learned to listen to the rush. Without my help, he had to rely on his instincts. He tried to smell the animals in the woods, but the water made it impossible to track them. He listened and made out four feet hitting the floor. He set out in that direction. It was animalistic; the adrenaline raced through his whole body, and his instincts flared up. Giving in to himself, he had become an animal. He chased a boar. It was agile, but Rafael had my blood running through his veins and was quicker. He wrestled it to the ground. The animal's heart pumped so fast that Rafael couldn't restrain himself from having a taste. Maybe more than just a taste. Only then did he realize the extent of his thirst. He carried it back to the car.

"Baby, wake up, I brought you some food."

He looked at me wide-eyed and the clear shock was written all over his face. I glimpsed at the mirror and I understood why. My skin had turned gray, and my eyes held some deep purple bags. I looked deathly ill.

"Babe, what can I do?"

"I need to feed." I wrapped my arms around his strong neck and was brought to the animal. As the blood touched my lips, I began feeling the color returning to my cheeks. I knew it was only a matter of time before my skin fused itself back together. I sighed in contentment and relief. I was able to walk back to the car where I changed my shirt, throwing the old torn one to the curb. I hadn't packed that many shirts and felt annoyed at having to throw away one.

"Where do we go now?"

"We continue tracking Malcolm. Keep following the empty cities."

"And then what?"

"Then, hopefully I can figure out how to tap into William's power, I kill Malcolm, and finish this." I silently prayed that the Universe let it unfold that easily. It wasn't the lack of wanting to. But I hadn't known a war was brewing and I had just spent the last few centuries trying to quiet my power instead of learning to develop it.

CHAPTER SIXTEEN

2008

Alia remained in the shade although a growing urge to run into the light engulfed her. She watched while they brutalized the girl, a newborn vampire. Three middle-aged men against a confused newborn seemed hardly fair. They dragged her into the sun where she began shrieking. They pushed her onto the ground and beat her with an inhuman cruelty. Yet vampires were considered the animals. Alia wanted to help but she couldn't. She hadn't fed in too long and the sun was at its highest. Two men, the two sidekicks, held the girl while the third took a knife out from his jacket. She begged for her life, begged for them to let her into the shadow as her skin began to blister. They wouldn't hear her. Her body trembled so hard the men had a hard time keeping her down.

"I wonder if you bleed red. You got to drink our

blood to survive right? So it has to be red. I say we check."

He stabbed repeatedly as her shrieks and pain echoed throughout the parking lot. She begged them again to let her go. Alia was horrified. How could they? She was only standing in the shadows when they attacked her. When they finally had their fill of fun with her, they released their grips and stood by watching the radiation burn her to death. She screamed until her vocal cords melted, then she convulsed on the ground until the end came and her entire body broke down to ash.

Alia's anger peaked. Creeping in the shadows, she followed each man home. Watching and learning. She wanted revenge, and knew she wasn't fully ready for what she was about to do. Her demon was going to be set free.

She waited for the sun to set and broke into each of the sidekicks' houses respectively. Luckily, they didn't live far from each other, and it took no time at all. Each household met the same exact fate. She ripped the wives' throats out first, making the husbands watch them drown in their own blood, and after toying with the men for a bit, she finally bled them dry, taking her sweet time and savoring them. The other one, the one that had stabbed the baby vampire again and again, taking pleasure in it, received a much worse treatment. She knocked on his door, asking to use his phone to call a tow truck for her car.

He looked her up and down, a grin spreading on his face before moving aside to pass the threshold. Unsurprisingly, he did not have a significant other, but lived with his mother who seemed to be just as prejudiced as him, if not more. The apple did not fall far from the tree. She watched a heavy anti-vampire propaganda channel, spewing venom at the television, talking about all vampires needing to be rounded up and disposed of. And that's when they realized the mistake they had made, letting her inside their home. She grabbed him by the throat and threw him in the air. He crashed down onto the floor and begged for his life. She quickly knocked the other woman unconscious and began working on the piece of garbage at her feet.

"You didn't stop when she screamed in pain or when she begged you, so why should I?" She kicked him in the mouth.

He lay flat on his back, breathing heavily. She seductively straddled him, brought his hands above his head, and licked his neck. Growling like a lion. He shivered, whimpered, and tried to break free of her grasp, but she was stronger.

"What color do you bleed? A monster like you couldn't possibly bleed red. We're not the monsters, people like you are."

"Go to hell!"

"You'll make it there first. You won't kill any more of us after tonight."

The power in her legs stopped him from wiggling around; she kissed him deeply and bit his tongue off. She drank the blood gushing from his mouth so he wouldn't drown in it. He shrieked from the pain. She pierced and broke every single major vein in his body, enjoying the taste of his blood on her fingertips. The man was seconds from passing and had stopped fighting it. His eyes displayed nothing but fear. He knew it was over.

"Do you want to die?" she asked.

"No, please no."

Whether he knew what he was agreeing to or if he thought she could heal him did not matter. She quickly rushed her essence into his mouth. She then tied his unconscious mother to a chair, gagging her tightly, using a knife to cut little slashes across her skin. Just enough for a very thin layer of blood to form.

"When you wake up and the thirst takes over, feed on your own mother," she whispered in his ear. "And when you hate what you've become, then take a walk into the sun."

She was always the first one to preach about human rights, but she had exhibited a cruelty Malcolm would have been proud of. Everything always went right back to Malcolm, and she scolded herself for it. Vampires wouldn't remain unknown anymore. They were coming out to the public whether humans liked it or not and she would pave the way.

Others had tried before her but had been either ridiculed and unbelieved or murdered by people like those three men. Right now, the big two questions in America were "Do we believe vampires are real? And if so, what do we do about it?" It would have been easier if all vampires came out at the same time, but for the time being, only a few brave ones had attempted it.

She would do it for them all. She talked to the news, proclaiming to be a real-life vampire and at first, she was viewed as a lunatic, searching for her five minutes of fame. But she persevered. And while they didn't want to believe her, she cut her arm open live on the air, and healed in front of thousands of eyes, just as she had done to convince Jenn. Everyone lost their minds, feeling fear and excitement, and the ball began rolling fast. She went on talk shows, on the radio, and was invited to talk at big events. She made enough noise about herself, claiming to be a spokesperson for all vampires, that a year later, after being investigated dutifully, she was eventually invited to the Capitol for an audience with the congressional floor.

This was a dream come true. Not many people, human or vampire, had been given such an opportunity. And although she didn't have the support of all her kind—she had received a ton of angry, threatening letters—she walked up the Capitol building stairs holding her breath. This was history in the making. She showed the guard her badge and was led inside and showed to the House Chamber. She wore a two-piece gray pants suit with a white undershirt and darker gray strapped heels. Her long hair hung in loose curls and a golden necklace hung above her cleavage. She wore no makeup except for dark eyeliner around her eyes. The assembly room was full; everyone was in attendance that day. She marched down and stood at one of the desks at the forefront of the room. Everyone was quiet; you could hear a pin drop. They had not wanted her to be present for the matters that did not concern her. She had only been allowed to come into the room for part of the session. She was just glad to be given an audience.

"Ms. Henry, thank you for being here today," said the Speaker of the House.

"Thank you for having me."

He looked down at the papers in front of him, frowning. "Let's get right to it, shall we? What is it you want?"

"Rights, the same rights as any American citizens. What we want is freedom. Vampires are not violent, we are not what the media has portrayed, not what you've seen in movies, or TV shows, or read in books." So what if she was downplaying their nature a bit?

He seemed astounded. "Not violent? Do you not drink blood after all?"

"We do. But we're not savages. We have control of ourselves. We also don't actually *need* to drink human blood; animal blood can sustain us just as well. As a society, we can work together to come up with regulations and laws."

"I'm sorry, Ms. Henry," he said, taking off his glasses and rubbing his eyes. "I just have a hard time believing you are being honest when you say you're not a violent species."

"Well, I'm sorry to point out, Mr. Speaker, that humans don't have a record of keeping the peace amongst themselves. There's very little difference between us; we are just as violent of a species as you are. There are some people who have done very bad things, but you still believe in the general goodness of your species. The same can be said about mine."

The room erupted in chaotic and furious whispers, the noise rising steadily. Alia had to regain control of it. Her voiced boomed out, automatically quieting everyone.

"The fact is," she spoke out, loud and with confidence, "that we are no longer going to be hiding in the shadows remaining a secret. We will no longer hide ourselves to protect the ego of men. I am standing here today to ask for your help in transitioning us into a part of society. We have been here for decades, some of us centuries; there are hundreds of thousands of us worldwide. We pay our taxes like everyone else, and you never even knew what we really are. Nothing is going to change. We are intelligent, sentient beings and we deserve to be known. We deserve to live our lives like the rest of you do." She turned her back on the audience leader, making eye contact with as many representatives as possible. "Make no mistake, while we would prefer to choose the path of least violence, if you refuse my proposal, my cry for help, we will do what is necessary to reach our goals. And quite frankly, it would be more beneficial to work together."

"Is that a threat to our nation?"

She turned back towards the Speaker.

"No, of course not. But we are coming out regardless of your decision today. The manner in which this is received by the public, the manner in which we come out, depends on you all. And it is happening. You cannot put this knowledge back in the box."

Alia had them by the throat. They knew it, and she knew it. She received a nod of approval. The room was now entirely silent.

"Very well, Ms. Henry, what kind of regulations do you foresee in place?"

"First and foremost, please understand that we will not be studied without consent. We are not lab rats. We want the same rights as all humans. If a vampire submits for case studies, they are to be compensated for their time. Secondly, I agree that no vampire should drink human blood without consent."

"And how do you propose we monitor that?" someone asked behind her.

"My team and I have developed a database where donors can register themselves. Their driver's licenses will then showcase it. Exactly like an organ donor. I believe you were presented earlier with a manila folder of mine. In it I highlighted all the ideas I have to make this coexistence run smoothly. I am available with any questions you may have."

She took her leave, walking out on a shocked audience. They would do their best to accommodate vampires, she knew it. What other choice did they have?

W e tracked Malcolm through different cities and states, but he always seemed one step ahead of us. I shifted through the radio stations. Most were just static now as more and more people sequestered themselves at home and refused to go to work anymore. A few were still operating, and the news was grim.

"And where is Alia Henry? She was the vampire spokesperson about thirteen years ago, and now she's nowhere to be found on these matters. I distinctly remember her advocating the species' non-violence..."

"Oh my god, all of my hard work!" I groaned and turned off the radio.

I had bought a map and marked down the areas Malcolm had left me "presents." While his victims never attacked me, Malcolm knew I would feel guilt over their deaths, and did it just to taunt me. He was following a direct trajectory and after racking my brain, I had an idea of where he might be going, but I hoped I was wrong. That place meant very bad memories for me, and I wanted to intercept him before he got there. Unfortunately, we didn't.

Somewhere, abandoned in the middle of Virginia's Blue Ridge Mountains, stood the remains of a psychiatric hospital. The purposely-lit fire of 1912 had killed all 153 patients and the staff. Part of the roof had caved in during the blaze. The building was dilapidated but looked as horrifying as it had the last time I set my eyes upon it, minus the flames. Part of the vaulted ceiling that was intact still had beautiful molding spiraling across it. I heard noises inside and knew we had to go forward. The windows had shattered from the blaze's intensity and glass still covered the floor. The walls had been tagged with various obscenities and garbage littered the floor, along with what seemed to be half the forest's worth of dirt and leaves.

Breathing heavily, we advanced down the dark corridors slowly and silently. The wind shrieked outside the walls. At the edge of a mental breakdown, I squeezed Rafael's hand tighter.

"This place —" he began to say.

"Many cruel things happened here. This building is filled with vengeful spirits. I can feel them breathing down my neck."

We walked past an old dormitory filled with overturned metal wire box springs. We continued down the hallway and I glanced inside a room, stopping in my tracks. I knew Rafael couldn't see the two apparitions in there. One was lying on a reclining chair with electrodes attached to his forehead and a gag in his mouth to bite down on. The second man who was standing up turned a machine on and watched as the other began convulsing. The chair and the device, though old and useless, were still physically in the room.

"What's wrong?" Rafael whispered.

"I let some really awful things happen here. I could have stopped it all if I hadn't been so scared of Malcolm."

He walked inside and inspected the machine. I stayed back in the hallway. "What did this used to be?"

"Before vampires became known to the world, they used to send the unlucky ones who came across our kind here. People thought they were crazy, talking about vampires. Malcolm liked paying them visits and torturing them into utter psychosis. That," I said, jutting my chin forward, "was used to shock the crazy out of them. Eventually, Malcolm got tired of playing with them and set the whole place on fire; I watched it ablaze and heard the screams." The memories flashed across my mind.

A cold feeling invaded us. The spirits knew I was talking about them. They remembered me standing by and doing nothing to help them. Malcolm was here; I could smell him, which meant he knew we were here as well. We had to keep moving, stay unnoticed, and get him alone. We kept walking and with no guards in view, I relaxed a little. The commotion seemed to emerge from the basement. Rusted metal railings and stairs led us down, and luckily for us, a veranda overviewed the whole cellar. It held no doors and no windows and had been renovated to look like a common room with couches and tables. With no electricity, candles and oil lamps lit the space, which I found to be relatively dangerous, given the asylum's history. Two staircases led upstairs but were blocked off by gates. Down below, a group of people huddled together in the center of the room.

"What is this?" Rafael whispered.

"I suppose this is where he brings the missing people."

"But there's only about forty people here! Where are the rest?"

"Already dead."

"We need to help them."

"We will, but we need to be smart about this."

The humans looked nervous and scared as the vampires surrounded them, snarling. Malcolm's new family—how nice. There were no Astaroths here and I wondered where he hid them. Finally, one launched himself at a woman, grabbing her by the hair, and the rest followed his lead. This was a feast and a massacre. I was repulsed and couldn't help but look away. Malcolm appeared from a dark corner.

"Everybody, stop!" Each vampire slowly raised their head, eyes full of wonder. Malcolm smelled the air and scrutinized the shadows. I pushed Rafael and I further back into the darkness. I put my index finger in front of my lips and motioned for Rafael to remain quiet. "Alia, are you here?" Malcolm asked. "Wonderful! Why don't you come down?"

He sensed I was present, just like I sensed him earlier, but the smell of blood was covering our scent.

"Everyone out!" Malcolm screamed. The vampires reluctantly dropped their victims and exited up the staircases—some coming close to us but paying no attention. Malcolm stood still, alone among the humans. His eyes searched for me. I motioned for Rafael to stay put while I walked down the stairs. His eyes flashed surprise and anger, but I was already down before he could grab my arm.

My ex's gaze turned in my direction. "There you are. What do you think of the new asylum?"

"Still smells like burnt flesh to me." We locked eyes. "I'm not going to let you do this, Malcolm."

His eyes turned to hate. "You won't be here much longer to stop me."

"Maybe not today, maybe not tomorrow, but I will kill you." I felt confident of this.

He grabbed my throat and a deep growl emerged from upstairs. "It's okay, Rafael!" I called out. I quickly pulled myself out of his reach. With William's knowledge of martial arts, I had an advantage Malcolm didn't expect. "Things have changed; I know I can take you."

He smiled. "The question then is why haven't you done so yet?"

He jumped at me, mouth open and ready to kill, but Rafael intercepted him, tackling him to the floor. It was like two cement blocks colliding. Rafael had him pinned down by the throat and I knew we'd only have a few moments with this advantage. In his struggle Malcolm spilled an oil lamp—I suspected purposely—and the basement quickly filled up with smoke and flames. The humans cried out in terror.

"Get them out of here. I will deal with Malcolm," I ordered.

"Alia, the fire..."

Exasperation hit me. "Please just do as I ask you. Get them to safety." I stood in between Malcolm and the humans.

They all followed Rafael out the same way we had come in,

some helping others walk, and Malcolm's hateful gaze remained on them. Smoke began to fill my lungs. Malcolm and I circled around each other, waiting to attack. My eyes watered and the heat was sizzling my skin, but I was ready to end this once and for all. He punched and kicked, and I blocked. I figured out how to tap into William's power. It was as though all this power was trapped inside a bubble deep in my chest inside a separate compartment. It got brighter and hotter as the adrenaline flushed through me. All I had to do was push the door open.

I went on the attack, landing more blows than I would have before, but even with all this new power, I wasn't comparable to Malcolm. He healed faster than I remembered. The fire had gotten pretty bad, and I attempted to push him in. Beams, along with pieces of the roof, fell in between us and I jumped back just in time to avoid being crushed. The building wouldn't be standing for much longer; I couldn't even really see Malcolm in all this smoke anymore. I ran up the stairs, fire brushing against my skin, and down the hallways. I heard Malcolm roar his disapproval—guess he wanted to finish this just as much as I did. I exited out the front door. I had no time to feed and heal myself; it would have to take however long it took. Although my lungs were filled with smoke, I tracked Rafael's scent down.

He stood on top of a hill looking down at the burning asylum and heard me come. His senses were already growing stronger. "Oh Alia, your skin!" He brushed his hand over it and I shuddered in pain.

"It's alright. My arms will heal. Where are the other vampires?"

"Most, if not all, left the premises as soon as the fire broke out. The others probably went back inside to help Malcolm out."

"Hah! Guess this was more than what most of them

bargained for." Rafael looked at me expectantly and I knew what he wanted to know. "I couldn't kill him. I'm... not strong enough. We need to leave now; we can't be lucky enough for him to die in a simple fire."

We ran for miles through the mountain and its thick forest which was hard for all of us, not being used to this terrain or the elevation. I led the way with the humans behind me, and Rafael secured the back. The humans quickly became tired of our fast pace. I didn't care and didn't want to stop, but Rafael felt more compassion towards them than I did. All wouldn't survive. The slowest would be sacrificed, giving time for the others to escape. They were cold, but a fire would have revealed our location.

Rafael wanted to keep watch the first half of the night, but I wouldn't let him. As tired as I was, my senses were still sharper than his. I walked away from the camp and sat comfortably at the bottom of an oak tree, soaking up its energy and slowly healing my burns. I stayed awake for most of the night and didn't bother waking Rafael. I fought against the numbness in my body and mind. I don't know how long I was asleep but, when I heard a branch crack, I was immediately on my feet. I gazed around the trees looking for the noise's origin and held my breath as I watched the shadows advance slowly like a dark river. Astaroths. I ran alongside them, deep in the forest, and returned back to the camp, not nearly as fast as I could have. I was still clearly exhausted. Rafael heard me and met me half-way, worried. I woke the humans, shoving and pushing them.

"Get up! They've almost caught up to us." I hurried them.

Tired or not, they had to push themselves harder if they wanted to survive. Our pursuers were right behind us, but luckily, we were near a town. It had been completely blocked off by a cement wall. We had to jump it. I pulled myself up and looked around. One after the other, the others struggled to pull themselves over after me, but I wasn't looking back to check on them. I was already jumping another fence. Most of the humans decided to wander off their own ways and that was fine by me. I had gotten then to a more secure location; now they had to fend for themselves. The Astaroths hadn't caught up to us yet, which led me to believe they were not pursuing us with fervor. This was all a game of cat and mouse. Rafael felt the need to give directions to the humans with us.

"Find food quickly. The next town over is about twenty miles south. Keep moving until you reach a big city. You should be safe there."

My arms were getting tired and pulling myself from fence to fence was beginning to hurt. Rafael and I had to remain unseen. It was of the outmost importance. I ran faster and faster, pushing my body to extremes. I felt Malcolm was getting closer until I heard his echoing footsteps behind me. I didn't need to look back to know it was him although this town was filled with people going about their days. I slowed my run into a walk as I entered the town's crowd and frantically looked behind my shoulder to see if my assailant was still on my tail. I didn't see Rafael anywhere. Somehow we had lost each other, and I found myself alone. I put my jacket's hood on and quickened the pace. Still, I heard Malcolm's steps behind me, and I immediately broke into a run. I shoved, pushing people out of my way, and jumped into the first building on my right. The hotel lobby's elevator was just about to close when I raced in. The two-minute ride gave me enough time to catch my breath, and I knew the humans were giving me inquisitive looks. The elevator slowed down, and I prepared myself for another chase. I couldn't be sure he had seen me enter the hotel, but I knew he wasn't far away. I ran to the rooftop and jumped off the fire escape. I landed in a back alley.

"No, no, no," I muttered.

I couldn't stay in a dark alley. Malcolm feared the same

thing we did: being ambushed by a mob of humans. He was strong, but how many could he fight off at the same time? I needed to mingle with them. While they wondered if I was human or vampire, they'd be my shields. As I walked out into safety, a hand pulled me back into the darkness. Malcolm slammed me into the wall. He pushed his elbow into my throat so I wouldn't be able to scream out. I managed to push him off me, but he quickly slammed me back. My head hit the wall, hard. Where was Rafael?

"Let go of me," I snarled.

"Or what? What are you going to do?"

"Let go of me," I repeated louder, bringing some human attention in our direction.

"Listen to me, bitch, we are going to do things my way."

Rip his fucking head off a little voice said within my mind. *Don't let him talk to you that way!* A shade of red invaded my sight, and I began to shake angrily; the beast in me was taking over. I said nothing, merely looked at him. His words made no sense to me; they no longer touched me. I had to keep my calm. I began praying that Rafael would magically turn up and take me away from this situation. I continued struggling against the elbow pressed on my throat and soon, I perceived Rafael's head above the crowd. My heart jumped. My savior had arrived. I forced the beast back under. He quickly heard or smelled us, and his eyes narrowed as he saw the position Malcolm had me in. He looked statuesque as he shoved bodies out of his way and a second later, he was behind Malcolm. He twisted Malcolm's arm behind his back. No matter how strong he was, if he fought for release, he would dislocate his own limb.

"Let go of her before I rip your arm out." Rafael growled and his strength told me he must have just fed, and for once, I could honestly say I should have taken the time to as well.

A few humans were watching, whispering among themselves, and pointing at us. I heard a crunching noise; Malcolm winced. I moved away from the wall and pulled on Rafael's arm. "Not here and not now. We have to leave."

More humans gathered now, including police officers who pulled their guns out. The three of us broke out in runs and before I realized it, Rafael was no longer behind me. I didn't know where I was headed, just turned street after street, corner after corner. I had lost my breath and a stitch was forming in my side. I slowed down. This time I ended up outside a cemetery gate which was locked. As I snuck from above once more, a hand grabbed my foot. I slipped down on the other side and fell flat on my back. I looked up and dodged an ax coming at my face. Malcolm was covered in human blood, which explained where he got the weapon. His foot met my nose.

I lay on the floor in pain as Malcolm advanced towards me. I raised my head, looking at my attacker. My nose was definitely broken and bled heavily. My eyes continuously watered no matter how much I blinked. My body would not respond to my commands anymore—I was too weak. I did not want to give up. My anger had turned into determination, but in this moment, I truly thought it was the end.

"Do me a favor," I struggled to say through the blood running into my mouth. "Let him live."

"Your lover boy? I don't understand what you see in him."

"I love him more than I ever loved you."

"You'll see him in hell."

He grabbed me by the throat, raising me up and titling my head to the side, ready to plunge his teeth into me. Suddenly, someone attacked him from behind. He was grabbed by the shoulders and sent flying through the air. Rafael stood snarling like a beast. He seemed to have no trouble getting in touch with his predator side. He pulled me by the waist and helped me walk, which wasn't working very well, and had to carry me in his arms.

"Everything will be okay, babe. I'll take care of him," he assured me.

"If I can't do it, you won't be able to either."

"You're not using all your abilities. You're a powerful witch. Why can't you use your powers against him?"

Lightning struck the air in a series of spiderwebs and thunder rumbled right above our heads, the crashing reverberating through our chests. I felt so depleted. He carried me to a patch of woods, leaning back against my dead weight. He was worried for me as I appeared unable to heal. But I was, extremely slowly. He sat me against a tree, and I painfully cracked my nose back into place. I pondered what magic I could use to our benefit. I had no tools, no time to meditate or beg the spirits for help. I dug my fingers deep into the earth, inhaling slowly, and drew energy from the soil in order to rejuvenate myself. In a matter of minutes, my wounds were healed, and I felt better than I had in days.

"Do you smell that?" I asked.

"It smells like fire. He wouldn't go as far as setting the whole forest on fire, would he?"

"To flush us out? I wouldn't put it past him."

We tried reaching the edge of the trees but were rapidly completely surrounded by bright orange-and-red flames. Embers flew through the air, stinging our skins. This was not an enemy we could fight, only one we could flee from. The hot wind already burned my skin and sizzled my hair.

"There's nowhere for us to go," he said in disbelief. My thoughts were whirling inside my head, trying to find a way out. There had to be a way out—I just had to find it. The fire was creeping steadily closer. I was beginning to hyperventilate when he pulled me into his arms and placed his chin on my head. My arms went around his waist and we both closed our eyes, awaiting our deaths. *It is just energy. Tame it. Take it. Use it.* The voices whispered furiously in my ears. And it dawned on me exactly how I could use my powers in this moment. I felt serene now. I turned my head towards Rafael and smiled, my long hair twisting around my face and body. He looked back at me, confused and unsure.

"Alia, what are you doing?"

I extended my hand to him. "Just take my hand, Rafael. Follow my lead," I answered in a low, almost too-calm voice.

"No." He looked panicked, and it broke my heart to see him so fragile.

"Take my hand; trust me."

"What are we going to do?" he barked harshly.

"The elements are just energy waiting to be gathered and dispensed."

My hand was still extended in the air, and he took some time before holding it. I closed my eyes, placing my other hand on the ground, and inhaled sharply as I focus on absorbing the fire's energy, ounce by ounce. As much as the earth was grounding for me, fire felt warm, energetic, exciting, and even a little chaotic. This source flowing through me little by little was wild and unpredictable. It was frightening. I felt a big bubble of power forming deep in my belly and I became filled with more life than I had felt in years. The blood in my veins pumped rapidly. My muscles shook with the effort of staying in control and around us, the blaze began losing its strength, as though I was suffocating it. This was so much power for one to absorb. I funneled some directly into Rafael through our joined hands, watching his face illuminate with vigor, and then released the rest back into the ground in a big shockwave. Trees that hadn't burned yet, exploded when my power reached them.

The ground and the air were heavy with ashes. My own

skin was dark and cracked from the fire, but already healing from all this energy absorbed. I glanced around and saw the blaze had turned down to cinders. I stood up, breathing heavily, and looked at the desolation, taking in all the destruction. The forest had been consumed entirely. Yet in the middle of all this death, in the very middle of a meadow, a bush remained. Although the tree was obviously dead, a bright red rose stood. Somehow it had been conserved. I didn't dare pick it off, just bent down and smelled the sweet aroma. Within all this devastation, there was one remaining rose. The universe was sending me a sign. Hope.

Taking William's essence had allowed my powers to grow to a whole new scale. I had just learned of its extent. While I always played with nature's energy to some degree and took just enough to rejuvenate myself, I had never thought to turn it all into a weapon. Absorbing as much as my body could handle, holding it for a little while and then releasing it back into the world. For the first time, I felt we stood a chance.

CHAPTER SEVENTEEN

1903

Alia hadn't seen Liz in a few hours and the last time she had, her friend hadn't seemed like her usual happy and carefree self, but instead had been preoccupied and worried. She hadn't told her so, but Alia had felt it as her maker. William was hunting outside the mansion's property and she just knew something wasn't right. She walked to all the spots within the house she would have expected to see Liz— her bedroom, the kitchen, dining hall, billiard room—and still did not run into her. She wasn't exactly worried about her, but she also wasn't at ease. She just needed to make sure she was alright.

Alia opened the large glass double doors that led to the balcony and leaned over the railing breathing deeply. That was when she picked up on Liz's voice, and she strained to hear where it was coming from. It sounded distant. She walked through the yard, being led by it, when she heard clothes rustling and soft grunting. She hid behind a tree and sneaked a peek. What she saw turned her blood cold, jealousy gripping her quickly. Malcolm had Liz in his arms and was kissing her passionately. Or what seemed to be passionately at first. Liz didn't appear to be enjoying it nearly as much as Malcolm was. She kept her arms tightly pressed against his chest, trying to push him away and turning her face from his.

"Please, Malcolm. I can't," she begged.

"Why? Because of Alia? What she doesn't know won't hurt her."

"But I don't want to. I love William. They'll smell it on us."

"So then go away for a few days."

He had an answer to all her refusals and refuse him she tried. Alia wondered how many other women he had forced himself on, or how long this had been going on. She was frozen with shock, her world crashing down. As deranged as he could sometimes get, he was her everything.

She looked again and he had her down on the grass. Her skirts were raised and he was straddling her hips. He held her arms above her head with one hand while fidgeting with his pants with the other. Liz was openly crying, and her body shook with the effort of attempting to throw him off her. Seeing her struggle pushed Alia into action. She couldn't stand here and let Liz go through this. Alia grabbed a thick branch off the ground and whacked Malcolm across the head as hard as she could. She hit him with a strength she didn't know she possessed and had he not been a vampire, she surely would have killed him. The impact made a sickening sound and blood spurted from his gash as he fell from Liz on his side. Alia helped her friend from the floor and made to hit him again.

"Don't you lay a finger on her!" she screamed, beside herself.

Kneeling and massaging the back of his head, he grabbed the branch out of her hands, throwing it across the field. Alia placed Liz, who was still crying, softly behind her, protecting her with her body. He cocked his head at the sight of it and chuckled.

"Who do you think you are, giving me orders?" he asked, circling around them.

"I am your queen, and you will not touch her again."

Much faster than she could perceive, he had her by the neck and pushed her against a tree. But she had counted on his outburst of violence. She had been with him long enough and had, just as quickly, grabbed the sharp letter opener she kept tied to her thigh. It was now angled upright at his own throat. He slightly released the pressure on her and she smirked, keeping her weapon in place.

"Liz, go to my room."

"I can't leave you here."

"I'll be up in just a moment. My *king* and I are just going to have a little chat."

His eyes narrowed and she saw Liz run back

towards the house. Malcolm and Alia's gazes remained locked.

"Do you really think this little blade is going to do you any good?" he growled.

"I don't. But I could shove it so far up your brain it would take you a long time to heal. Too long for you to be sure I wouldn't finish the job. I can guarantee you I would cut off your balls. I doubt those would grow back."

"Nicely played." He released her, walking back a few feet. He sounded impressed.

"Here's what's going to happen." She kept wielding the letter opener in front of her, half expecting another attack. "You will never force yourself on Liz again." He raised his eyebrows. "And as much as I let you push me over, I promise you if you touch her again, I will end your life. Even if I die too."

He clasped his hands in front of himself. "Deal." He looked at her a moment longer; was it pride she saw? Then he began walking away.

"How did we get here, Malcolm?" That stopped him in his tracks. "I thought you loved me and now I find you trying to rape my closest friend. If I'm your queen, why have you been abusing me since you turned me?"

"You think I've been treating you differently?"

"Yes," she whispered, feeling the tears building up.

"Alia, you didn't want to acknowledge what kind of beast I was when you were human. You pretended I had any sort of humanity left when I never did. And I never hid that from you. You've brainwashed yourself into making me the bad guy when I've been the same person all along. This is your fault."

A knife to the heart would have hurt less than his answer. "Have you ever loved me then?"

He smirked, shaking his head. "Does a lion love his lionesses? I am an animal with primal needs. I view you and all other women in this household as my pack, as my mates. Nothing more. And you, you are weak. You like being called the queen but look how long it even took you to speak up."

She raised her chin higher, resigned to not let him see how much his words affected her. She should have known better than to open herself up to him in this moment. He walked away and she waited until he was out of sight before making her way back to the house.

She found Elizabeth waiting in her room as requested, and she was still visibly shaken up from the altercation.

"Has it happened before?" Alia asked after closing and locking the door, afraid of the answer.

Liz shook her head no violently. "This was the first time, I promise you."

"You didn't seem well this morning. You must have known."

"He was making comments all morning. I was afraid he would take it further, and he tried."

They hugged, fiercely. "I need you to tell me if he ever does something like this to you again. Do you understand me? I would kill him for you, Liz."

William came home just a bit before sunrise and the girls decided to keep the events from him, lest he get himself killed out of rage. When Alia was reassured Liz would be safe with her lover, she headed to Malcolm's office. She was far from done from letting him hear her mind. She was about to knock on the wooden door when she heard voices inside: Malcolm and the head of his security. Jonathan had recently been introduced to the family as being in charge of staying one step ahead of any danger that could come their way. If any evidence was left at a crime scene that would lead back to the clan, he was in charge of making it all go away.

"Central America?" she heard Malcolm ask. "Are you sure she's hiding there?"

"Positive."

"Well, that's a large area. Can you pinpoint where?"

"We tracked her all the way to Costa Rica in the Guanacaste region. We lost her then."

"And how do you propose we go there?" Silence. "It doesn't matter. Isn't there an active volcano there? Oh, she's smart, the volcano's energy is shielding her. She doesn't want to be found. Hopefully, she stays lost. I don't have the time to hunt her down there."

Alia had no idea who they were talking about, but suddenly the door swung open and Malcolm's hand was once again at her throat. Her feet were raised a good foot off the ground. For the briefest second, he seemed disturbed she had heard this exchange. Was that fear she smelled?

"Alia dearest, it's now my turn to issue a threat. If I ever smell or find you eavesdropping on my business again, how did you put it? 'I will end your life.' Do I make myself clear?" He banged her head against the wall a few times.

He dropped her to the floor where she coughed earnestly. Malcolm and Jonathan stepped over her and walked away into the house without a backward glance. She paid little attention to her throat that was on fire. Instead, she replayed the conversation in her mind. She didn't believe Jonathan was a simple security man anymore. Who was he tracking? Who did Malcolm fear so much?

I woke up with a gasp, half raising from my lying position and not fully understanding where I was. Slowly, yesterday's events returned, and my memory began catching up. I was lying across the backseat of a car that Rafael was driving. We had found this vehicle abandoned alongside the forest and it smelled like an ashtray. It was the second time I dreamt of this, and I knew it had to mean something. My spirit guides were nudging me towards Costa Rica.

"I know where we must go," I said, crawling forward to the passenger seat. I received a curious look. "Playa Hermosa in Costa Rica," I finished.

"What's there?"

"Our way of getting rid of Malcolm."

"And what would that be?"

"I'm not sure yet," I said, hesitating, "but I know it's there."

He remained quiet for a long time. "Okay. But how do we get to Costa Rica?"

"I need to charge my phone and make a call and request one last favor."

We pulled up to the first motel we came across and it was despicable. One of those motels with a half-working neon sign. It was late at night and the concierge was too afraid to refuse us; besides, there were only two other cars in the parking lot. The room was a disgrace for the eighty dollars we had paid, but we would only be here momentarily. I checked the mattress for bed bugs and when that passed the test, dropped my duffel bag on the ground. I reached for the wireless phone, dialed a number, and began pacing. It rang for a long time and when I thought it would go to voicemail, the other end finally picked up.

"Nicholas? It's Alia. I'm sorry to bother you so late, but I need your help one more time." I listened to his protests. "I understand." More protests. "You will be paid generously, and I promise you this will be the last time I call you." Money drowned out the objection. "Please grab one of my private jets; you have the gate's code. We will need to head to Costa Rica as soon as possible. We are at the Inn Motel in Durham, North Carolina. There is plenty of space for you to land in a field behind the motel. I'll send you our exact location. How long until you arrive?" I sighed. "Okay, we will see you then."

I hung up and threw my jacket on the bed, kicking off my shoes. "Get comfy. We will be here for at least forty-eight hours."

"What are we supposed to do meanwhile?"

I massaged my temples. "Remain undetected. No one must know we are here."

"And food?"

"I strongly advise against it."

He was annoyed and flipped angrily through the channels. Slightly amused, I watched him watch the television until I fell asleep. When I awoke, the curtains were wide open, and Rafael was no longer in the room. I ran into the rain, screaming his name. Unable to find him and in an immoderate panic, I returned to the room. I knew he was alive. I awaited his return, sitting on the bed, and checked my text messages and voice-mails in the meantime. Detective Thompson had tried to get a hold of me, and I was glad to see he was still alive. His texts went from worried to pure fury as he was unable to reach me. I sent him a brief reply, trying to update him as to what I knew of Malcolm's plans and explained my reason for heading to Costa Rica where I would not have service. I hoped this would be enough to somewhat help my name from being associated with Malcolm for the time being. I then called Lidia, feeling over-whelming relief when she picked up. We spoke briefly but she and George were safe, far away from the main city and its crazi-ness. My heart felt a little less worried when she and I hung up.

Rafael soon walked in, flinching as he saw me awake.

"What's up?" he asked. He had fed. I could smell it on his breath. At least it was animal blood, and I was relieved.

"'What's up?' What part of 'remain undetected' do you not understand?"

"I understand but I only went out for a quick bite. I can't continue starving myself. I figured you'd go yourself when you woke up." I was about to start arguing he was far from starving with the energy transfer I had given him. "No one saw me," he added. "You have to relax a little. I know we went through a lot, and we are fighting for our lives, but we can't constantly live in fear this way."

Maybe my paranoia was getting out of control, but it seemed to me it had kept us alive on multiple occasions. Or maybe this really was no way to live at all. He agreed to appease my mind by staying indoors for the remainder of our stay. I caught up on some dearly missed sleep, constantly going in and out of consciousness. I was more mentally than physically exhausted, my body still buzzing with this newly attained energy, yet I could barely keep my eyes open long enough to check whether Rafael was near me. He paced around the room, watching television and watching over me. We extended our stay one day at a time and finally, a few days later, we heard an airplane flying over the motel. We gathered our few belongings and waited patiently in the lot for the small aircraft to land. The plane appeared in the distance, becoming more apparent as it lowered down. The night's darkness made the landing a little more complicated than it should have been. The jet jolted a few times, bouncing from side to side, when the wheels touched the ground and began slowing down.

Finally, the door opened, and the pilot emerged.

"Ms. Henry, I wish I could say it is good to see you."

"Well, I certainly can. It's good to see you, Nicholas," I said, entering the aircraft and settling down in one of the four seats.

"Ms. Henry, with everything going on in the world, this has to be the last time I help you. At least until the world calms down. My wife will leave me if I involve myself again."

"I understand. Why don't you keep this plane for yourself. Sell it, keep it, do whatever you will with it. Do you have a piece of paper? I'll transfer it to you right now."

I jotted down all the information I could remember, and Nicholas was now a $75,000 plane richer. The ride was long and uncomfortable, and I spent some time studying Costa Rica's geography from a map. Nicholas was not in a talking mood, and I knew he just didn't want to be involved in anymore vampire business. We traveled over the Guanacaste province with its vast, green mountains and landed into a valley. I bid Nicholas farewell and we began walking deep into the forest that bordered the ocean. I had never been to Costa Rica, and I was slightly taken aback by its suffocating, humid heat; my body was immediately covered in a thin layer of sweat. I had no solid idea of where to go apart from what I had heard what felt like a lifetime ago and followed my intuition. We seemed to be walking aimlessly. Rafael's annoyance and my anticipation grew.

As I walked on, now bordering the water, I was aware my body felt different. I grew progressively more tired, my skin was numb to the touch, and I felt detached from my surroundings, the sounds around me muted. I attempted to hide it from Rafael to the best of my ability by pretending to look at the map once more. I was confused and disoriented.

When I turned around, I saw Malcolm holding Rafael above the ground by the throat before plunging his teeth into my boyfriend's flesh. I screamed and watched as he dropped the dead body to the floor, laughing. I smelled fire and an overwhelmingly strong scent of sulfur. All my senses came rushing back in at once, sounds and sensations, as I took a deep breath. I realized I was actually screaming, and Rafael stood in front of me, holding me in his arms.

"Babe! What is happening?" he shouted over me.

I looked around, afraid and baffled at what I had just experienced.

"I... I think I had my first vision from William's powers."

"What did you see? Fuck, I don't think I want to know!"

"I saw Malcolm attacking us." I would keep the details to myself. I did not need to worry Rafael. I relaxed in his arms a little, letting my head rest on his chest. If that is how all of William's visions came to him, I could comprehend that it drove him mad. And again, I felt guilt and shame over how things ended for him, but I also found a deep place of love within me reserved for him. He was with me, always.

All of a sudden, I laid eyes upon an old, short fisherman. The singularity of this encounter left us speechless and staring at each other. We had been walking for a short amount of time but had seen no other human beings apart from him.

"What is he doing here?" Rafael whispered.

The man pointed behind himself. "Ella está esperando por ustedes."

"What did he say?"

"She is waiting for us," I translated for Rafael.

"Who is?" he questioned.

I shot him an annoyed glare. How was I supposed to know who "she" was? I was as clueless as him. We walked slowly past the little man who resumed his activity and moved down the path. In the distance we noticed an old church built within the mountain's rock. The voices whispered encouragingly for us to move forward.

"We have to get inside," I said.

"Why?"

I shrugged. "Maybe this is where we will find out how to kill Malcolm."

I half expected to be struck by lightning as soon as I opened the door. I laughed to myself; I was kidding. Mostly.

"What is this God-forsaken noise?" Rafael asked, covering his ears.

The high-pitched ringing screeched louder the longer we stayed. "Interesting choice of words. We are the forsaken ones. God does not want us in his house."

"So, God exists?"

"Of course. A higher power mixed with old magic created life, but the way humans have it portrayed is completely wrong."

"How do you know that?"

"I spent two centuries traveling and studying the old texts. Studying the inconsistencies within all the modern translations. Also studying the similarities within the originally translated texts." I shrugged again, "It's only my take on it."

"Why aren't we wanted here?"

"God created life. We are the walking dead, mistakes that escaped him. A disease. Humans are meant to be safe here, and the noise is meant to drive us out."

"What will happen to us if we die?" He seemed panicked.

The fresco paintings were mostly faded and hard to make out, giving us an idea of just how old and forgotten this church was. I advanced towards the small altar and knelt in front of it as I had been taught to do when I was human. The mosaics' saints seemed unpleased by our presence.

"I don't know, Rafael. I only died once and didn't make it to Heaven. Let's think about this another time. We need to figure out what we are looking for." I looked around. Maybe it was a relic? A weapon? A book?

"You are looking for me," said a female voice from above.

As she jumped off a balcony and landed perfectly on her feet, I had the time to take a good look at her. Her petite figure seemed fragile. Her bright green eyes lit her entire oval-shaped face that was framed with shoulder-length, straight black hair. What surprised me the most was what I heard: a heartbeat within a vampire. She stood a few feet from me quietly.

"What are you?" was the first thing I asked.

"I'm much like yourself, yet very different." She remained still, arms at her side, while I circled around her, studying her.

"You are not completely..." I trailed off.

"Dead? No, I am, not. I have the need to drink blood, but my heart still beats."

"How is that possible?"

"I was unwillingly turned. Cursed to an in-between life. Half vampire, half human."

I scoffed. "Those are legends."

"Yet here I stand before your eyes."

Still unsure of her intentions, Rafael stood ready to attack.

"You can tell him to stand down. I made sure you kept dreaming of that same memory so you'd come here, so we'd finally meet and fight him together. I asked your spirit guides to bring you here."

I knew she meant Malcolm. The screeching never ceased and intensified the longer we remained inside. She didn't seem to have any issues with it, and maybe because she was half human, it didn't affect her quite the same. She seemed aware of our discomfort and led us outside to continue our conversation.

"How do you know him?" I asked.

"I knew him when he was a new vampire. He created me sixty years before your time."

I stopped investigating her and returned to Rafael's side,

putting a hand on his arm. "What do you want with us?" he asked, finally relaxing his stance.

"I want revenge on Malcolm for what he has done to me. I have been waiting over three hundred years. Patiently awaiting the day we'd gather forces to put an end to his reign of chaos."

"He has an Astaroth army with him."

"They will all be exterminated," she answered with conviction. "You should rest here. We will leave in the morning."

"Where are we going?" I asked.

"I've had a long time to create a vampire sanctuary over the years. We are going to meet them." And with no arguments from us, she walked back into the church.

The vibrantly green grass a little farther in the jungle was abundant and thick due to the constant moisture in the air and, along with the moss, made for a great laying pad. The crickets and frogs were out in forces, and I relaxed on the ground, feeling myself doze off. This humidity was taxing.

"Do we trust her?" Rafael asked in a low tone.

"I don't think we have another option, but I think we can. My senses aren't alerting me of any danger. I feel really calm around her, like this is where I'm meant to be."

We were asleep for a bit when I felt as though I was being watched, and we were. The girl nodded for me to follow her. I trailed a few feet behind her as we walked down to the ocean. She sat down on the black sand, and I did the same, putting my feet in the water. It was surprisingly warm; I had always been under the impression that the Pacific was cold.

"You never told me your name," I said, burying my feet in the wet sand.

"Eloise." She stared at me with a curious intensity, and I held her glare. "I have waited for this day to come for so long. Now that it's here, I don't know how to handle it," she said, laughing and looking away.

I didn't reply.

"Do you fully understand what it means to be unwillingly turned?"

"No, I don't."

"And I assume one of the very first rules he taught you was to never transform anyone without their consent, correct?"

I nodded.

"He and I met when I was a human. We were friends, and then his persona changed. He was barely over a century old, and he made it clear from the beginning just how lonely he was. I accepted him for what he was, yet I knew he was an abomination, and I did not want to become one myself. Close to my twenty-fourth birthday, I fell terminally ill as people often did back then. He came to me minutes from my passing and asked me whether I wanted to be turned. And through the pain, I said, loud and clear, 'no,' but he still bit me. My transformation was harder than a regular vampire's. I was lost within the darkness of a void. I felt my soul being pulled by demons. Each inch of my skin was burned off by the fires of Hell. When I awoke, I was submerged by anger, hatred, and a need for vengeance. The curse for ones like myself is to have this uncontrollable need for vengeance. We do not feel a minute of peace as long as the one who violated the law still breathes. I am the first and the last person he has ever turned unwillingly, and I am the only one who can kill him. He is afraid of me and has tried killing me. I will only be truly allowed to die once he is dead."

She paused for a moment. I thought she might be done. "Are you saying you're invincible?"

She chuckled. "If you want to call it that. I bleed, I hurt, I die, but I always come back. And I always will. I cannot die unless he dies first."

"Why haven't you killed him yet then?"

"He and I are connected in a way that makes it absolutely impossible to launch a sneak attack. I sense him at all times, and it is amplified by the wrongness of what he did to me. I've tried to get to him many times, but he is cunning and a coward who lets others die in his place so he can escape. I just need to get my hands on him."

"And the volcano energy shields you from him?" She raised her eyebrows in surprise. "I heard him talk about it in passing years ago," I explained.

As if a light bulb shone above my head, it all became so clear to me. "This is what the war is about, isn't it? He's doing all that he can to become powerful enough. He wants my powers to get rid of you somehow. With you gone, he has nothing to be afraid of ever again, no limitations. Only then can he be sure to rule the world with no obstacles. I just got caught in the middle."

"My goal was never to involve anyone else and much less kill other vampires in his place. I gave up hope of ever destroying him and getting peace, I just..." She paused. "I just didn't want to kill any more of us."

"I used to feel sorry for him," she continued, "knowing that he was alone figuring out how to be a vampire. His sire died right after turning him and he had to learn everything by trial and error. But then what type of person forces this onto someone else?" She shook her head. "He was never good to begin with."

"He's always been power hungry."

"I made my peace with feeling this way and letting him get away with it. But then I had a vision of the future. Us three together will be the end of him."

"What exactly did you see?"

I could tell she was careful choosing her words. "I saw us on the winning side. I felt the ability to die again, and that can only mean Malcolm is no longer alive."

"And was Rafael on that side?"

She looked down and said, "You had a vision of him? Did you see him die?"

"Yes," I replied, and my voice was a whisper. "Are you ever able to alter your visions?"

"I'm afraid they aren't simple psychic visions. They are glimpses of destiny."

"We are masters of our own destinies."

She got up and walked away a few feet. "Some events have already been set in stone. Your friend William understood this although it took everything from him," she said over her shoulder.

I looked back onto the dark water and felt a pinch of sadness thinking of William. Had I been too hard on him for the decisions he made? I felt the tears fall down my cheeks. I refused to believe I couldn't change my destiny. I would save Rafael, no matter what it took.

CHAPTER EIGHTEEN

1923

Alia stood leaning against the bar, pretending to like her martini, and minding her own business. Tonight was her night off; she wasn't expected to hunt for the clan or find possible recruits. She could just enjoy herself, whatever that meant anymore, and that's exactly what she would try to do. She was mentally exhausted. The last century and a half had beat her down. The speakeasy was full of patrons, some dancing near the jazz band on stage, most sitting at their tables and some, like her, hovering by the bar. She wore fox fur around her slim, naked shoulders and a long glittering gown that plunged down her cleavage. She looked like a movie star. She was one of the few who hadn't cut her hair into a bob and she'd be damned if she let anyone touch her long, beautiful curls. She held an unlit cigarette between her fingers, keeping her gaze on her drink, deep into her own thoughts, when she heard the scratch of a match and a light sulfuric smell floated in the air. She inhaled deeply, loving the feel of smoke filling up her lungs. Upon turning her face, her gaze met with a stranger's, although he was about a full foot taller than Alia and well above six feet tall. He had a devious smile and sharp cheekbones under bright green eyes. His black suit jacket was impressively fitted to a strong but lean body type. He looked like a swimmer. And he was a vampire.

"Why, thank you," she said, offering a small smile and taking another drag off her cigarette.

"You are very welcome, miss. I've noticed you haven't touched your drink."

"You've been watching me?"

"Only a little." He blushed.

She fully angled her body towards him now, narrowing her eyes and studying him.

"Do we know each other?"

"Only in passing, and only through what others have to say about us."

His face did look familiar, but she couldn't quite place him yet. The band had slowed their songs down progressively and were now playing slow and sultry music.

"Would you like to dance?" he asked.

She gave him her hand and let him walk her to the dance floor. She had never seen him before, but his smell... where had she smelled him before? He placed his hands on the small of her back, bringing her closer, and she put her arms around his tall neck. He had to lean forward, curving his body for her to reach. They glided over the dance floor, rubbing their bodies on each other in what could only be described as sensual. He twirled her, encircling her waist with his arms and swaying her from side to side, smelling her neck. Her body filled with tension, finally recognizing his scent.

"Do you think Mr. Istvan would appreciate this scene?" he asked.

And she chuckled. "I know exactly who you are, Mr. Landon, and I do not care what Malcolm thinks. It is you who should be afraid."

They didn't stop dancing, but he did move her around so he could look into her face.

"You know who I am?"

"Of course. So why don't you just tell me what it is you want so we can stop playing this little charade and resume our nights?"

"You are a curious creature, Ms. Henry. You control the biggest vampire clan in the city and yet you hate it."

"I do not control anyone."

"Well, you are his right-hand woman. His queen, as he likes to call you." She scoffed and stopped dancing, standing still in the middle of the dance floor.

"You have exactly sixty seconds to tell me what you're after before I walk away, and trust me when I say you will not get a second chance at getting this close to me again."

"I want to take you away from him. I want to offer you and actually provide you with all that he's promised you and never delivered. We have a very different culture in my clan. One that I think you would be happier with. One that resonates more with you and your eating habits."

Music to her ears, but there had to be a catch. "And why would you do that for me?"

"Because you would provide me with information. Bank accounts, alliances, names, and all his other weaknesses. We plan on removing him and it'll be much easier with your help. Come with me tonight."

"How long ago were you turned, Mr. Landon?"

"Please, call me Joshua. I was turned twenty-five years ago."

"And you've already made yourself clan leader? That's impressive. But I am not for sale." She made to turn away, but he grabbed her arm.

"I am offering you your freedom."

She quickly pulled out a small, sharp knife from her dress and angled it at his heart. "I do not need you or anyone else to grant me freedom. We are infinitely older than you and I have been with him 150 years. What makes you think I would follow you? You came to me because you think I'm fragile," she whispered quickly. "You think I'm helpless and the weak link in his armor. What you don't know is that I don't need Malcolm and I am vicious enough on my own. You made a mistake coming for me tonight."

He took a step back, putting his hands up. "I came here tonight because I saw how sad you looked. It's an honest offer. We share a similar problem; I only offered to take care of it for the both of us. Think on it."

"What about the rest of my family?"

"The offer only stands for you, I'm afraid."

"And you're so sure I'll accept it?"

He brushed his hand along her jawline. "Haven't you suffered enough?"

The bar's metal doors banged open with a loud crash and police officers stormed the place. The bartender turned a hidden lever that dropped all the liquor bottles down a chute and began smashing bottles that were on the bar. The jazz band didn't stop playing. As far as they were concerned, music in a bar was legal. This put the conversation to an end as patrons, Alia included, ran to avoid being arrested. She reached the street sidewalk and slowed her walk, pretending she had not narrowly escaped detention. She spent a long time thinking about Mr. Landon's proposition as she hailed a cab and made her way back to the house. She walked up the stairs, down the corridor, and knocked on Malcolm's office door.

"Ah, Alia, light of my life, how was your night?"

He was in a rare and bright mood tonight, gesturing for her to come sit on his lap. As she reluctantly did so, he inhaled sharply. "Who were you with?" he asked.

"Joshua Landon." She searched his eyes for any trace, any sign of jealousy.

"Is that so?" He laughed. "And what did the fella want?"

No matter what he had done or how he treated

her, this was her home, this was her family. She wanted to think she cared for her family's well-being more than anything, but if she was quite honest, she hoped her loyalty would impress Malcolm and make him see how valuable she was. She didn't care to have his love anymore, that ship had long sailed, but she still wanted to feel appreciated.

She picked up a letter opener, playing with the sharp end while he rubbed her thigh absentmindedly, which was surprising since they had not slept together in years. "He wanted me to betray you. Tell him all of your secrets so he could remove you from the playing field and take me as his."

"And you didn't go for it?" He sounded surprised. "You could have been rid of me for good if Landon had succeeded! Your level of masochism will never cease to amaze me." Her heart crumpled before returning to its numb state. She stood up and walked to the door.

"I thought you'd be proud of me," she whispered.

"Alia," he began, about to say something, then seemed to change his mind, sighing. "Please close the door behind you."

She stepped out, then turned around, one hand on the door. "What will you do?"

"He wanted me out of his way, and you just gave me the upper hand. He'll be handled."

She knew this meant Joshua Landon and his clan would be dead before sunrise and felt guilt over it. Malcolm was a monster, but she wanted nothing more than to please him even after all these years, and she hoped her loyalty would ease some of the tension between them. The following evening when she awoke, she heard the news that all members of that other clan had been completely eradicated and everyone attributed it to her meeting. They were still alive thanks to her. They applauded her. Then why did it feel so wrong?

"You murdered them all," she said, entering his office. She didn't know why she was so baffled by his actions anymore, but she hadn't expected an extermination.

He looked up from his paperwork. "You know he would have done the same to us."

She shook her head side to side, as though this was only a bad dream. "I'm sure you didn't consider sparing any."

"I couldn't just take out the leader while he had already trained his followers to have the same mentality as him."

"You told everyone it was thanks to me."

He looked at her strangely. "It's eating at you, isn't it? The guilt?" He stood and came to stand in front of her. "Let me do you a favor on this one and take this off your shoulders..." He slightly leaned into Alia, whispering near her ear, "I knew about your meeting before you came to me. I knew about Landon's plans before he tried recruiting you."

"How?" she gasped.

His eyes burned intensely into hers. "Haven't

you learned yet? I am always one step ahead." He returned to his desk, sat in his chair, and shuffled the papers he was previously looking at. "I have eyes on you and your friends at all times. Do you really think it was a coincidence that you ran into him? Who do you think has been whispering rumors about your allegiance?"

"But why?"

"I wanted reassurance. It had been a while since I was sure of where you stood with the clan. You're always trying to leave me or fighting with me. I thought I'd kill two birds with one stone."

Of course this had been a test. "I'm getting really tired of your games, you know," she said, turning away.

"Love, you and I are far from being done with my games!" He laughed.

A shiver ran down her spine as she slammed the door shut behind her. She couldn't shake the terror his words put in her.

When I dreamt of my past, I always relived the same emotions and I was actually shocked at feeling this deep sense of loyalty towards Malcolm. It always took me some time to get over this. It was like dreaming your partner cheated on you and waking up mad. I hoped Eloise didn't know of this, and I, of course, omitted telling Rafael. However, my wish was soon crushed as she cornered me while I was washing my hands in the ocean.

"I need to know your heart is completely into this."

"What do you mean?"

"Let's not beat around the bush. I know what's coming. If I'm not the one to do it, will you kill Malcolm when the time comes?"

"Of course she will. He has put us through enough," Rafael intervened.

"That's not what I've seen!" she screamed.

Rafael's arm slipped from my shoulders. "Come again?"

She ignored his question and remained looking at me. "Are you wasting my time, Alia?" Her eyes flashed fury.

"No, it will be done. They are just memories, you know that."

The conversation was over. Eloise walked away and so did Rafael. I caught up to him and grabbed his arm. "Wait up."

He jerked away so quickly I stumbled. "Why would Eloise doubt you, Alia?"

"You don't even know what she was talking about. It was just a dream, a memory! How should I know?"

"Be honest with me. Do you actually still have feelings for him?"

What an absurd question, but maybe a tad of truth lay in it.

"How could you do this to me, Alia? You could have let me

die. Instead, I'm now a vampire and learning my girlfriend is still in love with her ex."

"In love? Far from it. I have history with him—he and I are tied. He is a part of me as much as I am a part of him."

His anger dissipated. He was thoughtful. "No one else dreams like you do. If you are a part of him, could he be sending you these memories? To mess with you?"

"I don't know." I paused, dumbfounded. "Theoretically and logically, if Eloise can make me have the same dream multiple times, then I suppose if he's gathered the power, he could too."

I had always thought my dreams were associated with my witch powers and because of my guilt, but Rafael could have a point.

"When did these dreams start?"

I instinctively wanted to answer "as long as I could remember" but that wasn't quite true. I walked a few feet away, racking my brain. I wasn't reborn this way and now that I thought long and hard about it, it absolutely started after the massacre I escaped. Was he really doing this to me? To keep me weak, anxious, and traumatized until he came for me? I would be so glad to be rid of these nightmares once I killed him. Now I wanted to know if I could return the favor and give him a piece of his own medicine. I just didn't know if it would take more power than I possessed.

Eloise had trained herself on this issue and thought I could absolutely achieve it in no time.

"All you need to do to send another vampire visions, dreams, or whatever else you want to call it, is to focus on them and break through their walls. Envision yourself inside their safe space, sending them orders through their mind," she explained.

"Could we even see what he's got planned?" Rafael asked.

"Entering someone's mind is never easy. You may not like

what you see in there, but if you can get him to feel safe, he could tell you whatever you wanted."

This was so wild to think about. Ninety-six years of believing these dreams were normal, to finding out Malcolm very well could have been manipulating them all along.

"Do you want to work on raising your mental shield first before we head out?" Eloise offered.

"What will it entail?"

"Would you want to meet your inner child? I think that would be a good place to start. We could work on letting go of some of your guilt so Malcolm can't have so much control over you. I'll need to access your mind."

I swallowed hard and nodded my approval, very uncomfortable with the idea but also curious about it and the process. It would feel great to not carry so much shame around. She led me to a soft spot under a tree where we sat cross-legged and Rafael stood by a few feet away, watching us. The sky was overcast, and the humidity coated my skin with sweat.

"Close your eyes and do what you must to connect to your deeper self." I dug my hands into the grass. "Take a deep breath and let me do the rest."

I took a breath, the deepest breath it felt I had ever taken, and opened my eyes. I found myself in a completely dark place. The floor was made of concrete and my footsteps echoed but I saw no walls or windows. Just continuous darkness. There was no sound and I smelled nothing; it did not feel like any place I had ever been to before. And I could not tell whether I was indoors or outdoors. I walked cautiously, not afraid but not trusting either. Unsure whether I was going around in circles, I began feeling anxious and frustrated.

I saw a weak light, heard faint crying in the distance, and followed the sound until the light was so close, I could see a small child kneeling on the ground, hunched over, hugging herself. Her crying had turned into big, ugly open sobs and I could not see her face through the dark hair draped over her.

I put a knee down next to the small figure and placed a hand on her shoulder. "It's alright, child. Why are you crying?" I asked in what I hoped was a soothing voice.

She looked up, her face streaming with tears and I jumped up and away from her with a gasp. My heart was hammering against my chest. The little girl in such deep distress wore my face. What I looked like as a small child, maybe eight or nine years old. She seemed to be in so much pain, but I was just so taken aback, I did not even attempt to calm her down again. I looked up, trying to figure out where this light shining down on her like a small spotlight was coming from, but could not discern anything.

Her crying had slowed down and when I lowered my eyes again, I was disturbed to see black, inky claws circling her throat. I was then feeling actual fear for her, for myself, as I could see someone hiding behind her in the dark. All I saw were the whites of the creature's eyes.

"Who are you?" I asked. But it did not answer. Instead it kept its eyes on me and leaned into the small girl's ear, whispering. I heard it as loud as if it were spoken directly to me.

"You broke your father's heart. You deserve to suffer for what you've done to him. He died alone with no one to care for him. Had you just listened to him he'd have lived a long, happy life and for that, you do not deserve to know what true love is." The literal black venom dripping from its mouth, turning into words, pierced my heart. My smaller version, as I understood her to be, began crying again and I felt our pain deep in my soul. I felt the shame pouring out and the guilt overtaking me, us.

The claws grew tighter on her throat, and I felt myself suffocating. "We were so young," I responded unconvincingly, sobbing softly. "We had no idea what we were doing, the impact it would have."

The demon continued its bullying. "You brought Elizabeth and William into your world, just to hand them into the hands of a lunatic that destroyed everything he touched. They should have never been changed to begin with. You destroy everything you love, including yourself. You're no better than Malcolm in that aspect."

"I destroy everything I love," my eight-year-old self whimpered.

"That's not true!" I half cried, half shouted. "I did what I thought was best for them!" But I damn well knew I did not fully believe it in my heart. It had been out of selfishness and not wanting to deal with Malcolm alone.

"Then is it our fault?"

"No, of course not," I breathed out.

I began noticing a brick wall building itself around us, appearing out of nowhere. With every vile word the demon spoke, a few more bricks emerged, slowly closing in around us, trapping us inside this wall of toxicity. The girl began to crumble on herself more and more. I could feel her tiredness in my bones, her will to block it all off and shut down her feelings.

The raspy voice didn't miss a beat. "You are so stuck in playing the victim. You could have prevented some of it, if not all of it, just by standing up to him. But your need for his approval, his love, turned you into a pushover and it was just so much easier to let him have his way. You could have saved them all, had you had the guts to do what was needed. You are as responsible for all of it as he is. Malcolm knows he's evil, but you pretend to not be and that makes you perhaps the worse one."

"I am evil. Why didn't I try saving them? Why didn't I stand up for them?"

I once again kneeled down next to the child and held her hands in mine. "We are not evil. We were never evil. It just took us a very long time to feel confident in ourselves. We could have done a lot of things differently, but we didn't know we could yet. Now we are strong enough." I could feel myself losing tenacity, the numbness from crying overtaking me as well.

The creature's hands were still wrapped around her neck, but they were no longer tightening up. "You and your skills are just not good enough. How in the world can you think you'll beat him? Why even try at all? You will fail. You're not strong enough. You don't have what it takes. You're better off just letting him take your life, like you took William's."

I knew that I needed to exit this negative space, that I was very close to getting trapped here. And that was when I stood into my own power, rising from the floor with a roaring, "*That is enough.*"

The demon stood with me, finally releasing younger Alia's throat, and that was when I realized that she was just another version of myself, a much uglier, scarred, and demonic version. Her skin bore long, thinly-raised gashes where it seemed she had been broken and put together time and time again. I felt sadness for little Alia who never stood a chance, listening to this abuse that I willingly let us be put through. I even grew a little angry. Who would we have become had I been my own best friend? Who would we have become had I not allowed Malcolm to make me believe I was weak?

"I know what you're doing to her, to us," I said, drying my tears while she watched me, cocking her head to the side like an animal. "And it's not going to work anymore. We don't *need* you anymore." I quickly got down next to the child and pulled her into my lap, holding her tightly to my chest. "I love you. I am here for you. I am going to take care of us now."

My demon roared its fury. "Where would you be if it weren't for me? I am the only one that saved us. I was our only savior!"

"I thank you for protecting us and I am sorry you had to become this person to keep us safe all those years, but it's over now. We are *safe*. We can be truly happy. You have no more power here. You have filled our head with lies, but you're the one who's weak. You're the unlovable part of us. You're cold and scared. And that's not us anymore. I am letting you go."

Light began pulsing through the shadows as I rocked my younger self. The wall around us started falling apart, one brick at a time.

"You'll need me again because who are you without me? If you're not the angry, sad victim of your story, what is your identity then?"

I whispered in my younger self's ear, still holding on to her tightly. "Don't listen to her. She's wrong and she's scared. Look inside you. You know you don't truly believe her. We can be happy without all the heaviness she brings. I'll take good care of us."

"I am a part of you; you can't just remove me."

"I don't plan on removing you. I am accepting that you are a part of me and will always be, but you will no longer control my fear and actions. You are no longer going to be the worst part of me. We are no longer going to fight each other."

The demon was now just a faint image, disappearing in the bright space around us as I continued whispering, "I am worth all the love and success the world has to offer," until I started believing it.

When I came to, facing Eloise once more, I burst into tears of overwhelming relief. I had never faced my demon before, had never communicated with this side that I had refused to acknowledge although it was causing me so much pain. I felt light, as though an enormous weight had been removed from my shoulders. Leaning forward on my knees, I hugged Eloise fiercely. "Thank you so much," I whispered.

She smiled and wiped the tears off my face. "He should have a harder time messing with you now."

I stood and Rafael walked up to me, crushing me in a tight embrace, kissing my temple. "I know that was hard. I am so proud of you." I returned his hug, feeling so much freer.

We packed our bags and began migrating by foot from Playa Hermosa to the province of Alajuela. Rafael and I looked at each other after walking for a little bit, and I knew exactly what he was thinking.

"Are we going to walk all the way there?" I asked.

"Yes," Eloise simply answered.

"Wait, what?" Rafael and I both almost exclaimed at the same time.

"Having a car in Costa Rica is a privilege. It is incredibly difficult to buy one. And with the way relations between humans and vampires are going right now, it'd be in our best interest to not force our luck asking for help. Don't you think?"

"Couldn't you have had us meet you closer to where we are going?" Rafael half joked.

"You would have never been able to find the camp's location. The church was a nice and secured place I've used many times."

Our walk to La Fortuna would take a day and a half to two days, and that was only if we stopped for a few short, casual breaks to hunt and bathe in rivers. With the wildlife roaming around, the forest was more treacherous than the last and also much more humid; we had to be very careful where we stepped. I especially kept my eyes open for the famous eyelash viper that Eloise warned us could often be found next to flowers, awaiting their next kill. A bite could be lethal to humans if not handled immediately, and although it wouldn't kill a vampire, it could seriously slow one down, and we just didn't have any time to waste. Even without Malcolm's doing the sun hadn't been out in months. This was the rainy season. The sky was muggy, a thick mist was constantly spraying, and it was even darker under the trees, their tight rows making it impossible for any clarity to appear. The jungle was filled with sounds I had never heard before. I was taught and heard firsthand the distinction between different species of bird calls and howler monkeys. The latter seemed to enjoy following us over the next few miles and I kept my eyes on them out of caution. I wiped the sweat from my forehead and heard a buzzing around me. A little shape, too small and fast for me to really make out, was flying around my face in circles. I tried keeping my eyes on it as it zigzagged into the air. I kept seeing flashes of deep emerald green.

"Oh!" I exclaimed. "It's a hummingbird! I'm sorry little bird, I'm not a flower!"

It landed on my left shoulder, and I held my breath while we looked at each other for a little while before it took off in the opposite direction. What a neat experience. I had never seen one this close before and I doubted many people had. We emerged from the jungle, followed the almost empty roads, and traversed small towns. A lot of people seemed to live in makeshift metal sheet shelters, and others in homes made of wood or whatever other scrap metal they could find. The lucky ones got to live in houses made of concrete with electricity, but they were few and far between and all had bars on their windows, if not barbed wire fences. Animals roamed freely, from wild packs of dogs to undernourished cows and horses. But the few people we saw seemed happy, sitting in their front yards with their families. Their riches lay elsewhere, in their tranquility and way of life. While we did our best to remain inconspicuous, the towns weren't very lively to begin with and were practically deserted.

"What happened to the people here?"

"They're hiding deeper in the forest. They're afraid. The vampire scare reached us even here. We're pretty secluded from the world, but they all heard about vampires snatching people away, emptying entire neighborhoods in America. They didn't want to be next."

We had been walking for an entire day and night, leading into the next morning, and were determined to reach our destination rapidly. Rafael was by my side and Eloise leading in the front. We were more often than not quiet but there was so much to look at that it wasn't an uncomfortable silence. The cities had turned into farmlands, the deep green of the jungle changing into bright green grass and hills rolling into the distance. It seemed to be a richer area soil-wise but also civilization-wise. The few houses along the road all had nicely decorated yards and most had cars.

We continued bordering the roadway and climbed much higher, our legs burning with the effort. When we turned a curve, we came upon a cliff and the scenery took my breath away. There it was, the massive shape of the Arenal Volcano rising into the sky, its peak covered by a thick layer of clouds. At its base, Lake Arenal spread across miles and miles surrounded by luscious green grass and forests. It was an impressive sight to behold. We stood there for a moment, enjoying the scene before resuming our walk down.

The morning fog rose quickly and so thick that it became impossible to trek at the same pace safely. We stopped to wash our faces and cool our bodies down at the lake. Although the water was far from chilly, it was welcomed anyway. Our clothes were soaked through with sweat, and we enjoyed the water.

Through the fog, I saw something take shape on the water and focused on it.

"Do you see that?" I whispered, getting deeper in.

Eloise pulled me back slightly. "Careful, there are crocodiles in these waters."

The fog cleared slightly, the wind moving it along enough for us to discern the shape was in fact a small, shipwrecked sailboat. Nature had begun to claim it over some time ago as trees grew through the mainsail and around the mast. The water surrounding it began moving and we decided to continue on our journey before this creepy scene claimed us as well. We walked upstream from a hot spring that seemed to be our guide and a few hours later, seeing the volcano getting closer, stopped following the water to walk back into the forest where the air was surprisingly cooler under the canopy. I spent some time studying the new floras, examining up close new plants and some of the brightest colored flowers I had ever seen.

We passed a wooden archway that I guessed signaled the camp's entrance and I walked in a circle, taking it all in. An entire village had been built, complete with countless wooden huts and wooden showers closed off with bamboo and fire pits. Above ground were dozens of tree houses and mesh bridges connecting them all. About 520 vampires occupied themselves with everyday life tasks. I dropped the duffel bag to the ground.

"Are they all going to fight?"

"Most will. The rest are just hiding, living here in peace."

"This isn't enough." I was panicked.

Eloise placed a comforting hand on my arm. "This is all we have. They're not the ones we need to win the fight. You are."

"How long are we to stay here?"

"Take some time to relax and eat. When you are ready, come find me, and we'll solidify a plan."

We took residence in a vacant hut. I stood by the door and

watched the others. Maybe we did stand a chance. Rafael and I walked around, meeting our new friends and sharing a few words, some in Spanish, most in English.

"What do you do for food around here?" My boyfriend asked a man he'd helped cut wood.

"We harvest pigs, raccoons, and other mammals. Some of us would rather hunt, although there isn't much other than critters, birds, and reptiles, and maybe, if you're lucky, a puma or two, but those are rare. It depends on your mood."

Rafael just wanted to grab some food and crash. I, on the other hand, needed to hunt and clear my head. I went back to the thermal river and waited, listening. The scenery was breathtaking. I finally broke away from my fear and found peace. I heard paws echoing on the earth and closed my eyes to perceive the direction. I raced after it. I must have been tired. I found myself unusually slow, and the animal gave me a hard time chasing it. Perhaps I should have followed Rafael's lead. Instead of being naturally relaxing, this turned out to be exhausting. Bolting between the trees, left, right, stop and go, I finally just threw myself on the animal and tackled it to the ground, biting into the flesh. The blood flowing through my throat sent a bolt of rejuvenation through me. I walked back to camp, enjoying nature and the breeze.

Rafael was fast asleep, and I lay next to him. The comforting scent of hay reminded me of the Renaissance era, of living though simpler times, and I smiled to myself.

CHAPTER NINETEEN

I had been here before. Dreamt of this memory multiple times in the past, but I was aware of it now being just that—a memory. I was watching this scene replay in front of me while I stood on the outside of it. I was in the mansion Malcolm had built for our family, in our old bedroom. In my memory, I was laying on the bed wide awake while he was fast asleep on my left. This was the night before Liz, William, and I attempted to escape him. I held a knife in my hand, clutching it tightly to my chest. I wanted to use it on him. I wanted to end his life and return to my own. I wanted to be free. I raised myself, leaning on my elbow, and turned towards him. Could I do it? The knife began shaking in my hand as I placed it to his unsuspecting throat. It would be so easy to apply a little pressure, slit his skin and take out his heart before he finished healing. So why couldn't I do it?

Because I was weak and a coward. That's all I had ever been and would ever be. How dare I think of myself any other way? I lay back down, hiding the knife under my pillow, and pretended to be asleep when he stirred.

And as I stood there, watching this scene unfold, I recognized the limiting beliefs that had plagued me my entire life.

"That is enough," I said, and the scene froze. "Hello, Malcolm," I greeted him.

The Malcolm lying in bed opened his eyes. Then, the scene changed, and it was only present-day Malcolm and me standing in the darkness of his own mind.

"Hello, Alia. Finally figured out my little trick, huh?" He seemed so proud of himself. "I can't believe it took you this long." He chuckled. "I do believe it came from Liz."

Her power. That was her power. "You no longer have any hold over me, Malcolm; your little mind games are over."

"Take a walk with me." I felt that he couldn't physically hurt me in this astral realm and went along. There was a banging in the distance and as we approached it, I could see a man standing inside a metal cage, much like the ones used to go diving in, throwing his body at it, trying to break it open. No, not a man. Malcolm's demon. The feral look on its face shocked me. My own demon hadn't looked this animalistic.

"How do you reel this thing back in its cage

when you let it out?" I asked, not entirely expecting an answer.

"It's easy. I let it have its fun enough that it just listens to me when I tell him to get back inside. It knows it will come out again. I tried teaching you, but you fought me at every turn."

The beast ceased its noise and when I turned around, a little boy stood in its stead. His deep blue eyes held my gaze defiantly, but he also shook with fear.

"Why is your inner child so afraid, Malcolm?"

"I have done a lot of terrible things. I know that. And it was with selfish interest, most of the time. But our adventure is reaching its crescendo, I think. It's scary to think it is coming to an end one way or the other."

He seemed almost amicable today and I looked at him. This man I had loved so much once.

"Why are we doing this, Malcolm? You could have told me what you were building your clan for. You could have been honest with me from the get-go. We could have found a magical solution together to free Eloise. Who knows where we would be now?"

"Ah, so you've met Eloise, and I imagine you're with her now in Costa Rica. I knew it would always come to this. You're not the only one with insecurities and it wasn't any of your business. I didn't want anyone being handed my weakness."

"We could have helped you release your link to her had you just been good to us all."

"Or you would have used it against me. A

gazelle doesn't expect a lion to be nicer to it. A lion is a lion, and I am who I have always been."

"How do you think this is going to play out exactly? You can't kill her."

"I don't mean to kill her. And with all the powers I have accumulated over the centuries, there are now different ways for me to trap her and make sure she never stands in my way again."

Different scenes from his memory flashed in the background in quick sequences. I saw him as a small child in Hungary, emaciated and hungry, begging for money in the streets. A man kicking him in the back, bringing the child to his knees, shouting at him to try harder or he wouldn't get crumbs for dinner. I blinked and saw the woman who must have sired him, her unparalleled beauty and elegance. The way he worshiped the ground she walked upon and his need for her. I felt his fury and despair when she was put to death, his need for vengeance, and I understood it. I tried not to focus on his memories too much. It wouldn't do me any good.

"And me?" I asked him then, returning to our conversation.

"I really wish things could have been different between us. When I turned you, it truly was to be my mate, but you could never embrace the changes and lifestyle. You always tried to change me and you always attempted to get in the way of what I wanted to do. I grew tired of it, but felt your power grow so much and knew I had to keep you close by. Then it became clear that you alone would give me the power I needed against Eloise, and I had to have it. But that wasn't my intention from the beginning, you know. I was hard on you, but I had to distance myself from your love and expectations of me so I could do what I had to do."

"Well, that makes me feel better."

"I did care for you. I really did. But then my own preservation kicked in and you became a means to an end."

"I noticed."

He chuckled. "Always a pleasure, Alia. It'll be over soon, one way or the other." He took my hand and kissed the top of it, breaking the connection.

I had slept for twelve consecutive hours, knowing it would take Malcolm some time to make his way here—if he knew exactly where we were. I walked around lazily and found Rafael mingling with other vampires, communicating with his hands as he did not speak Spanish. I put my hand on his arm and as he turned around and saw me, a large smile appeared on his lips. Forgetting what he was doing and with no additional word, he followed me to the log cabin bathhouse. The water must have come directly from the volcano and was almost too hot. His excitement for me constantly comforted my mind, and I felt how hard he was as he hugged me from behind, one hand massaging my breast, the other finding its way in between my legs. I didn't bother keeping my moans quiet as he inserted his middle finger in and out of me. I turned around, and he lifted me directly on his erection, pressing me against the wall. I held on tightly as he bounced me up and down, water flowing down our bodies. I groaned into his mouth as I came moments before he did.

We dried off and then met Eloise outside her hut stroking a fire.

"I trust you've slept well," she said.

I nodded. "Do you think Malcolm will come here? You do realize if he does, most of your friends, if not all, will die. How can they possibly survive an Astaroth attack?"

She smiled and I knew something was up. "He'll most certainly be coming here, in just a few days in fact. As for my friends, those who will fight fully understand the risks they are taking."

"A few days?" I repeated. No, this was too soon. We were finally getting a break. We were supposed to be shielded from him here, safe.

"I planted in him a vision of us losing to his army. Him

drinking you and releasing himself of me. His ego will not let him pass up this opportunity."

"You don't think he'll know it is a trap?"

"If he finds it strange, he shows no care for it. Maybe he believes himself and his army powerful enough to win the battle, or perhaps he thinks it's time to bring it to an end."

"So what? We just wait here until he shows up and massacres everyone?"

"Of course not. Those who do not wish to fight can leave. And since you've fought Astaroths before, you can teach the rest how to kill them so that the three of us can focus on Malcolm."

"What do you want me to do?" Rafael asked.

"Nothing," I replied in Eloise's place. "I don't want you here."

"What are you talking about?" He seemed confused.

"I need you to leave. I can't fight this battle worrying about you." I hugged him.

"I'm here to fight. I can help."

"I know, and you'll help by being safe. That way I can focus on what needs to be done."

"He needs to be here, Alia," Eloise interfered. "We need him. He was in my vision. Everything will change if he's not here playing his part."

"We'll find another way." I was getting angry. "I am not going to let you do this. He will not be sacrificed for your quest!"

"Sacrificed? What are you talking about?" Then he remembered my vision when we first arrived in Costa Rica. "You hid this from me?" He looked hurt. I tightened my grip on him. "How will it happen?" He was looking down at me, his face soft and serene.

"I don't know," I lied. "It wasn't very clear to me."

"How will it happen, Eloise?" She hesitated, afraid answering him would change the future. "Tell me or I walk!" He knew I wasn't honest.

She sighed. "I see Alia against Malcolm one-on-one. He's about to kill her but you stop him and while he's distracted drinking you, I kill him."

"Oh." He exhaled and gently pushed me off him. I looked at him walking around in circles.

"You don't have to do this, Rafael," I sobbed.

He looked up at me, brows furrowed. "But I do, because if I don't, you'll die, and Eloise won't have the opportunity to kill him." He stood silent, and I felt as though the oxygen had disappeared from the world. "When exactly will he be here?"

"Two days." I felt Eloise's uneasiness and empathy for us.

"We will be ready for him," Rafael answered with conviction.

She nodded and walked away, awarding me a glance. She regretted having to do this, and I hated her for it. I remained defeated, looking at Rafael. Tears of anger rolled down my face. I didn't want him to accept his fate because I refused to accept it myself.

"Come here," he said, attempting to embrace me in his arms.

"No!" I slapped his hands away. "Don't do that." He circled my waist. "You've got to fight this," I cried.

"Calm down, it's okay, babe. I don't believe in fate."

But I did, and within a few days he would be taken from me. "Please let's leave; we can keep running."

"For how long? Forever? I can't. He'll hunt you wherever we go. That's not a life and I'm not a coward. I refuse to be known as that."

"Who cares what people think? I need you alive so I can live myself! I won't survive your death!"

"My mind is made up, Alia."

"You've killed us both then."

"If that's the case, then we shall learn if there's an afterlife together."

The peaceful atmosphere of this area suddenly became suffocating. This wasn't paradise. It had become a jail where I awaited my lover's death.

I spent a few hours teaching a workshop on Astaroths— their weaknesses and their strengths. One-on-one, I helped develop each fighter's skills, but I felt this was a futile effort. Not many were actually gifted, and they didn't have many actual weapons that hadn't been carved out of wood. Rafael watched us from afar. Finally, once alone in our hut, I sat next to him, kissed his lips, and looked out onto the village as they got ready to fight.

"Are you scared?" I questioned.

"Yes, I am. It's not like I want those visions to be real."

"I could do a protection spell on you. Give you a little bit more of a fighting chance."

He chuckled. "If you really think it will help, then sure, why not?"

"You find this funny?" I was becoming quite exasperated.

"Of course not, but if there is such a thing as fate, I doubt your spells and magic will save me."

"It doesn't hurt to try."

I sat in front of him, peering into his eyes, placing my right index and middle finger on his forehead, while touching my own forehead with my opposite fingers.

Friendly Guardians here I preach,
Keep him out of harm's reach,
With this blood, safe into your care
And guarded through the despair.

I bit my finger, using the blood to draw a pentagram on his forehead.

"That's it?" he inquired. "That easy?"

"It's the best I can do with no supplies, but it will work."

I walked down to the river where I washed myself and the few shirts I had brought, more out of habit than a belief I would get to wear them again. I cried and took out my anguish into the rushing water. I was losing control and my chest felt so tight I could hardly breathe. I felt trapped. After a few moments of feeling sheer panic, I forced myself into relaxing by practicing my skills of energy absorption and release. I had done it with fire and while water was not any calmer, it felt less chaotic and more stable. I returned to the village feeling full of power and pretending I hadn't just had a meltdown; I had another workshop to lead.

Fewer people attended this time as those who did not wish to fight had evacuated the grounds. I spent the next day secluded from the others, practicing my control over the elements, combining water, earth, fire, and air together. I could suffocate a fire by absorbing the air around it and that led me to believe I could take the air out of someone's lungs, but I refused to try that on anyone within the village. I could even draw energy from the volcano's deep underground lava. Rafael and I spent the remaining hours of our final day in each other's arms. And while I wanted nothing more than to show him how much I physically needed him, I didn't think I could focus long enough to enjoy being intimate.

Eloise came to find us, knocking on our door. "It is time."

I tightened my hold on him. "It isn't too late to rethink this," I said.

He observed me, brushing my face with his hand. "Come on, let's get ready."

Eloise, wishing to give us more time, had already placed her troops within the forest and given her last orders. She watched the battlefield from above a cliff.

"Where do we go?" I asked.

"We stay here, together. If Malcolm appears, you two go first and occupy him." *She means Rafael needs to die.* "Then I'll emerge and kill him."

"You really think he's going to come out in the open?"

"He's here for your blood. If he won't come out, then you will lure him out."

The forest was unnaturally still; the animals hid, and the air did not flow. We awaited their arrival. My partners by my side, their emotions washed through me. Eloise's excitement was palpable and so was Rafael's nervousness. I took his hand and squeezed; his palm was sweating. My own heart beat uncontrollably fast. Somewhere, a branch cracked. From our position up top, we saw the Astaroths advance.

"Here they come," Eloise murmured.

Shadows fled through the trees and were met by our forces, but they were so many that putting up a fight seemed ineffective. Weapons clashed against claws, but we were already and very apparently suffering a defeat. There was no hope in this battle. Our only chance stood with Malcolm. Part of me was giving up.

"Alia, go in." I didn't like being ordered.

I looked at Rafael and shared his anguish. Assuming the visions were correct, this would be the last time I would see him. I absolutely was not ready to leave him. My breath was caught in my throat. I studied his face one last time, forging it in my memory.

"Go." He attempted to have a reassuring smile. "I'll see you after the fight."

No, you won't. We're not meant to. I nodded, returning his fake smile, and jumped off the cliff into the ongoing battle.

I immediately dodged blow after blow and picked up a fallen soldier's ax. I sliced into backs, heads, arms, legs, and anything in my reach. For the first time in my life, I needed to and let the beast take over. I took a deep breath and opened the cage that controlled my inner demon. I let it take over my every move, surpassing my own skills, and felt its joy at being freed. My personal enemy and I working hand in hand for a greater goal, and it felt so rewarding. It was as though I had become a vessel of frustration and rage. By letting it loose, I was exceeding my own expectations. But I was also a witch, and I absorbed the elements around me. With the volcano nearby, there was so much ready for the taking. I felt the power within my heart accentuate, and I knew the energy I was creating would soon explode. I was no longer master of my body; I was being manipulated by a foreign force, but I trusted it completely.

Only half aware, I slowly marched within the heart of the battle and gave in to the power. It detonated as a bomb, sending a shock wave in every direction and injuring only my rivals. I came to and was amazed by the outcome. I felt drained, but I knew there remained much more power where this came from. With only a gesture from my hands, I sent bodies flying through the air and walked to another Astaroth-infested area. My teammates were having a tough time overcoming the assault. Using the earth as my source of strength, I handled a thick log to hit the ground with, dispersing another shock wave. I was left panting and gasping for air; it would take some time before I could use this power again. I noticed Rafael in my peripheral vision fighting some distance away and struggling to keep his own. I watched in horror as the Astaroth pinned him to the floor, putting its rotting foot on his chest. I tried pushing through the crowd to reach him but was unable to make it very far. I dodged a few claws, stabbed through a few bodies, but it seemed the world had turned to slow motion. I think I even screamed his name as the corpse went to plunge its claws into Rafael's stomach. The protection spell worked as a shield at the very last minute, and I let my breath out of my lungs with a victorious laugh.

A hand grabbed my arm and slammed me into a tree. My skull hurt. And it wasn't who I thought it would be.

"What the hell was that?" Eloise screamed. "You cast a spell on him? How the hell is my vision going to come true now?" She held me against my will with her elbow pressed firmly against my throat. Although she was shorter than me, my skull bled freely, and I could not break free.

"Of course I did! We'll occupy Malcolm another way than with Rafael's death!"

She was furious, and I thought she might strike me until the wind picked up. "Wait! I smell him. Malcolm is close!" She finally let go of me and looked around.

The wind came from the east, and indeed there he was, watching us from above a precipice with a mixture of anger and shock on his face. Then he ran. In the same rhythm, Eloise and I thrust ourselves after him, using all the speed our legs were capable of.

I rejoiced in seeing this fearful side of him and let the beast loose once more. It liked to chase. Eloise ran by my side, and I realized Rafael was not following us. I smiled to myself because her vision was wrong and focused on increasing my speed. I wanted him for myself, to drink his blood before she could. He wasn't far from us but remained a good distance away. I dodged trees, branches, and boulders, and while I was getting closer to him, I fed off his fright. We were far from the campsite and out of the jungle. Almost out of breath, I resolved to tapping into my powers once more. I reached for the earth and detonated it under his feet as though bombs went off. The explosions momentarily decelerated his rapidity but not enough for Eloise and me to catch up. I became aware that she was falling back, and as much as my lungs screamed for a break, I couldn't let him get away. I gave a shot at syphoning the air out of his lungs and that seemed to work. I felt his emotions and perceived his thoughts. I was one with him, inside his head. Although afraid to suffocate, he didn't think of me as a threat still, but was extremely frightened by Eloise, and I was somewhat offended by that. I was so close I could smell the sweat off him and touch him. Subsequently, the connection closed, and I felt like a door had been slammed in my face, the shock of it feeling like a gut punch. I came to a halt, my hands on my hips and gasping for air. Within a blink, I lost him. I looked in every direction, listened, and smelled for him, but he had vanished.

"Damn it!" I gasped. How in the world could I have let him disappear this way? He had done it again. The coward had escaped and could be miles away already.

I crouched on the floor, putting my face between my hands, and screamed my frustration. Suddenly, a pair of hands circled my neck, crushing the bones and throwing me to the floor. "It is time to end this," he grunted.

Malcolm stood above me, choking the air out of my lungs. I kicked and squirmed to break free but felt myself wither; I had used too much power. *This can't be it.* Where was my beast when I needed it? Finally, when one of my blows landed him square in the chest, I catapulted myself on my feet and made for an escape. I didn't get very far. He threw himself at me, and we slid down a cliff. I felt the bones in my leg break and cried out. His fervor was tenacious, and I found myself only surviving due to magic. I dug my fingers into the earth and attempted to rejuvenate myself some, trying to rely on nature to come to my help. I blocked his blows with a force shield, but my nose began to bleed, and I knew I was in trouble. Magic was draining my life, and it became obvious that I would not outlive this fight. I didn't want to hide from him with magic tricks. He had seen me too fearful my entire life. I chose to die honorably and no longer shrink from him. I fought him, but my pace was slow and tired. I was no match. My face was bruised and bleeding. My body was broken and shattered. Adrenaline did little to mask my pain anymore. He kicked me hard, and I flew backwards through some trees, landing on my back. I felt my spine break.

My life didn't flash before my eyes like I expected it to or had wanted it to. The only thing I saw was the condensation of my breath in the air. The only thing I felt was regret. I didn't feel sorry for the way I was dying. I had prepared myself for it. However, I had never thought it would end this specific way. And the pain, the pain was the most bothersome and unbearable. I couldn't move or feel my legs, but the burning sensation in my chest made me cringe my teeth. As I lay back, I looked at the sky and felt as though I saw it for the first time. The beauty of it took my breath away, and sadness lingered over me as I understood I would never be able to gaze at the stars again.

Then, out of the corner of my eye, I saw Malcolm come my way. I gasped and tried to drag myself away, but the pain prevented me from getting far. Overwhelmed and panicked thoughts plunged through me like a trapped animal knowing death was imminent. There was nothing more I could do to protect myself. I was scared, and tears rolled down my cheeks, but I wouldn't beg, and inched away ever so slowly. I continued breathing hard and closed my eyes, for I knew he was standing above me. I awaited the end of my being.

And in that moment, in that split second, so much became clear to me. I hadn't lived at all—almost three hundred years and I had merely existed. I didn't want it to be over. I rejoiced in feeling pain because it would be the last thing I ever felt. To feel. To live. I just wanted another chance, again.

Rafael was not intervening. Eloise's vision was wrong, and this brought me happiness. He would survive.

Malcolm spun me around by the shoulder and I felt the spike entering my chest and the fire rushing through my veins, causing me to scream out in pain. My blood flowed, my breath became short gasps, and my mind was shutting down. I wasn't completely dead yet since the spike, which he still held in my torso, had not been shoved all the way through my heart. But it was just a matter of seconds. Malcolm looked down at me with a victorious smile.

"What are you waiting for?" I wheezed.

"I'm contemplating the meaning of your life." He laughed, shaking his head. "It really had none. You left no mark on this world."

I was coughing up blood, and his words no longer affected me. The burning fire returned as he impaled me deeper into the ground so I wouldn't be able to move when he drank my essence. Rafael appeared behind him, and my fear suddenly became a reality. Malcolm was thrown backwards, and the spike taken out of my chest. I felt the agony of wood splintering in my flesh, and I grasped at my consciousness. Rafael was by side, but I could not hear his words. His survival was all I thought about. Then, I realized the events were proceeding as the vision foresaw and I was utterly helpless to stop it.

My body shattered, I watched in horror as the prophecy became fulfilled. Malcolm hit him a first time and was met by the spell's shield, but as I was seconds from fainting, the shield grew thin and weak. It only took Malcolm a few more tries before obliterating it. They exchanged a few blows, but Malcolm was a much more skilled fighter. I closed my eyes, not wanting to see what came next. I felt my lover's physical pain and desperation. Then, I just didn't feel him anymore and I became astonished at how strange of a feeling it was. Feeling my mate die felt entirely different from feeling my friends leave this world.

When I opened my eyes, I was not surprised but was nonetheless heartbroken to see Rafael lying inert on the ground. Eloise had Malcolm by the throat. She glanced at me, trying to decipher whether I was still alive. He fought to be released. She raised him higher off his feet, and his neck cracked louder.

"Hello, Malcolm." He struggled against her grasp. "So here we are again!" she said to him.

"Just get it over with."

Her fingers tightened around his esophagus. "In a moment. I want you to fully realize this is the end for you. Drown in your stupor."

He threw a punch, she blocked it. He growled and thrashed, but she violently slammed his back against a tree and took advantage of his stunned state to bite his neck. He cried out and attempted to get her off, but she was onto him like a leech. I could see the gradual weakness overcoming him, and this was all so hysterical to me. As painful as it was, I laughed wholeheartedly, bringing her attention back on me. Still drinking his blood, she brought him closer to me and gasped as she forced her lips off his flesh.

"You're too frail to heal; let me help you, Alia. There's not much left, but it might be just enough."

What was the point? The one reason I had to keep on fighting lay dead a few feet from me. My body was broken, but even that pain was not comparable to the heartbreak I felt. Everyone I had ever loved had died, more or less by my fault. Rafael had been the last casualty I failed to protect. And as much pain as I was in, I knew a great deal was suppressed by my extreme weariness. "I just want to die," I whispered.

"I'm sorry. I can't let you do that. It isn't your time just yet."

She forced Malcolm to bend his neck so the blood would trickle onto my mouth. At first, I moved my head slightly from side to side, as stirring caused me excruciating pain, but once the blood touched my tongue, I could not resist the urge. Was it because he was my creator or because I despised him? Whatever the case was, his essence was the greatest I ever tasted. Even with the amount of power in his blood, the pain my injuries were putting me through was too much to handle, and I felt myself slip into darkness. My vision blurred out completely, but not before seeing Eloise rip Malcolm's heart out of his chest.

CHAPTER TWENTY

Versailles had always been a place of happiness for me. I had been here many times throughout my real life, but this wasn't real. It had to be a figment of my imagination, and I walked around the corridors unable to figure out a date. I looked down at my body. I was wearing the most beautiful, royal, Renaissance gown. The palace was utterly empty, and I believed I found myself in the Salon de la Guerre. It looked as I imagined it would in the daylight, for in this fantasy, I was a day walker. The walls were covered with marble panels and golden statues. The high-vaulted ceiling, from which hung a beautiful crystal chandelier, glorified some military victories. I heard laughter echoing and moved to the next room, the Hall of Mirrors. Before noticing the room's beauty, I observed the people dancing in the middle of the gallery: Liz and William. Her full skirt swayed with her movement while he wore colorful tights with a shirt and coat. They were finally able to get that last dance after all. My heart tightened in my chest, and I choked a sob down. Upon my arrival, they stopped twirling and watched me. I remained frozen in shock. Finally, she hastily came to embrace me, and I could smell her perfume. It felt as real as ever. When I was released from her arms, I continued looking in disbelief between Liz and Will's faces.

"I found her," he said, and she laughed.

"Is this real?" I asked, incredulous but also hopeful.

Her smile turned sad. "It's as real as you make it."

I looked around and was astonished by the splendor of the seventeen mirror arches, again seeing this for the first time in the daylight. I could see the reflection of the gardens in them. The walls around the arches were made of marble and decorated with France's symbols. I remembered the history that took place here, the births and weddings, as well as the kings and queens who walked in this enormous room. The ornamentation was exquisite with golden tables, golden statues, massive chandeliers, and as always, painted high-vaulted ceilings.

As beautiful as this wall was, it could not keep my attentiveness from my friends. I turned my eyes back to them. "How are we here? This is not real."

"You brought us here, Alia," William spoke.

"So, we can stay forever?"

Liz shook her head. "No. You have a decision to make."

"A decision?" I was so glad to see her. I barely paid attention to her words. But what she talking about?

They looked at each other and pain crossed their eyes. "In the real world, you are hurt. Dying. You need to decide whether to let go or keep fighting."

I laughed. "Well, that's simple, I want to stay here with you."

"It doesn't work like that." She seemed about to cry. "This, this isn't real. And we aren't really here. Your magic helped us meet again, but if you let go, your powers will die with you, and I can't promise we will see each other again."

I exhaled slowly. Defeated, I walked to the window, looking at the garden. "I wish I could retrieve the time that we lost," I said.

She circled my waist from behind, putting her chin on my shoulder, and looked out with me. "And I wish you would stop blaming yourself for events that were not of your doing. I am so proud of who you have become. I wish I had gotten to say it more often."

I looked at her and cried because her clemency was what I had always needed to hear. I was finally awarded atonement.

"Alia, you must decide," William pressed.

My weeping intensified as I panicked about

losing them. "Don't leave me, not yet. This is too soon."

She grasped my face between her hands and kissed my tears. "I cannot guarantee that I will find you when you finally cross into our realm, but William and I found each other, and I will keep looking for you, sister. But only when your time comes. For now, you have work to finish."

I wished people would let me decide when I would die. I was so tired.

"Be strong, sister; you always have a part of me within you," William whispered in my ear.

I was deeply distressed but found an inner peace at the very same time. "I love you," I whispered and smiled.

"As we love you."

I opened my eyes and blinked hard, once, twice. I was lying on the floor. I was so tired, and the sky was completely overcast but yet so bright that I was having a hard time keeping my eyes open. I felt the rain on my face and relished in how refreshing it was and listened to the sound of it falling onto leaves. I opened my eyes once more and focused on the palm leaves swaying in the wind overhead. It took a while for my injuries to heal completely, but time was meaningless at this point. When my bones had finally all agonizingly cracked back into place and I was able to get to my feet, I saw Malcolm's lifeless and pale body on the ground. Admittedly, I might have considered kicking his corpse for a little while and the intense satisfaction the idea brought me felt almost shameful. I saw Rafael's body and all my need for vengeance leeched out of me, replaced with breath-taking grief. I lay down and remained with my head on my lover's chest for a long time until the tears stopped coming. I had failed him. My eyes felt heavy, and I could have easily gone to sleep right there. My mind was tired to a point of utter numbness. I stared straight ahead at nothing in particular. No thoughts coming in, no thoughts coming out, just a lifeless husk. I stayed in this stupor for a long time, and then I thought of Eloise.

I had a hint she would finally want to end her long existence. With Malcolm's death, the sky was beginning to clear up, the rain had stopped, and a sun we hadn't seen in months was peeking out from behind the clouds. After all we had been through, I couldn't let her end it alone. The sky's clarity let me know that I only had a few minutes and I was running out of time. I dragged Rafael's body underneath the trees, making a mental note to give him a proper burial later. I tracked her with no difficulty, her scent forever ebbed in my mind, and met her at the edge of a cliff overseeing the lake. Her back was turned to me, but she knew I was present.

"You shouldn't be here," she said. "The sun will rise soon."

I walked to her side and held her hand tightly. She remained looking down at the lake, but a faint smile crossed her lips. The black water's intensity pulled me in, and I couldn't stop the sobs from surfacing.

"Are you sure you want to do this?" I asked. "You're finally free of him. You can live your life."

"Oh, I'm sure. I have seen and explored the world for centuries. I am no longer interested in what it has to offer. I have wanted to end it for so long and now that I can, I know it's the right decision for me."

The rising heat stung my skin, yet I didn't want to leave her. My hand blistered on top of hers, but I wasn't letting go.

"Walk away," she ordered through gritted teeth.

I stayed looking at her. Finally, she turned her face towards me and repeated, almost pleading, "Walk away."

Her eyes portrayed every feeling imaginable: anticipation, remorse, pain, fear. Most of all, relief. Crying, I retracted to the tree's shadows but kept my eyes on her. The sky was pink and orange now. Eloise lifted her arms by her sides and welcomed the flames covering her body. She didn't cry out, she only let it consume her. With her final breath, she took a step over the edge of the cliff. I knew she'd be dead before hitting the water.

I closed my eyes and listened to the wind howling. The way it made the trees dance and sing. A bird cried out, and my gaze followed the animal. My stare dropped back to the water. This reminded me how jealous of the ocean's freedom I had been at one point, but not anymore.

What was I to do now? What had become the purpose of my life? I walked back to Rafael's resting body, and I didn't know why I bothered carefully avoiding the sunlight. What did it matter now? Emotions no longer affected me; I did not feel them. However, alarm submerged me when I did not see his body. I frantically paced around. Perhaps I was not in the right area. I checked and rechecked, but a while into my search, I had come to terms with the fact that I would not find him. Perhaps I had not hidden him from the sun well enough. It was another failure on my part. I'd add it to the list. Or perhaps, he could... still be alive? But I actually had seen him die; I had felt him. This was not like the Malcolm situation. He was dead, wasn't he? I screamed his name repeatedly, just in case, and laughed at myself when I didn't receive an answer.

Staying in the shadows, I headed back to camp in hopes of finding some life, some meaning. Disappointment met me once again. My brows furrowed and my eyes couldn't believe what I was seeing. I walked down the path of destruction, and my breath caught in my throat. How could this have happened? One of the burning fire pits had propagated and burned some of the village down. The rain had turned the fires to embers, and I felt the surrounding heat burn my flesh. My hair flapped violently around my face, but I didn't mind. I wished it would have kept me from this desperate scene. Mutilated bodies lay about everywhere I could perceive. We had won this fight alright, but at what cost? For me to be the only one to survive a massacre, once again.

CHAPTER TWENTY-ONE

Thinking back on my life and all the things I should have done differently, I sat there desperate and alone with not one soul to care whether I lived or died. I was not angry anymore. I felt relaxed and at ease. Anger kept me from feeling other emotions such as pain. Now that I had let my anger go, I let my walls down. Without my shield, I began to feel and grieve. I fought with everything I had, and it wasn't enough. I lost everyone who ever mattered in my life, and I just didn't have it in me anymore.

I listened to the washing of the water onshore, to the wind's melody in the trees, and I felt the breeze on my cheeks. I opened my eyes as my past came to haunt me with all the possible different outcomes of my life, had I been stronger.

I couldn't remember ever seeing anything as beautiful as this. I had been lost in the darkness inside my soul for so long, I forgot how simple yet stunning it could be. A burning ring of fire in the sky, although still slightly covered, was all it took to take my breath away. Humans took the sun for granted. I knew I couldn't handle any more spiritual torture; this world had nothing more to offer. My family and my lover were all taken from me. When I had been about to die, I had hoped for another chance, but without Rafael, this second chance meant nothing. My spirit and soul were now broken and would take another lifetime to mend. I just did not have the strength or the willpower needed to put myself back together, and time was running out. This was it for me.

I'd taken the decision and in a matter of minutes it would be over. Sweet death would deliver me from this pain. I felt and saw my skin peeling off. The physical pain took my mind off my broken heart, and I was so grateful for it. I felt my energy seeping out of my pores and being released into nature.

I had the strange sensation that I was being watched, and out of the corner of my eye, I noticed a figure in the distance, standing in the shade. My powers were diminishing, and I couldn't see that far anymore, but I heard my name being called.

"Alia, stop!"

It almost sounded like Rafael, and this must have been my mind playing tricks on me. My imagination, grasping at a happy memory to battle the pain death was bringing on. I did not move, but I thought of him and smiled.

I felt myself seized, moved into the shade, and I did not understand how I was seeing him so clearly. He panted, bent over his knees. I touched his face and his chest; he felt so real. "I almost didn't think I would find you in time," he gasped.

I was so shocked that I couldn't speak.

"Alia, are you okay?" He raised himself and embraced me.

"You're alive? How? I watched you die. You were dead!"

"Not dead but on the brink of death. You fainted, then Eloise fed me Malcolm's blood right before my heart stopped. It healed me. She foresaw all this and warned me you'd be here. I took a chance and trusted her vision. When we were alone, she told me I wasn't really going to die, but I would come really close to it. She lied to you so you'd fight him with everything you had."

"I couldn't find your body. I called your name. Why didn't you answer me?" I was shaking with the tension I had been holding in.

"I'm sorry." He squeezed me tighter, cradling my head in his hand. "I woke up and came over here directly, waiting for you, but she didn't tell me exactly where you'd be."

I was so relieved to see him alive, but I had difficulty grasping the notion that my distress had been foreseen and brushed aside. He looked at me as though I was not burnt and scarred. "Is it all over for good?" He brushed my hair behind my ear.

Hugging him back, I felt my skin heal. I suspected that with Malcolm's power now inside me, I would need no more help healing. "Yes, it's really over."

Circling my waist, he put his chin on my head. "Where do we go from here?"

"I can only guess how hard it will be coexisting with humans again. It will be a while before the world goes back to normal, but we can help it."

I kissed him then, deeply and passionately. I had gone through so many emotions, and I was exhausted. I needed to sleep for a week. For now, we decided to take a much-needed vacation before finding our way back to America where a ton of work awaited us. Starting over wouldn't be easy. It would take a long time and a lot of efforts to reestablish a peace treaty. It would take a lot for vampires to be trusted once more. But I felt up for the challenge. I had done it before and could do it again.

There was no need for us to return to the campsite. I knew what would wait for us there and I thought it best to avoid the sight. We slowly made our way towards the next major city, hoping someone there would help us get on a flight, but mostly enjoying our time alone together. I found myself understanding what this country had to offer and why everyone called it "Pura Vida": the animals, the weather, the ability to survive off the land. I appreciated how not much was needed to be happy here and I was in no rush to return home. As we walked through the jungle holding hands, needing that physical touch, I found myself falling deeper and deeper in love with this beautiful man who sacrificed everything for me and to be with me. I was now convinced everything would be fine. Rafael and I would live, love each other, and rebuild our world. For the first time in months, I knew he and I had a place in the future.

CHAPTER TWENTY-TWO

R afael and I ended up spending another four months in
Costa Rica, rebuilding ourselves and decompressing
from all we had endured before making our way back to America. That in itself had been as big of a struggle as I imagined it
would be. Although far from broke, we had no IDs or bank
cards on us to book a flight home. Without Malcolm's control
over the weather, we could only move across the land at night
or on overcast, cloudy days. It made our trek slow. But then
again, we were in no rush.

Surprisingly, back in the United States, vampires who had
gone into hiding during this whole Malcolm ordeal started
rallies and peaceful walks to express their desires to coexist
with humans once more. These happened in a lot of the major
cities: New York, Chicago, Philadelphia, and even on the other
side of the country, Los Angeles and San Diego. Vampires were
being proactive and being heard.

By the time we found safe passage on an American couple's
private jet, a lot of the public relations hard work had already
been done for me. Rafael and I stayed briefly at his house

before selling it and moving to Washington, D.C., where I purchased an apartment for the both of us. We moved Rafael's furniture into it, and although I wanted to change it all to something the both of us liked, there were more important matters to be concerned with. I was in the process of selling the club and purging myself of my old life.

I stood by the floor-to-ceiling windows overlooking the downtown area, nibbling on a fingernail. I found myself stress biting my nails more often these days and had no idea where this habit came from all of a sudden. Rafael turned the TV off and came to stand behind me, encircling my waist with his arms and putting his chin on my shoulder.

"What are we looking at?"

"Nothing, just staring off." I scratched my throat.

"Are you nervous about tomorrow?" he asked, kissing my neck.

"No." That was a lie, and he knew it. "Yes. I just really, really want this job at the Department of Control. I want to help them rebuild and improve human-vampire relations. I want to be involved."

"But forcing vampires to come out and to register in a database or suffer the consequences... I don't know, it sounds like a dictatorship to me."

"I know you don't agree." I exhaled. "But it's the only way we can return to a normal life."

I could see his reflection in the glass and saw the moment he frowned. "Are you sure you're ready for this?" he asked. "You've been through so much. I really think you could use some more time off. Your panic attacks are—"

"Getting better," I cut him off. "Please, I need your support in this and I need to do something with my days. I can't stay here anymore, replaying everything that's happened and all the people we lost."

I turned around to face him and he hugged me tightly. "You'll always have my support. Just don't lose yourself in your pain and block me out," he said. "I still want us to attend therapy, talk to someone about our trauma."

I knew what he really meant was *my* trauma. I pushed myself slightly off of him, forcing him to look me in the eyes. "We will go, and as long as I have you by my side, I can do anything. Now, let's fix the mess Malcolm made."

He smiled at me and just like that, I thought with this man's love and strength, we would reshape the world. I felt I was finally allowed to breathe and live. But I had spent my whole life being naive, and it would appear I had not yet learned my lesson because nothing turned out the way I thought it would. My pain was far from done; I should have known better.

ABOUT THE AUTHOR

Leslie Cardix was born and raised in the south of France until the age of 12. A single child, she spent much of her time imagining impossible adventures to undertake in the deep forests that engulfed her home. When her parents decided to move the family to America, her imagination only intensified and reading and writing became new friends in an unfamiliar country.

Now Leslie lives in North Carolina with her husband, their baby girl and their 3 dogs. When she isn't writing or reading, she can be found running her CrossFit gym, working out or hiking.

lesliecardix.com

26166906R00184